FETCHENKO

By

Duane Schwartz

Argus Enterprises International, Inc
North Carolina***New Jersey

A-Argus Better Book Publishers, LLC

For information:
A-Argus Better Book Publishers, LLC
Post Office Box 914
Kernersville, North Carolina 27285
www.a-argusbooks.com

ISBN: 978-0-9846195-1-1
ISBN: 0-9846195-1-8

Book Cover designed by Dubya

Printed in the United States of America

Also by Duane Schwartz

Calumet

Cobb's Landing

Little Cicero

The Winds of Change

Available at
www.a-argusbooks.com

DEDICATION:

This novel is dedicated to all those who *'took the blame'* for acts they did not commit. Hopefully, it was not to the extent of the characters in this work of fiction. But also—hopefully, you managed to get even in the end.

More so than writing, the author's most difficult job is in promoting his work. It has been this author's fortune to have a wife whose diligence in that area far exceeds the term "beyond the call of duty". It is also this author's fortune that I can thank her publicly for her sacrifices. So... I thank you, Betty. And I want you and all those who read this to know none of this would exist without your contribution.

On that same note, Betty and two friends of hers organized and hosted an event at our local community center. Another huge sacrifice—a great success. And I have two more to thank, Barb Linder and Mia Stockey. So... thank you Barb and Mia. Your efforts are appreciated and will be long remembered.

A hefty thank you is owed to my good friend, Ed Svegal, who gave countless hours at his computer editing my work, correcting my spelling and punctuation, and offering suggestions that made this novel better in the end. Your efforts, my friend, will never go unappreciated or unnoticed. And the same gratitude goes out to Rachel Olson who gave of her time and talent to read a proof copy of this work and offer her own editing expertise.

Chapter One

Florescent orange leaves from the maple lined Main Street of the quaint out of the way village floated like feathers in a breeze onto the hood of the '56 Studebaker Flight Hawk. Autumn had arrived in the little mining community. The old car angled into a parking space just south of a fifties-style café sporting a sign that bore the name ALBERT & SUE'S. A quick glance at his watch told its driver it was seven a.m., and a roll of the window brought on a shiver. "Christ," he said, "it is freezing."

"Give it time," his pretty passenger told him. "It's early. It'll warm up."

"When?"

"Soon. Go inside. Get us a table. I'm going to that little pharmacy to turn in your prescription." She gestured at a storefront behind them.

"No real hurry," he said as he looked up the narrow street. One rust-riddled jalopy filled two parking spaces half a block away. "I'm sure there'll be plenty of open tables." She smiled at him, winked, and then stepped out of the car. "Order us coffee. I'll join you in a few minutes." She turned and walked toward the little drug-store.

He opened his car door and began the painful process of stepping into the street. "I bet they won't stock my medicine," he yelled after her.

"Coffee," she ordered softly as she waved a thin, gloved hand over her shoulder. "Order coffee — decaf for me."

He took another glance at the ancient front of Albert and Sue's and said, "I doubt they're that up to date. It'll probably be Sanka."

He watched his lady cross the street as he searched behind the seat for his cane. Her limp, slight but obvious, even though it did lend a poetic motion to her walk, served as a reminder of her pain. It was his fault; it was he who had caused her injuries — him and his lifetime of building powerful and dangerous enemies. He straightened and planted the cane on the pavement. He turned and headed toward the café.

Inside the store, she looked back at him and watched his labored movements. Sadness crossed her pretty face. A tear welled in one eye. She brushed it aside and turned to face the pharmacist.

In the café the man chose a table in a far corner where the light was so dim he would not cast a shadow. Albert Shaw, a light haired, balding, slightly overweight and shabbily attired man in his early sixties, approached. "What kin-ah-git-cha?" he asked.

"Two coffees."

"Two?"

"Yes, two," the man said. He checked out Albert's puzzled look then added, "My wife will be joining me." Albert's questioning gaze changed to one of relief. His guest smiled in amusement. "Make hers decaf."

"All I got is Sanka," Albert said.

The man grinned broadly. "Just make it two regular."

"Will do. Say, don't I know you?" Albert asked.

"Unlikely."

"Sure look familiar."

"I'm not from around here," the man said. "The name's Walker, Jed Walker. I'm from back east."

"Seems you got the accent," Albert said.

"Eastern?" Walker asked.

"Nope! Midwest."

The statement set Jed Walker aback. He knocked his cane to the floor. Its silver top popped loose, skidded under the table and stopped at the boot of Albert Shaw.

He knew Shaw alright; at least he had when they were kids. Shaw hadn't been bright then, and, it seemed, he hadn't developed much intellectually since, so Shaw's ability to pick up on a local accent in his speech felt out of place to Walker. He chose to let the whole thing go, hoped it would fade to nothing. "What's with that?" He pointed at a portrait on the wall. It was of an older, distinguished looking man. The painting was framed garishly and covered in a thick layer of dust. The figure within sported a dart in his left eye.

"Why, that there's Governor Thaddeus Frank," Albert said as he looked at the painting. "What the... ? Them goddamn kids!" He approached the painting and reached out to remove the dart.

"Leave it," Walker said. "It looks good on him — political jewelry."

Shaw smiled. "He was kind of a jerk as I recall. I'll get them coffees Mr. Walker."

Behind a long counter cluttered with restaurant equipment, most of it dirty and in bad repair, a humungous coffee percolator stood. Walker watched as his host grabbed two mugs and started filling them. This ought to be tasty, he thought.

The door opened and a stringer of bells announced the newest patron's arrival. A slender lady entered, and along with her, a cold blast of early morning fall air. Walker shuddered. He tried to focus. Was it his lady?

Albert Shaw watched attentively. Pretty, he thought. Red hair, tight blue jeans, very pretty. My kind of girl. Not sure I agree with the turtleneck though. She made her way to Walker's table. He noticed her slight limp. "Boots must hurt," he whispered to himself. Albert guessed her age in the late forties. His eyes followed her. But when she lowered herself into the chair across from Walker, the coffee he had been pouring began to overflow onto the counter. "Shit!" he said and jumped back.

"Albert!" a woman called through a serving window near the coffee maker. "Put your eyes back in your head and do your job!"

I'll be damned, Walker thought. Susan Langley. He wondered if she would recognize him. Not likely. Susan was considerably younger than him and had traveled in different circles when they were teens. She wouldn't know him; frankly, he shouldn't know her either. Hell... if Tony Copeletti hadn't had such a crush on her back then, he wouldn't. But... Tony did... and talked about her constantly. So much so that he and Henry Tyler, the third member of their childhood trio, were so sick of the name Susan Langley they came to agree that if Tony mentioned her one more time they were going to beat the shit out of him.

Albert made his way to the table with the two coffee cups. "You must be Mrs. Walker," he said as he placed one of them in front of her.

"I... er... well, I guess I must be," the pretty redhead agreed.

"Get-cha anything more?"

The Walkers both chose a light breakfast and Albert was off to place their order.

"Mrs. Walker?" she asked as soon as Albert was gone. "Then who are you?"

"Mr. Walker, of course." He snuffed out a smoldering cigarette that had burned to the filter. "I thought Walker sounded good. It reminds me of that old television show about the ranger. I liked that show and the guy who played in it."

"Does Mr. Walker have a first name?" she asked.

"Jed."

"Jed?"

"Jed," he repeated.

"Jed. I guess I could get used to it. What about Mrs. Walker? Does she get a first name too?"

"Ima," he proudly announced.

"Ima!" she said, a bit too loudly. She lowered her voice. "Ima Walker? Not on your life. Why not Hooker? Then I could be Ima Hooker."

"How about Leona?"

"Not as bad as Ima, but still... a terrible name."

"I like it. Leona. It's kind of an old fashioned name. It fits." He smiled.

"Fits who?" she demanded. "It damn sure doesn't fit me."

"The name Walker," he explained. "It fits with the name Walker, Leona Walker. Now doesn't that sound good together? Jed and Leona Walker. It has a ring to it."

"Ring, hell. It's a gong! It's clatter. It's loose change falling on a table. I refuse."

"Well, how about we shorten it," he suggested. "The full name will be Leona Walker, but we'll call you Lee Walker. How's that?"

Albert Shaw returned to the table, a plate in each hand. Surprisingly, the food had appeal. Susan Langley was obviously a good cook. The meal outclassed its atmosphere by miles. "Enjoy," Albert said. Then he left.

"Lee Walker," the woman mused aloud. "That doesn't sound too bad." She took a bite of her food. "This is good. By the way, what do Jed and Lee Walker do for a living?"

"They're retired." Walker said.

"From what?"

"I haven't a clue," he admitted. "I haven't thought that far, besides, nobody's asked yet." He took a bite from his plate. "Excellent!" he said. Then they ate in silence. Albert came by their table once to refill their coffee cups, but otherwise left them alone.

When they had finished, Lee Walker suggested they go home and do whatever it is that old retired folks do in little mining towns, smiled at Jed, and stood. Jed, although he did not know what retired folks did in little mining communities or anywhere else, agreed to go do it anyway.

He rose laboriously and tried to reach for his cane. It still lay on the floor where it had fallen earlier. Lee silently walked to his side of the table and picked it up for him. She snatched its silver top, stuck it in Jed's jacket pocket, and handed the cane to him. She glanced at the painting on the wall, the likeness of the older, distinguished man with the dart in his eye.

Jed dropped money on the table, enough to cover the meal and a generous tip, and they left the café. The bright morning sun, after the cave-like darkness of Albert & Sue's, nearly stopped them. The attack had left him with only one working eye and a diminished tolerance for light. His head began echoing his heartbeat.

Lee Walker was not bothered by bright light. It was the rise in temperature that made her wish she could be wearing a spaghetti strap top like she wore before she had been left with the hideous scar above her heart. She hung tightly to Jed's arm and guided him to their car. "Who's the guy in the painting, the one with the dart in his eye?" she asked as she opened his door.

Jed Walker slid in behind the wheel and tossed the cane in the back seat. "My grandfather," he said.

Chapter Two

Jed Walker had come full circle like many folks, that journey that takes one from his roots to another seemingly foreign life out in a world that could not previously have been imagined. From there they travel through some mystic process in which all of life's secrets are taught and learned — handed down by the elders one encounters in this alter universe. Inevitably it all turns to bullshit and prompts the recipient to return to his roots. His story, however, is not like most other folks' — not at all. The reason his story is different is its beginning, those facts of his early existence that caused him to venture out. His return, none the less, had to come. It was nature. When one runs into trouble, serious trouble like Jed Walker ran into, one returns to his roots to either hide from or repair the damages caused by that trouble. Sometimes it's both.

Jed Walker had been born Arthur Fetchenko. He was born in the same northern Minnesota mining community where he and the love of his live, Lee Walker, ate this morning's breakfast. Lee was born Elizabeth (Liz) Harmon in New Creek, West Virginia. She would be the exception to the rule. She would never be able to return to her roots. Both of them would die if she did. Her new root in life would have to be for now and forever, Arthur Fetchenko's roots. There was no other avenue for either of them to take.

The story of Jed and Lee Walker is not one that can be told from beginning to end. Its complexities will not allow that. And it cannot be told starting with its whole ending. It must take up in the middle. It must start with Henry Tyler. After all, it was not only Jed and Lee Walker who suffered from the fate of Arthur Fetchenko and Liz Harmon. There were others, Henry Tyler among them.

* * *

Eight months earlier:

Henry Tyler contemplated suicide from the edge of his office chair while watching traffic roll by on the street three stories below. His father had done it. It was in him to take his own life. He carried the gene, if there was such a thing as a suicide gene. It was not common sense that was stopping him at this moment. It was fear. But that fear was not of death, after all wasn't that the purpose of suicide? It was fear of botching, of ending up a vegetable or worse.

He watched the little people and their little cars in the street. They seemed to scurry about without direction and reminded him of himself, of what he had become. He felt lost. "How did I let things come to this? How did everything get so far out of hand? Where did I lose control?" he asked himself aloud.

"Excuse me?" Susan Burton thought Henry had been addressing her as she entered.

"Oh! Ah... sorry, Susan." He turned to face his assistant. She was a slender, pretty blond in her mid thirties and Henry had hired her a year earlier largely for her looks. It had surprised him to learn she had talents which made her indispensable. "You caught me talking to myself again." It happened too frequent of late, ever since he heard his old friend, Arthur Fetchenko, was coming. "What is it, Susan?" he asked, still facing the window.

"It's time, Judge Tyler. Court is ready whenever you are."

He looked back at her. "I'll be just a minute, Susan. Thank you." She turned and left his office, and he directed his attention once more to the street below — his thoughts to how the little creatures and their tiny automobiles reminded him of himself. Then two cars collided in the intersection. "Figures," he said. He took aim at a slow-moving housefly that had been making its way across the window sill, snapped it with his thumb and middle finger into the air at rocket speed, and told it, "You would have died if I hadn't taken the screen out, you son-of-a-bitch." Then he rose and put on his robe. He would button it as he walked down the long hallway that took him from the safety of his office to the public eye, which awaited him on the other side of the courtroom doors. And as he arrived at those doors it occurred to him that he harbored resentment these days for the duties with which he had been charged. Or possibly it was with he who had charged him with those duties, Arthur Fetchenko. Maybe it was the combination that disillusioned him, the trio who so many years ago ran wild through the streets and back alleys of the little mining community. There was him and Arthur and the nephew of a Chicago-land gangster — an all but out of control young ruffian named Tony Copeletti. That was a bad combination then. It is a bad combination now, bad but powerful. Dangerous. Henry paused for a time outside the courtroom. It was during this quiet moment that he remembered he had seen Tony the other day walking along the street in front of the courthouse. Of course he had seen him as he saw everything else, from three stories up, so at the time he could not be confident it had been Copeletti. He knew now though — it had been him — and he also knew seeing him was responsible for his recent bout with depression. He leaned against the wall for a moment, drew a deep breath, and gathered his thoughts. "Too many memories," he said.

He was a tall man, six-foot-one, with thinning blond hair that he wore so short he was often mistaken for bald. Long hair, he had reasoned, made him appear ordinary, close cropped and he looked professional. His right eye drooped a bit from a poke he had taken from a tree branch during childhood, a flaw he didn't mind since he thought it added distinction, something valuable given his station in life. And the robe? Well... the robe was Superman's cape. And now as he smoothed wrinkles from it he vowed that he would demand an audience with Arthur Fetchenko as soon as this was all over, and he would break his ties as a member of that trio forever. He threw open the massive doors.

"ALL RISE!" the deep voice of the bailiff's rang out.

Henry Tyler took his position at the bench. He inventoried the room's occupants, a habit he had developed over the years, one that yielded specific results. It let him know that everyone who should be present was indeed present, it made him aware of anyone who was there who shouldn't be there, and it gave all of the courtroom's occupants a sense that the judge was in full control, not them. This morning he looked over the defendants' table — two defendants, two lawyers. Then he looked at the prosecutor's table. There were three, Mike Sweeney the prosecutor, Arthur Fetchenko, and Tony Copeletti.

Arthur Fetchenko had more than a casual interest in the case. One of his men, a Cherokee Indian named Jacob Rain was personally involved. Arthur was there for Jacob. And Tony Copeletti, well... he was where Arthur was — always. Henry Tyler was there because Arthur Fetchenko had ordered it, and he had done so to ensure that justice — the Fetchenko form of justice — was issued. Henry too, like it or not, worked for Fetchenko, and because he did, certain duties could and would be demanded of him from time to time. This was one of those times. Henry knew only too well that he was what he was and enjoyed the position in life that he now held because Fetchenko had handed it to him. For that he hated Fetchenko. But for the sake of history — his, Arthur's, and Tony Copeletti's — he loved Fetchenko. Henry Tyler lived with an internal struggle.

The case being tried was not the case of the century, although it did have its attractions. It was a history maker. The two defendants worked for the Wisconsin Department of Social Services and they were being tried for, well... really, for bad judgment. They made a poor call which resulted in a young man's drug addiction, which in turn led to a life of degradation ending in a horrible death, and all for a very wrong reason. And now, providing they lost of course, they were about to be held liable for their poor choice. But they would lose. That had been predetermined — by Fetchenko. The young man at the receiving end of their wrongdoing was Jacob Rain's only son.

Henry Tyler was torn — understandably so. There are many in his position who would have given a left nut to sit where he sat right now. History was about to be made. The future for all public employees would soon hold responsibility for their actions and decisions, and for the judge who sat in judgment over the verdict that was about to be handed down the future held a reputation as the common man's hero. Many a judge would envy him, but to them he'd say, "Have at it. I don't want it." And he would say that because the decision would not be passed by him; it would be passed through him. Imagine the wrong party getting a hold of the underlying truth of things here. It may take more than one nut to fix it, and Henry Tyler wanted to keep his — both of them. And there was that other thing — integrity. So long as Arthur Fetchenko passed judgment in Henry Tyler's court, Henry's was gone. Let someone else risk it. That was his take on it.

Henry looked over the remainder of the room. No Jacob Rain. Perhaps Arthur Fetchenko did not want him here. He thanked God for that. Rain could be unruly should any of this go wrong. To him, this would not be about government employees being responsible; it would be about his son — his dead son.

Tyler was surprised at the depth of preparation on the part of the prosecutor, and astonished the defense's lack in that area. He supposed the defense thought the case frivolous and that Tyler would throw it out anyway, and truthfully, there had come a time when Henry considered stopping the proceedings and demanding that the defense prepare, but a stern look from Arthur Fetchenko made him change his mind. In the end the trial unfolded in such a way that Henry Tyler made an important discovery. He learned that he and Arthur Fetchenko were in agreement concerning this case. These two public servants had overstepped their authority by miles, and they had broken the law on many plateaus in the process. You see, Jacob Rains' boy's mother was deceased, and although her new husband was never found guilty of any wrong doing, he had been a strong suspect in that investigation. The general consensus was that he had escaped prosecution on a technicality. However, a ton of evidence had been handed to the two public servants on trial, evidence that, in the opinion of Henry Tyler, demanded a close look at the stepfather regarding that incident as well as in his treatment of the dead teenager. The real icing on the cake though, came when it was told by one of the prosecution's witnesses, a white-haired lady named Beasley, her account of a conversation between the two defendants. Jacob Rain had paid them a visit to request their help in preventing more harm from coming to his only son. The conversation in question took place as soon as Rain departed. And Mrs. Beasley's account of it brought it into the light.

"What is it you do at the social services office Mrs. Beasley?" the prosecutor asked.

"I clean, Mr. Sweeney," she answered.

"Do you know who Mr. Rain is, Mrs. Beasley?"

"Yes Sir, Mr. Sweeney. He's that nice young Indian fella, one with the nasty scar runnin' down the cheek —

used to live over on Fourth Street. I've known him for years now, and I knew that boy of his before he died."

"Were you in the social services building when Mr. Rain visited the two defendants?" Sweeney asked her.

"Only one of them." she said.

"Excuse me?"

"Only one," she repeated. "He only saw one of them. That one there," she said as she pointed a long bony finger at the younger of the defendants. "Other one comes in after Mr. Rain left."

"Well, that's mighty interesting, Mrs. Beasley," the DA told her. "Can you tell the court what went on during that meeting?"

"Not much," she answered. "Mr. Rain was just telling what he knew about the boy's step-daddy and things, and about how he, Mr. Rain that is, knew that the man had something to do with the woman's death and all that. The man in the office, Mr. Thompson there," she pointed again in the direction of the defendants table, "he didn't say nothing at all, just uh-huh'd a bunch and let Mr. Rain do all the talking till the end when he said he'd look into the whole thing."

"Then what happened?" Sweeney asked.

"Why, Mr. Rain left," Mrs. Beasley said.

"I mean after Mr. Rain left the office. What took place in the office after that? Were you in the area? Were you close enough to hear what went on then?"

"Oh, yes. Well, Mr. Sweeney, I was close enough to do more than just hear what went on. I was all done cleaning out of the hallway and moved on to the office to clean the bathroom at the back of the office when that man," the bony finger shot towards the defendant's table once more, "Mr. Nellis there, come in to Mr. Thompson's office. I guess he didn't see me though, because he just started spouting off like an angry old tea kettle or something."

"And what did Mr. Nellis say to Mr. Thompson?" Sweeney asked Mrs. Beasley.

"Well none of it was nice," she said. "It was mostly foul language, nothing I can say out loud, front of all these folks."

"I'm afraid I need you to repeat what you overheard — exactly — in Mr. Thompson's office that day." Sweeney told her.

"I can't do that, Mr. Sweeney. The Lord will send me straight into the fires of hell if I was to start talking like that," she objected.

"Your Honor?" the DA begged Henry Tyler.

"Mrs. Beasley?" the judge said.

"But, Henry," she complained.

"Mrs. Beasley, you must tell the court what you heard," Judge Tyler instructed. Then he added just to comfort the old gal, "The Lord will allow it since it's for the sake of justice, Mrs. Beasley. I assure you."

"Are you sure?" she asked, a discerning eye aimed at Henry Tyler.

"Yes, Mrs. Beasley," Henry told her. "I'm positive."

"Well, ok then." She paused a long pause, drew a deep breath, then went on. "Mr. Nellis there said to Mr. Thompson, and this ain't me talking you understand, Mr. Sweeney, it ain't me."

"I understand," Sweeney told her. "Go on."

"Well, Mr. Nellis said he didn't want Mr. Thompson to go fuckin' 'round with any of Mr. Rain's affairs, to just ignore it all and let it go," she said, looking into her lap.

Sweeney checked with the members of the jury to be sure they had all heard the old woman, and then continued. "And what did Mr. Thompson say to that?"

"He said that there was no way," she looked Sweeney right in the eye, "there was just no way that he was about to help some useless, no-count, goddamn Indian and as far as he was concerned they should all be shipped back to the reservation where they belong. 'Let their own kind deal with their crap', is how he put it."

The two defendants, William Nellis and Arnold Thompson, along with the two attorneys who represented them, turned their heads in unison, almost robotically, in the direction of the jury. There sat five God-fearing matronly-appearing middle-aged women, the pastor of the First Baptist Church, and six other jurors of obvious Indian descent. All four of the occupants of the defendants' table realized at once that their case had been eternally lost.

A feeble attempt by one of the attorneys for the defense to dissuade the jury from returning with the inevitable guilty verdict, and the whole show was over. The jury adjourned to discuss the fate of the defendants. The bailiff dragged Nellis and Thompson to a holding cell in another part of the courthouse. The two defense attorneys retired to the cafeteria on the first floor where they would pitch in and buy Mike Sweeney a victory cup of coffee. Tony Copeletti, after a brief and private conversation with Arthur Fetchenko, left the courthouse to deal with some other affair. Arthur Fetchenko approached Mrs. Beasley, embraced her affectionately, and then sat her down for a quiet talk where they would catch up on old times. And Henry Tyler returned to his chambers where he would await the return of the jury and perhaps stare a bit more at the little creatures on the street beneath his window while he further contemplated suicide. He chose, since he knew Fetchenko would be in town for a few days this time, to delay his meeting with him, the one where he would detach himself from the two childhood chums who now seemed to control him and everything around him.

Chapter Three

Arthur Fetchenko rose at first light. A quick shower, a room service breakfast, and he was off to see Henry Tyler. He knew Henry would hold a grudge — he always did — but once he pushed him past feeling that his integrity had been compromised, something Henry constantly fretted over, he would settle down and they would both enjoy their visit.

Henry Tyler's office intimidated most who entered, but Arthur Fetchenko had always admired it for its ornate, turn of the century, rich wood paneling and full wall bookcases filled with leather bound volumes of law books and American classics. Henry's desk stretched wider and deeper than any other Arthur had seen, and was stained dark-walnut to match the rest of the wood in the huge room. As always, everything was polished to a foot deep shine. Henry had been, even when they were children, a neat-freak, and his office showed that he hadn't changed. A speck of dust — something out of place — unlikely in Henry's chambers.

Henry Tyler was parked in a wooden swivel chair, his back to the door as he gazed silently out his window when Arthur Fetchenko arrived. "I see you still got Senator Beckworth's old chair," Fetchenko said. The chair was one of Tyler's most treasured possessions. Beckworth had occupied it at the United States Senate from the age of twenty nine until he died of heart failure while sitting in it at the ripe old age of eighty four. He was Henry's uncle on his mother's side. Henry's big dream in life was that he

would one day take that chair back to the Senate and oc-
cupy it himself until he too, died in it.

"Morning Arthur," Henry said. "You know, you really should dump that aftershave. I can smell you coming
for miles."

"I see you're still your same cheerful self. Pouting?"

"Nope! Pissed," Henry Tyler said.

"Uh-oh. And what is it you're pissed about, or
shouldn't I even ask?"

"I'm pissed that my oldest and dearest friend doesn't
trust me to do my job, that he thinks I need watching, that
he thinks his place is to be screwing with the judicial system, that's what I'm pissed about."

"I wouldn't put it that way," Arthur said.

"Of course you wouldn't. You wouldn't be the great
Arthur Fetchenko if you did."

"Come on, old friend. You know what it is that we
do, and you knew it coming into the organization. I held
nothing from you then and I hide nothing now. We right
the wrongs, and yesterday we righted a wrong. That's all
that happened here," Fetchenko said. "Tell me I'm
wrong, Henry. Tell me we didn't right a wrong."

"Yes, but... we don't get this involved; we help the
proper people into power so they can right the wrongs —
not us."

"What's the difference, Henry? Who cares if we do
it or order it done by some limp-dick politician we put in
office? Who gives a shit, Henry? Long as it gets done."

"I give a shit." Henry knew the argument was lost,
and he also knew what he was getting into when he chose
to join his two childhood chums' battle against the injus-
tices of society. It had noble resonance to it then, and it
still does. But this was all new. Never before had any of
them taken this kind of action. Never before had any of
them taken any action, not personally. This case, though,
Henry Tyler had to admit if only to himself, Arthur
Fetchenko or no Arthur Fetchenko the decision would

have been the same. The two defendants were guilty, and worse than that where Henry was concerned, they were bigots. But still, "It was never personal before, Arthur. That's a line that should not have been crossed."

"We haven't had to before, Henry. I tried. We simply don't have the people in place for this sort of thing. But it was only time until it came down to this. You know that."

"Excuse me?"

"I said..."

"I know what you said. I just don't know where it's coming from. I thought our function was to help the right people get elected to office. I thought that they were, once in office, supposed to see to it that justice prevailed, not us."

"What's your real objection, Henry?" Fetchenko asked, tiring of the conversation. "Is it that the case involved Jacob Rain instead of a stranger? Because if it is, old friend, that's a piss-poor objection."

"Look, Arthur, tell me one thing and tell me straight. Are we expanding our parameters? Are we setting new boundaries to our operation?" Henry asked, his back still toward his guest.

"It's the logical next step, Henry."

"I should have left you in that reform school," he said. It was what he always said when he lost a battle with Arthur Fetchenko. The ancient senator's chair cried out in a squeal of protest as he swiveled to face his visitor.

Fetchenko straightened in his chair. He was not a big man, but he could intimidate. It came natural to him, and usually came involuntarily whenever Henry — or anyone else for that matter — mentioned reform school. His eyes, dark as coal, narrowed. His stare burned into Henry Tyler. Henry lowered his eyes.

"So what's next with this?" Henry asked.

"Whatever it is, you won't be here to see it. I need you back at the camp," he said. The Fetchenko outfit operated out of the east, from a secure compound buried in the mountains of West Virginia, near the little town of New Creek. Arthur always referred to it as the camp.

"I have a life here, Arthur," Henry Tyler protested. "I have a job to do. People around here depend on me."

"We'll get someone else to take over for you," Fetchenko promised, "someone good."

"But this is where I've lived for so many years," Henry insisted. "I hate to just pack up and leave. I've got roots."

"Oh come now, Henry. All you've been doing since Bess died is spending all of your spare time contemplating suicide." He watched the expression on his friends face turn from mild anger to shame. "Did you think you could hide that from me?"

Tyler remained silent.

"Henry, you need to come with me. I won't be able to live with myself if I leave you here and you wither away. Besides, I really do need you back east. Things are heating up."

"I should imagine it would with you stretching your powers like this. Who did you guys piss off with this one? Everyone?" Henry asked.

"Almost," Fetchenko said, "some, more than usual." There had been a recent movement among Arthur Fetchenko's critics to put limits on, or maybe even to put an end to, the growing influence he and his organization had on Washington. He was being pushed, and when pushed, Fetchenko always responded in kind.

"Who? Senators? Congressmen?" He studied Fetchenko's expression. "Not the White House!"

Fetchenko smiled. "I'm pretty sure. Word's out. We're looking at the presidency."

"Who you got in mind?"

"Jack Albrecht."

"That kid from New Mexico?" Henry knew who he was. He had worked with him two years before, when he began his career in politics. Albrecht was a different breed of politician: his ideas far from the status quo, his morals intact although thought to be marketable, his plan for the future as radical as those who founded this country, his resolve equal to those who fought so hard to take it away from England, and the real kicker, his backing exclusively Fetchenko. The kid was a shoe-in. All it takes is money, that and the backing of the right people. Fetchenko had money — lots and lots of it. And since most of Washington, the Democrats at least, were there through the assistance of Fetchenko's office, the kid would have backing. And the Republicans? Well... Albrecht is a Republican in the Democratic Party. Why wouldn't they back him?

"They'll kill you!" Tyler said.

"Well... that's the reason I need you."

"What am I supposed to do?"

"Find out who. Settle them down. Reassure them. Whoever's behind this, I'm betting they think we're trying to take their power away from them, and they're going to fight." It wasn't his entire plan for Henry Tyler, but, for now, it would do. Henry, brilliant that he was, tended to think things through a bit too much for Fetchenko. He would dole out information only as needed.

"Aren't we?" Tyler asked."

"Yeah, but, I don't want them to know it just yet, or, you're right, Henry — they'll kill me. The key will be in how well you sell Albrecht to them."

"You know what I see, Arthur? I see them killing me instead of you. That's what I see."

"Nah. I doubt it. We'll send you in as one of them." Fetchenko's untold plan was to get Henry Tyler's name in place on the ballot for United States Senator from his district in Wisconsin. It would be the same seat held by his uncle, Senator Beckworth. The chair, Henry's prize wooden swivel chair, would be going home. Arthur would see to it that Henry's competition for the office would be a nobody, an unknown without credentials. It should be a landslide like none other in history.

"Like a double agent," Henry said.

"If you insist," Fetchenko said.

"Not a chance. They kill double agents, too. Sometimes faster."

"Then we'd best have some protection for you. How about Copeletti?"

"Copeletti?" Tyler said. "Christ! I've never been around him when it didn't end in disaster. The son-of-a-bitch is a trouble magnet."

"Yeah. But you love him," Fetchenko said.

"That's because I have to," Henry said. "He's like a brother."

"I don't love my brother," Fetchenko said. He rose from his chair and began walking toward Henry's office door. "I'll see you at the mountain in a week, Henry. Take care."

"I'll be taking Bess with me," Henry Tyler insisted.

Fetchenko looked back at him. Henry was holding an urn under his arm. "Bring her," he said.

"And I'm bringing this too." Tyler shouted out as Fetchenko passed through the doorway out of sight. He dragged the old chair, screeching like a wounded cat, from behind the desk.

Arthur Fetchenko poked his head back into the office. "Only if you oil it."

Henry Tyler went back to his study of the little figures in the street below and allowed his mind to travel through his conversation with Arthur Fetchenko and the events of the past few days. Arthur was right. He did spend his time either working or contemplating suicide. That's no way to live, Henry, he told himself. Perhaps we do need a change. "Ah! What the hell," he said. "I can stay here and kill myself, or I can go to Washington and let a bunch of politicians do it for me."

* * *

The chopper's blades gained momentum; a rhythmic rocking signaled that the bird was lifting off. Arthur Fetchenko had not yet buckled in. Tony Copeletti reached a long, muscular arm out and slapped the pilot across the back of the helmet with a bear-like paw. Fetchenko's slight touch to Copeletti's forearm stopped him from hitting the pilot again. "I'm alright," Fetchenko said.

"Stupid son-of-a-bitch," Copeletti shouted at the pilots back. The pilot could not hear him, but a few seconds later turned to look over his shoulder, presumably to locate the origin of the smack. Copeletti flipped him a middle finger and yelled once more, "Stupid son-of-a-bitch!" The pilot smiled, apparently unable to read sign or lips.

"Let it go, Tony," Fetchenko said. The doors, powered by electricity and controlled by the pilot, began to close as the craft reached two stories from the ground. The high pitched whir of the engine and the whip, whip, whip of the blades gave way to quiet. "I hate takeoff — chopper ride's okay, but I don't like the takeoff." He leaned back in his seat and shut his eyes. The trip back to base camp would take several hours. It would serve as a good time for catching up on lost sleep. Arthur Fetchenko seldom left the estate; travel outside was dangerous — too many enemies, especially these days — therefore he didn't sleep on these outside missions. Home was nearly impenetrable. He'd sleep when he got back there. Tony Copeletti also gave up his rest on these excursions. Arthur was his responsibility and Tony, other than the occasional catnap, would remain awake until Arthur Fetchenko was safely tucked away within the walls of home, free from any danger.

* * *

Henry Tyler sometimes obsessed, his mind going trans-like, everything around him becoming opaque. Things he saw would be moving, yet, somehow remain still. His world would lose its depth. Today, as he watched the people below him in the street, he entered such a trance. His mind traveled backwards in time and seemed to take his body with it. He was a child again. He was ten years old and his father, who was a superintendent for the mining company, had moved him and his mother to a tiny town deep in the heart of iron mining country. For Henry, it was the edge of the universe. He knew no one. He was alone.

It was only through persistent prodding by his mother that young Henry ventured out to explore his strange new terrain, and had it not been for a mishap, he had tripped on a shoe lace sending him head-first into a mud puddle of the town's dirt main street — bloody nose and a black eye gained in the process — he might not have met the two onlookers who seemed amused by his misfortune. One of them was a skinny, dirty-faced, short Russian kid with the deportment of a strutting rooster, and the other was a husky Italian lad who, despite his generous height and weight advantage, seemed content following the smaller kid's orders. The Russian's name was Arthur Fetchenko, and the other boy was Tony Copeletti. They introduced themselves as the two guys who were about to kick the new kid's ass.

"Might as well," Henry said. "Nose is already bleedin'. Eye's killin' me. Can't hurt more than this."

Arthur smiled.

Tony Copeletti snatched Henry by his shirt collar, and dragged him to his feet. He drew a clenched fist back to let Henry have it. Arthur stopped him. "Leave 'im be," he said.

"Why?" Tony asked.

"'Cause I said so." Arthur brushed Henry off a bit. "You okay, kid?" he asked. He did not wait for an answer. "Who the hell are you anyway? Where did you come from? Wanna join our gang?"

"I'm Henry Tyler. I came here, just this morning, from Madison. That's a town over in Wisconsin. And no! I don't wanna join your gang. I don't wanna join no gang."

"Okay! Hit 'im, Tony."

"No! Wait a sec. Maybe I do wanna join. What's your gang do?" Henry asked.

"Nothin', really. We're just getting started. But we'll be doin' plenty, won't we, Tony?" He did not want or wait for a response from Tony. "I'm Arthur Fetchenko. This here's Tony Copeletti. He's a Wop."

"A what?" Henry quizzed.

"A Wop. A Ginzo. A Dago."

"A what?" Henry asked again.

"He means I'm Italian," Tony said. He narrowed his eyes and looked at Henry for a time. Then he warned, "Arthur here kin call me by those names, but don't you ever try it, cause I'll flat-out kill ya."

* * *

"Goddamn Dago," Henry said with a smile as he pulled himself back from his childhood.

"What?" Susan Burton asked as she entered Judge Tyler's chambers.

"Nothing, Susan. Come in. Tell me, Susan, how would you feel about going east?" Arthur Fetchenko was right. There wasn't much in his current life Henry Tyler could not do without, but Susan Burton? Now... her... he would miss.

* * *

The gentle vibration of the helicopter along with the rhythmic sound of its blades rotating overhead put Arthur Fetchenko in an almost coma-like sleep before the bird cleared Chicago. The smooth glide over Lake Michigan would pass unnoticed. The dream his extreme fatigue brought with it would not. It would take him back to a time he would just as soon forget, the days of a deplorable childhood spent in a tiny Minnesota mining town.

Chapter Four

Early fall held a chill. Darkness settled in, and along
with it — drizzle. Three boys slid into the bushes along-
side the entrance of the alley that lay between Colman's
Mercantile and the town's only filling station. It was once
the main path to the open mine pit that had, not so many
years before, provided virtually all of the little village's
income. But now, since the pit had filled with water and
the mining company was now extracting their ore at a location miles from this one, brush had taken over the alley
along with the three block long trail which once took
workers from their homes to their jobs. The boys' intention as they slipped into the bushes was to frighten the shit
out of the pretty young girl named Heidi Lang, who
would pass by at any moment on her way back from choir
practice at her father's church. She was who all of Arthur
Fetchenko's thoughts were about these days. The trio had
been together for three years now, Arthur and Tony and
Henry, and their interest in mischief had evolved into an
interest in girls, and Heidi Lang was the target Arthur had
zeroed in on. The noise they heard though did not come
from the direction Heidi would come from. It came from
behind them, deeper into the darkness. It was the sound
of a girl crying out for help and the sound of brush breaking under the pressure of a struggle. They did not know
who the girl was, or even that it was a girl for sure, and
they did not know who or what the attacker was. It could
have been man or beast. The boys hesitated. Then they
heard a man's voice — deep and eerie. But they could
not make out what he was saying. "Let's go!" Arthur said
quietly. Henry shot out of the brush and headed towards

the light of the street. Tony's fast hand landed in a firm grip on Henry's forearm and in one smooth movement swung him around and catapulted him down the dark alley toward the cries of the girl at breakneck speed. Tony Copeletti was large for his age, and strong from a long childhood of fighting off attacks from an abusive father. He sent Henry sailing past Arthur Fetchenko like a bullet. "Jesus, Copeletti," Arthur whispered, "don't kill the little son-of-a-bitch." He looked Henry over to see if he had been hurt. "You ok?" he asked. Then, after no reply, "Let's go. We gotta do something."

The three teens made their way through the thick brush, heading towards the sounds. Halfway between Main Street and the old mine the underbrush gave way to a clearing, an abandoned rail bed used nowadays by the town's youngsters as a path to take them to the water-filled mine — their swimming hole. Across the clearing from the boys lay a narrow path, beaten down from the constant summer travel of kids to the reddish-brown iron ore covered shoreline they called their beach. It was at the path's beginning they saw the girl and her attacker. He carried her, her long hair dragging the ground, her slight body limp, her clothing, what little there was of it, tattered. Henry began to sob. Tony covered his mouth. "Shh!" Arthur cautioned. Then he led his two companions down the edge of the opening, the dense brush keeping them hidden. They would go past the trail to another path only they knew of, for they had cleared it themselves early in the summer. It led to the edge of a bluff that overlooked the pit, a place where they could watch — unnoticed — skinny-dipping young girls; their summer's most cherished pass-time.

* * *

Turbulence dropped the helicopter abruptly. The air pocket's bottom felt like stone. Fetchenko snapped out of his dream. "Jesus Christ!" he shouted. "What the fuck did we hit?" He wiped a thin line of saliva from the corner of his mouth.

"Sorry, Mr. Fetchenko," the pilot said, "a bit of dead air. That's all." He gave his instrument panel a quick once-over to be certain it was only that.

"Can I kill him now?" Copeletti leaned in and asked Fetchenko.

The pilot joined them a few months before. Fetchenko thought there had been far more of these little disturbances since he signed on; the ride was always rough. "No!" he told Tony, "but you can fire him as soon as we get back."

"Assuming we get back." Copeletti said. Then he leaned back in his seat to relax. Arthur Fetchenko did the same. He would sleep, and he would dream his dream, the one he always dreamed when he flew. It was as though an evil serpent, an impiety from the past, lurked in the clouds. He knew that was where it lived because it was the only place it chose to show itself. So sleep would come, and along with it the dream serpent. It always did.

* * *

The moon, full and bright, pushed its way through the parting clouds just as the trio reached the bluff over-looking the lake's shoreline. Their view of the lifeless, pale girl and her assailant became frighteningly visible. "Fuck, Arthur," Henry Tyler whispered. "That's your grandfather."

The only grandparent Arthur Fetchenko knew was his grandfather on his father's side. He was a cruel, vulgar, aggressive man for whom Arthur harbored absolute hate. Most others around, however, loved and respected him — placed all of their hopes for the future in him. This was an age when the unions and the companies were bitter enemies on most planes, but where Thaddeus Malcolm

Frank was concerned, these two powerful enemies had become allies. Thaddeus Frank was the name he chose because his original, Fetchenko, was a tag placed on poor Russian immigrants with too many snotty-nosed and unintelligent children who tended to live a sub-common life in some shanty on the graces and charity of their betters. He considered himself far above all of that, so needed a name that set him apart from his humble beginnings. The party had seen value in him a couple of years before and began then to groom him to be the next governor of the state. He was the first candidate for that office that the party ever received support for within the powerful and respected mining companies. And even though he had been approved by the wealthy, the union also backed him. With both sides behind him, he became a shoe-in and the party's crown jewel. And this was election year.

Tony Copeletti was a bit on the clumsy side. Thaddeus Frank's head whipped around as though it was spring loaded when he heard the snapping twig under Tony's size eleven shoe. "You little shits!" he shouted as he spotted his three onlookers. He recognized Arthur immediately, and assumed the other two with him would be the Copeletti kid and Tyler, the mine's super's useless little urchin. "You little spying sons-a-bitches!" He wielded around and released his grip on the girl. He was a strong man, and when he let go of the girl's body, she sailed through the air and landed in the water with a splash that sent ripples in a circle that seemed to spread out to forever. Thaddeus Frank disappeared into the thick underbrush immediately, and the three boys bounced frantically down the steep slope and pushed on to the shoreline.

Arthur Fetchenko dove into the brisk fall water without regard for his own safety, thinking only about the girl, wondering if she were still alive. It would be only moments before he would be back on shore, her stretched across his lap, him looking down into her open eyes, shaking violently, not from the cold, from the tears. It was Heidi Lang. She was dead. Henry took off his heavy flannel shirt and handed it to Tony. Tony placed it on Arthur's shaking shoulders. Arthur snatched it from his shoulders and spread it over all that it would cover of his young love's lifeless corpse. He cried more. He cried for a long time.

Tony Copeletti dragged his friend to his feet after he took the girl from him and gently laid her on the ground. "We better go get some help," he said. "We better go see the sheriff." He waited a minute for Arthur to lead the way, then when Arthur made no attempt to move, Tony grabbed his arm and guided him towards the path his grandfather, young Heidi's murderer, escaped down thirty minutes earlier. "Come-on," he said.

The boys made their way to the sheriff's office and found it empty. They began to panic. "What do we do now?" asked Arthur. "We can't go to my folks." Arthur was a part of his family his family did not want, and he had always known that. His older brother they treated like royalty, even the cruel, hateful grandfather. But Arthur was different; he was an embarrassment. He had been a bed wetter, an unforgivable crime. It hadn't been that way until he was five when he was run over by a car, its front tire rolling over his midsection causing damage to his kidneys. It left him unable to make it through most nights without wetting his bed. But Arthur also had a sister, and his sister sided with him, leaving her on the outs with the rest of the family. Still, Arthur distanced himself from her, not because of her, because of how his parents punished him for his weak bladder. They made him wear her dresses if he wet his bed, and now, shear embarrassment keeps him from becoming close to her. Tonight, though, she was all he had. But what good would she be? Laura was only two years older than he. She would not know what to do. And what if his grandfather was there? He was Arthur's foremost trouble in life and had been as long as he could recall, for it had been his own grandfather, Thaddeus Malcolm Frank, who had been the driver of the car that altered five-year-old Arthur Fetchenko's life in the first place. "My folks won't help us."

"We could go see my dad," Tony Copeletti offered. His father had made a fortune during the war, his venture — the illegal sale of meats. Rationing took place as soon as the United States entered the war, and Tony's father capitalized. He sold his product, beef mostly, to anyone with money, with or without ration stamps, at prices tantamount to extortion. The family prospered. Families with children paid for it. His store in town and a farm in the country he worked with precision. He knew who did and who did not have ration stamps, and used the information advantageously, dodging the law by moving from location to location as they closed in, pretending to speak only Italian if they got too close, punishing anyone who turned him in by refusing to sell to them, stamps or not. A couple of hungry families and no one dared to turn him over to the law again. But as the war came to a close, so did his venture; his store fell, then he fell. He became a drunk who quickly burned up all of his ill-gotten gains on liquor. He took to beating his family and it fell apart. Tony's older sister ran away after rumor that her father had assaulted her, sex as his motive. Mrs. Copeletti, tired of it all, ran off with a salesman. Life, for Tony Copeletti, became fights with his father on the downside, his friendship with Arthur and Henry in the upside. His family reputation destroyed all hope of ever being respected or even liked by any of the local citizenry.

"Bad idea, Tony. I think we better go see my dad," Henry Tyler suggested. Warren Tyler, Henry's father, a relative newcomer to the north, was as much a misfit as the three boys. His crime, being a mining company supervisor rather than common like everyone else, put him on the outs with most folks. Upper class, that's what the Tylers were despite the fact that Warren was the only super in the town's rather small mine, did not mix with the lower class. They did not live near the labor class. They lived above, their homes built high on a hill overlooking all others, an age-old custom, but one still practiced. The Tylers lived a lonely life legislated by circumstance born of a social class system, a plight they suffered alone. Henry's parents, however, refused to project it onto their son. They allowed Henry's close companionship with the two other misfits of the town, Arthur Fetchenko and Tony Copeletti, simply because to do otherwise would have left their son with no one, alone like them. Besides, Warren Tyler saw within Arthur Fetchenko something his family, or any of the rest of the little town for that matter, neglected to see. He saw in the boy, great value, the future. And within Tony Copeletti he recognized an uncommonly ardent sense of loyalty. "My dad will help us."

The three boys agreed. Henry's father was their only hope. They would take their case to Warren Tyler.

The long steep hill that led to the Tyler place, with the heavy load of the girl's death weighing like an anvil on Arthur Fetchenko's young mind, seemed like a walk to the gallows. Yes, Mr. Tyler was hope, and in common troubles this would have eased his mind, but deep inside he knew that this night's trouble would be a lasting trouble. A girl was dead. This was not standard trouble, and Arthur knew there was more to come.

"I gotta get a hold of my uncle," Tony Copeletti said as they reached the halfway point in their climb. "I just got a feelin'."

"You got it, too?" asked Arthur.

"Got what?" Henry asked.

"The sense everything ain't gonna be okay," Arthur said.

"That's the one!" Tony said.

"Bullshit!" Henry insisted. "My dad can fix this." Henry had an advantage the other two boys did not have. He believed. He had parents who loved him, and who he

could trust. "You'll see," he said as they climbed the steps
to the front door. "You'll see."

Inside, the boys were met by the grim and sober face
of Warren Tyler. "Come on, boys," he told them. He led
them to a sitting room. Tom Hayes, the sheriff, sat glaring
at them from a chair in the corner of the room. In another corner sat Mr. Michael Phalen, Henry's father's immediate supervisor who had been in town on mining
company business. The stern look from his too-pinched
face sent shivers down the boys' necks. Leaning against a
wall was short, round, bearded man named Charlie John-
son. He was a union leader, and looked out of place in
this company. His presence told the boys the situation
was even more serious than they thought it might be. Arthur looked over his shoulder at Tony, and what Tony
saw in his friend's eyes told him it was time to make his
exit, that to do otherwise, to stay in this company, would
lead to trouble he would not be able to handle. He quietly
slipped from the room.

And there, behind Mr. Tyler's desk, his face buried
in his hands, his body shaking with the tears of grief spew-
ing forth as testimony to the deep pain of knowing his
grandson could do such a thing, that his own blood could
sink to rape and murder, was none other than Thaddeus
Malcolm Frank, the Party's, the mining company's, and
the union's hopeful for the next Governor of Minnesota.

Just as Arthur and Henry were escorted to a room
across the hall to the company of Henry's mother, another man entered through the front door. "Where is he?"
the man asked.

"Who is that?" Henry asked his mother.

A tear came to her eye. "That's Walter Dale," she
told him. "He's the leader of the local Democratic Farm
Labor Party."

"God damn it, Thaddeus. You got any idea how
much money went into your campaign. The election is in

the bag, now this. Has any one of you got an idea how we get around this?" he asked of all in the room.

Everyone looked across the hallway, at the room Arthur and Henry were in. Then the sheriff closed the door to Warren Tyler's study.

Henry, Arthur, and Henry's mother, stared at one another, Henry eyes filled with question, Arthur's with fear, and Mrs. Tyler with pity and doubt, pity for Arthur's plight because she knew the men in her husband's study would sacrifice Arthur for his grandfather's career, and doubt about hers and her son's future, because she knew that all of this was about to change it drastically. The Company, the Union, the Party; none of them was going to let the Tyler's become a liability. At best, they would have to relocate.

She was right on all counts. In the end, Arthur was charged with the crimes of his grandfather. Tony disappeared into the night to find his uncle who would take him in and save him from all of this, and Tony would carry with him always, the guilt of deserting his best friend in the dark of night like a coward. Henry would return to a life before Arthur Fetchenko and Tony Copeletti, and his family would leave the little town for a mandated new position with the company in another place. Warren Tyler's new job came with a substantial raise in salary in return for his cooperation with the company, the union, and the Party, and an undying remorse capable of causing him to eventually take his own life.

Arthur's trial would be swift, his guilt predetermined, and he would spend the remainder of his childhood in a reform school. Then, at the age of eighteen, the full price for his grandfather's sins was to be demanded from him. Thaddeus Malcolm Frank would become the next Governor of Minnesota and have a long and prosperous political career, but he would always know, deep within his black heart, that he had ruined the lives of many to get to a place he would know as a personal prison, no less confining than the one he had sent his grandson to, or the grave to which an innocent young girl was condemned.

Chapter Five

Dusk arrived with the chopper's descent into the man-made crater in a mountain near New Creek, West Virginia. The one time military installation, built originally as a secret location from which missiles could be launched in the event of an attack by Russia during the cold war, served Fetchenko and his people well. Arthur often found it humorous that a post for defending the country from the Russians was now occupied by a Russian. It was secure, more secure than the standard installation because it had been built into a mountain and had only two entrances, one by helicopter and the other by ground via a well concealed and heavily guarded tunnel through nearly a quarter-mile of rock and earth. At the bottom of the chopper's descent lay the courtyard of Fetchenko's estate. Tony Copeletti was on the job scanning every inch of the surrounding cliffs and the ground below for danger until the bird was safely landed.

Fetchenko opened his eyes as they touched down. He looked outside. Drizzle, he thought, the French Poodle of weather, more annoying than useful. Just rain and get it over with.

"Ready, Boss?" Copeletti asked, an overgrown smile on his face.

"You're lovin' this, aren't ya?" Fetchenko commented. Tony somehow seemed to derive pleasure from seeing Arthur drenched. Fetchenko watched him as he came around the helicopter and pulled the door open.

Tony popped an umbrella open and held it over Arthur's head. "Wouldn't want you to melt," he said.

Then he turned to the pilot. "I want you in the security office," he said. He didn't believe in putting off his duties. The pilot and his less than adequate skills would be history — in short order.

"I need to inspect the bird," the pilot said.

"As soon as you're done — in the security office," Copeletti said. He and Fetchenko began a dash for the ground level door to the courtyard, a door that led directly to security.

Inside, Arthur and Tony came face to face with Liz Harmon, a beautiful red-haired woman wearing tight fitting blue jeans, bare feet, a white spaghetti strap top, and a white baseball cap with a pony tail sticking through the its Velcro adjustment strap. She kissed Tony Copeletti's cheek simply because it seemed to embarrass him and she did so enjoy embarrassing him, then she threw her arms around Arthur's neck. "Welcome home, Boys," she said. "Come on. Dinner's ready."

"You two go ahead," Copeletti said. "I have something to take care of."

She and Arthur took an elevator to the second floor where offices and living quarters were located. Tony's guys were quartered on the ground floor, along with the security station, a parking garage, and the tunnel to the New Creek side of the mountain. The tunnel's outside access was through a garage-like room off the back of a little café called Ralph's Place, a building which used the mountain as its rear wall. Anyone who wished to leave the estate did so through Ralph's. But for Liz, Ralph's was a godsend. She often walked the tunnel and lunched or just had coffee there. She had been a local and had friends and some scattered family throughout the hills, and Ralph's was someplace where she could make a call and meet up with one of them. It saved her from being homesick. When she and Arthur became involved, Tony Copeletti nearly had a fit. She was a danger. Anyone who was close to Fetchenko was a danger. History had proven that. He had lost a wife to his enemies, and a child. So... since she chose a relationship with Arthur, Tony made the outside world an off limits condition of that choice. Liz Harmon had Arthur Fetchenko, the compound staff, the courtyard, and Ralph's place. That was her world.

"What's Tony got to do that's so urgent," she asked as the elevator came to a stop. "Kill somebody? I'm only asking because he looks too happy." She knew who Tony Copeletti was and what he was. She did not know all of the details, but she did know that Tony's uncle was a mobster from Chicago, and that at an early age, somewhere in his teen years, Tony had run off from the little Minnesota mining town where he and Arthur and Henry Tyler all grew up together, and went to live with his uncle, the Chicago mobster. She also knew that Tony was tough, extremely loyal to those he loved, and could unconditionally justify killing.

"No," Fetchenko said. "He just gets to fire somebody."

* * *

Hours east of New Creek a meeting took place in the back room of a little pub called *The Freedom Hill Speakeasy*, its name since prohibition days. It was a quaint, worn down wooden floored establishment, that served as the favorite meeting place of a small but influential group of senators, congressmen, and other political celebrities who called themselves 'The Veterans of Power', not because they were ex-military although some of them were, but the name was more a testimony to their long years of government service. The purpose of this meeting was to discuss how best to stop Fetchenko. He had overstepped this time.

Fetchenko was needed when this all began, him and his group a valuable tool to the Party, finding and shaping the right candidate for any office, then mentoring and grooming so that they would not only get the vote, they would serve the Party precisely how the Party wished. They all knew they were handing a converted enemy power beyond reason, but they felt the necessary controls were in place and the proper eyes were on him.

But someone had stopped watching, and while they were not watching, Fetchenko moved up and out of the reach of the Party. And now, rumor had it, he was all but in with the Republicans. Soon the whole of Washington, and many of the states, would owe their successes to Fetchenko. Frosting? America had become tired of the Democrats in the Oval Office. It happened — like clockwork. Two or three terms by one party and it was the opposition's turn. No mystery! But the right candidate had to be in place, and Arthur Fetchenko had the right candidate. And that candidate was for sale. The price? The same 'in' with the Republicans as he enjoyed with the Democrats. Yes! Arthur Fetchenko had to go. And this group of old-timers would see to it that he did.

"We should have gone further," Daniel Davidson, Senator from Ohio said. His comment came at the end of the conversation about Warren Tyler, Henry Tyler's father, and how he had hanged himself.

"And what should we have done?" Pat Ferelli, Minnesota Senator and Fetchenko's chief enemy asked.

"What we did to his old man." The reality was Warren Tyler hadn't hanged himself. These men had hanged him, or at least sanctioned it.

"We didn't do anything to his old man," Ferelli said, and looked around the room to see if they were being listened in on. "Besides, it's not Henry Tyler we have to deal with. It's Arthur Fetchenko. Henry's not a danger. He's one of us, or I hear he soon will be. Old man Tyler had it coming. Henry was just a kid. He didn't do anything."

For Warren, it had been his punishment for the aiding of convicted — not guilty, just convicted — murderer,

Arthur Fetchenko. Tyler had helped Arthur gain his freedom from reform school and had provided him with information which kept him from facing further charges in
the case of the young girl's rape and murder in his teen
years. That same information came in handy for use
against the Party later. In effect, Warren Tyler had sponsored blackmail and that's why he had to go. "Henry's
bidding for the seat his uncle, Alvin Beckworth, once
held. Hell... that should please you, Davidson."

"And why is that?"

"The last four who held that office, Beckworth being
the first of them, died while holding it. Henry Tyler will
probably follow that same tradition," Ferelli said and
grinned.

"I still don't see why we can't get rid of Henry Tyler," Michael (Mac) McArthur, congressman from Ten-
nessee, threw in.

"We got us a naïve one," Ferelli laughed. "You don't
kill a man like Henry Tyler — too many friends — too
high profile — all but in office already. Messing with him
will bring all of Washington down on us. Now Arthur
Fetchenko, he's another story. That's where we need
place our efforts. We take care of that problem and our
troubles are over."

"We all agree on that, but what makes you think we
can get rid of Arthur Fetchenko and not Henry Tyler?"
Victor Parker, D.F.L minority leader asked.

"Fetchenko's had so many looking to snuff him out,
nobody's going to know who got to him, and nobody's
going to care," McArthur said. "You might think he's got
friends, but make no mistake. A man helps others into
office, and then demands favors. That man didn't make a
friend. He's made another enemy. That's the way that
works."

"KILL THEM BOTH!" insisted the boisterous
Colonel Randal (Fergie) Ferguson, retired Army and avid
party loyalist who headed up security for this little group.

"Christ, Fergie. Keep your voice down," Parker demanded.

"You can't just kill everyone, Colonel. Weren't you paying attention?" Mac McArthur asked.

"I can kill anyone I wish," Ferguson said.

"All right! That's enough. Let's all just calm down, do some serious thinking, and at my dinner party we'll choose the how and when," Ferelli said. "Keep in mind though, the 'when' needs to be prior to his man taking the Whitehouse."

* * *

Tony Copeletti entered Arthur Fetchenko's quarters without knocking. His somber look told Arthur something was wrong.

"You okay?" Liz asked him.

He stood still and silent.

"Tony?" Fetchenko said. "What is it?"

"Two things, Boss."

"Well... let me have them."

"Sources tell me Ferelli, McArthur, Davidson, Parker, and that crazy Colonel, what's his name?"

"Ferguson?"

"Yeah, Ferguson. They're meeting tonight. Gonna come at us again."

"Well... that's nothing new. Henry will be here in a couple days. He can deal with them. Now, what else?"

Tony Copeletti bowed his head.

"What is it, Tony?" Fetchenko asked. He put a hand on Tony's shoulder.

"It's your sister ... Laura ... she's dead, Arthur. I'm so sorry."

Chapter Six

Nicole Carson stood in the rain and said goodbye to her mother. She silently scolded herself, *What a fool I've been.* It was a stupid argument, one they shouldn't even have had. Her mother had been right. She always was. But Nicole had that ridiculous pride and a stubborn side neither of them understood. But the fact was, they fought, she got pissed and took off, and now it was too late. Her mother was being laid to rest and she hadn't come home in time to say goodbye. So now her sorrows and her tears mixed with rain and slid down her cheeks unnoticed.

Eight years she had been with the D.A.'s office, since before she graduated law school, and she had been pleased with her career. Her mother had been proud. Judge Tyler, the most influential man in her life, had been proud of her. She even came to expect great things of herself, maybe even becoming the D.A. one day. Then that trial came along, that Rain thing, that whole mess involving the social services people, people she had known and worked with — her friends. Some powerful somebody comes along, hard-on for them or the system — maybe both — and that was that. *And Judge Henry Tyler, why him, why is he on board with this?* It had all been questions, unanswered, but without answers it was something she could not condone in all good conscience. Nicole Carson felt she had been right but wished she hadn't taken the steps she took. It had been the catalyst to the heated argument that separated her from her mother. And being right hadn't been worth the silence between them.

Henry Tyler stood beside her, supporting as much as she would allow. Uncle Henry, as she had grown up to know him, wasn't really her uncle, but he had played the role since she was in diapers. She wished things were different, that she could feel grateful for his presence now, but how could she. They had taken opposite sides. Maybe Uncle Henry could shut that off but she couldn't. She pulled away from him — chose to mourn alone.

A limo pulled to the curb along the edge of the cemetery and two giants in dark suits and sunglasses stepped out, one moving to the car's front and the other to its rear. There they stood — soldier like — all attention on the street. Nicole watched as two more men got out of the limo. The first, a rather large and muscular man (he too in black), dwarfed the second man, but the second man — she couldn't put her finger on it, perhaps it was simply the way he carried himself — most assuredly dominated this odd pair. She moved closer to Henry Tyler. "Who's that?" she whispered.

"He'll be at the house later," Henry told her. "I'll introduce you."

The preacher stopped his graveside sermon briefly as the new arrivals approached. The smaller man, the one apparently in charge, walked directly to Nicole and Henry. He shook Henry's hand. Henry nodded. Then he kissed Nicole on the cheek, and then he moved to the other side of the coffin, next to his huge partner. The reverend smiled and resumed his sermon.

"To God we commend the soul of this fine woman," the preacher said. "We shall miss her — always."

* * *

A small group joined Nicole at her mother's modest home, among them, the strangers from the cemetery. The big man walked through the entire home. "Security check?" Nicole asked Henry Tyler.

"Probably," he said.

"Are you going to tell me who he is?"

"His name is Tony Copeletti," Henry said, gesturing at the big man.

"No, the other one."

Just then the other stranger approached. "Arthur Fetchenko," he announced. "It's good to see you again, Nikki. It's been a long time. Your mother was a good woman. I owe her a great debt."

Nikki, she thought. *It must have been a long time. No one's called me Nikki since I was a little girl.* "Well, it'll be a little tough to repay her now, won't it, Mr. Fetchenko?" she responded without thinking. "I'm sorry," she quickly added. "That was rude. It was entirely uncalled for."

"Understood." Fetchenko said bluntly. "Go! Entertain your guests. We'll talk later."

"Forgive my curiosity," Nicole said, "but, who are you?"

"Fetchenko," he said. His eyes took on a hard gaze. "I thought I told you that."

Nicole Carson was not average. This son-of-a-bitch, whoever he was, was not going to make her back down. "That's not what I meant," she pressed. "Are you on old friend of my mother's, a business acquaintance?"

"Both." He smiled. "Your mother and I had some business dealings over the years, and we knew each other since we were kids."

"Are you from Minnesota Mr. Fetchenko?" She asked, remembering that her mother had talked of her early days in mining country.

"I was," he admitted, "but that was a long time ago."

Satisfied that she had not backed down, Nicole excused herself and moved on to attend to some of her other guests. From across the room, between pleasant conversations with a couple of her mother's neighbors, she pondered Fetchenko for a long moment. He was rugged yet sophisticated. From this distance the length of his hair looked right for him, not too long at all, and the hint of gray at the temples seemed to lend him an air of regency. He had high, strong cheekbones — Indian maybe. His slender nose showed signs of having been broken. He was broad shouldered for his height, and good postured. As she studied him she felt someone close in on her. She turned quickly and gasped audibly as she came face to chest with Tony Copeletti.

"Impressive, ain't he?" Copeletti said.

"Who?" she asked.

"The Czar," Tony said.

"Who?" she asked.

"The guy you been watchin'."

"Did you say...Czar?"

"Yeah."

She smiled in amusement. "Czar of what?" she asked.

"The whole freaking world," Tony said. "At least he will be one day."

Nicole smiled. She found him easy to be with. It was like talking to a huge puppy dog. He made her feel comfortable and safe. She didn't quite understand how, but that's the way he made her feel. She laughed out loud and stuck her arm through his. "Did you get some cake, Mr....?"

"Copeletti," he announced. "Tony Copeletti at your service, and no, I haven't had any of your cake. But I will, Miss Nikki, that is, if you're offering."

"Come," she said. "I'll fill you with sweets. Then you can tell me all about this Czar of yours." She guided him to a chair, and then brought him cake and coffee. "Now... just who is this Mr. Fetchenko? Is he an old friend of my mother's? Perhaps a business acquaintance?"

"Nah! None of those. He's her brother."

Nicole was taken aback. To the best of her knowledge, her mother had no siblings. "She never mentioned a brother."

"Not talkin' 'bout 'em don't make 'em not exist," he said with a smile.

"So... you're telling me I have an uncle," Nicole said.

"Not exactly." Copeletti said. He stood. "Gotta go check on my guys." And he was gone.

She looked, again at Fetchenko. He had been talking with her mother's next-door neighbor while Copeletti held her attention with conversation. Her gaze? Puzzled.

Evelyn Randolph, the neighbor, saw Fetchenko's smile fade. "What is it, Arthur?" she asked.

"I think Tony said something to her, something he shouldn't have."

"Like what?"

"Like who I am, or who she is, or both... I don't know. But from the look on her face, I'd best find out."

Evelyn looked at Nikki. "You're right. Let's go."

"Nicole, dear, I'm so sorry," Evelyn said as she cradled Nikki in her arms.

Nicole looked at Fetchenko. "Are you my uncle?"

"I... Ah..."

"Oh, for Christ sakes, Arthur. Don't beat around the bush. Tell her. She should have been told years ago and you know it. I don't know why Laura didn't," Evelyn Randolph scolded. She looked into Arthur's eyes. They told her he wasn't prepared. She turned to Nikki, held her by her shoulders at arm's length and said, "Nicole, Arthur Fetchenko is your father."

"Hah!" Nicole said, "You're kidding, right?"

"No. She's not," Fetchenko said.

Nicole Carson stared for a moment, first at Fetchenko, then at Evelyn Randolph, then back to Fetchenko. "I... ah... have to see to the other guests. Excuse me."

Tony Copeletti approached from behind Fetchenko, put a huge arm around him, and said, "Good job."

Fetchenko spun out of the big man's grasp and said, "Fuck you!"

Copeletti chuckled and walked away.

For the next hour Arthur Fetchenko saw Nicole Carson only briefly, at a glance. She busied herself talking to each of her guests and fellow mourners one at a time, thanking them for having attended her mother's funeral, and listening to their recollections of how good Laura Carson had looked in her casket, and what a nice job Nicole had done in picking out her mother's burial outfit. One of them, an elderly, outspoken neighbor who fed herself at least once a week by attending the funeral of someone she may or may not have known, actually had the audacity to suggest that Laura looked more alive in the coffin than she had in months. The ridiculous statement brought tears of laughter to Nicole's eyes, which brought a frown to the face of the audacious old bitch. While averting her eyes to avoid more laughter, or popping the old broad in the chops, whichever her roller-coaster of emotions might require of her, Nicole noticed that Fetchenko was sitting all alone in one corner of the room. She would take the opportunity to clarify.

"So... how is it you know Evelyn?" she asked Fetchenko.

"We were engaged, many years ago."

"Really! What happened?"

"Same thing that happened to you and me — my job. I do dangerous work. It started to overflow in yours and Evelyn's direction. That's all."

"So you threw us both over for your job. Is that it?"

"It's not that simple, Nikki," Fetchenko said.

"Nicole," she corrected. "What's not that simple? Why not just switch jobs?"

"I don't have a job you can just walk away from. It's complicated."

"What are you? Mob?"

"Much worse than that... politics," Fetchenko said.

His answer brought out a brief smile. "There. That wasn't so complicated, was it?"

He guessed it wasn't... that is if the girl was content in not knowing the details of his work. "I suppose not." When she made no further attempt at conversation, he asked, "We alright with this?"

"For now," she said.

"Where'd Evie go?"

Nikki Carson pointed. Evelyn was on her way to them, Tony Copeletti following behind. Just feet from them, Copeletti tapped her on the shoulder. "Evelyn Reynolds, the love of my life, aren't you a sight for sore eyes?" he said as she turned.

"Why, Tony Copeletti," she said. "I hardly recognized you. You've changed."

"It's old age, Darlin', just old age."

"Well it looks good on you. The older you get, the sexier you get," she said. She threw both arms around his muscular neck and hugged him hard.

With an ear-to-ear smile he glanced toward Nicole and winked. "When you're young, you hate liars. When you get a little older you learn to appreciate them."

Evelyn Reynolds hooked an arm through Tony's, and then turned to face Arthur Fetchenko. "Still writing poetry, Arthur?" She asked.

"No. Not anymore." He answered. "I leave all of that to the pros these days, guys like Bob Dylan." He smiled.

"*Go away from my window,*" she began to sing. "*Leave at your own chosen speed.*"

"I deserve that." He admitted. Then he changed the subject. "I was sorry to hear about Oscar, Evelyn," he offered.

"I thought you might have come to his funeral, Arthur," she scolded. "He was once a good friend of yours too."

"I gave it thought," he said. "I just felt it might be inappropriate at the time, especially considering that it hadn't been all that long since, well, you know, our little thing." She and Arthur, aside from having once been engaged (pre-Oscar, of course), had tried again to make their relationship coexist with Arthur's job at a time when it had looked like Evelyn and Oscar were over with.

"Our little thing?" she said indignantly. "For Pete's sakes, Arthur, call it what it was. It was an affair. Lots of folks have them."

He wondered briefly how things might have been, and then said, "So... still hot for me?"

"You bet your ass I am," she said. She reached over and grabbed both of his cheeks between her thumb and forefinger and pinched. "Always!"

"Let's take a walk," Fetchenko suggested, "just you and me."

"Not a chance, Boss. I'll be goin' along," Copeletti said.

"Then you stay back. Don't want you listening in."

* * *

Two blocks of silence in the fresh evening air, and silence gave-way to conversation, Evelyn initiating. "Do you have someone, Arthur?"

"There's a lady... back at the estate." The place had been the problem between them, Evelyn's need for freedom, her uneasiness at the thought of being a shut-in at the estate.

"I'm happy for you. I'm also a bit jealous." She pulled closer to him. "Is she nice?" *What a stupid question, Evelyn. Of course she's nice, or Arthur wouldn't be with her.*

Arthur smiled. "You turned me down. Remember?"

* * *

Tony Copeletti saw a glimmer of light from the alley ahead. "Time to go, Kids," he said as he clutched Fetchenko's shirtsleeve and wielded the couple around. "Vinny," he called to Vincent Gotto, one of his soldiers. "In the alley." Copeletti made a circling motion with a finger to let him know to approach the intruder from behind, and then grabbed himself first on one wrist, then the other — code for capture, not kill. "We'll head back."

* * *

"Colonel," Newton Ridgeway spoke softly into a cellular phone.

Vinny Gotto stopped abruptly. He listened.

"You were right. Fetchenko did go to the woman's funeral," he said. Then, "Will do, sir." He flipped the cell-phone closed and the light went out.

Gotto hit him hard from behind. He had the man disarmed and marching by gunpoint towards Nicole Carson's mother's house in a matter of seconds.

* * *

The guard who had been left to see to Nikki's safety was more than helpful. She learned her father was not mob, nor was he CIA or a member of any other three-letter government organization, although there was some sense that he did have connections in some of those organizations, and the mob for sure. And she learned from the young guard that she not only had a father she did not know, she had an uncle, one who the young man did not know the name of, or anything else about. "Now, that's

really all I know, Miss Nikki," the young man was saying
as Fetchenko, Copeletti, and Evelyn entered.

Copeletti shot the youngster a curious look, then
said, "I'm gonna check on Vinny."

"Call me," Fetchenko said. It was code for "Take
care of this outside the girl's view."

"I have questions," Nicole told Arthur.

"I'll bet you do. But I have to leave. Evie, can you
stick around?"

"Sure."

"Fill her in," he said.

"All of it?" Evelyn asked.

"All of it. Time she knew. I'll send someone." He
kissed both of the women on the cheek, grabbed the
young guard by the shirtsleeve, and left his sister's house.
It would be his last visit. He hoped, with Evelyn's help, it
would not be the last he would see of Nikki.

* * *

"So tell me. What'd you think of him?" Evelyn
asked Nicole.

"Honestly? I don't know what to think — about him
— about any of this. It's all so... I suppose odd is the
word." She went silent. Evelyn knew there would be
more. She waited. "I don't understand why he would, or
why any of you would for that matter, let me go through
life thinking I had no father."

"So you could go through life. Look, Nikki..."

"Why does everyone insist of calling me Nikki?"

"Okay, Nicole. There's something more you need to
know. You already know that Laura adopted you when
you were an infant."

"Obviously! Otherwise, I'd be a product of incest."

"Well... what you don't know is who your real mother was or how she died. Her name was Maryann, and she
and Arthur were married just out of high school, and they

were together for three years. Even at that young age, Arthur had enemies, some say he had been born with them, but that's beside the point. Anyway... your real mother died because someone tried to take out your father and missed. They thought they got you as well, but Arthur hid you with Laura. These secrets have kept you alive."

"What is he, anyway?" Nicole asked, trying for a feel of why all the cloak and dagger stuff was needed.

"He's a very good man who had a bad beginning and made the best of it. Now, really, Nicole, any more he'll have to tell you himself."

* * *

Arthur Fetchenko climbed into the helicopter ahead of Tony Copeletti. "What'd you get from our man in the alley?"

"He's working for Ferguson."

"Christ! If Colonel Ferguson knows, so does the rest of that pack of Washington parasites. Send somebody to watch over Nikki."

"Who you want me to send?"

"Your best! This is my daughter."

Tony Copeletti called Jacob Rain.

Chapter Seven

Arthur Fetchenko could not recall the last time the memory of his wife's murder surfaced. He used to pull it out once in a while, when he felt himself weakening, forgetting his goals and purpose. The scene, disturbing as it was, served to set him back on track. It would remind him who his enemies were, and why they were his enemies. He would fight sleep on this trip. Thoughts of that night would help fight it. And those thoughts would suffice; he did not need to dream it. Then there was Laura. He would miss her, always, despite their having been cheated out of a closeness they richly deserved. And what about Nikki? What about his daughter? Would Jacob Rain keep her safe? His thoughts ran deep — too deep — too random.

"You okay, Boss?" Tony Copeletti asked.

"Is Jacob Rain enough?"

"If you could come up with one son-of-a-bitch who you wouldn't want to run into in a dark alley, who would that be?" Copeletti asked him.

Arthur Fetchenko smiled, his confidence restored.

"Arthur?" Tony said.

"Yeah."

"You did all you could. You kept in touch with Laura, sent people to keep her safe, looked out for and supported Nikki all of these years. It's more than anyone else would've done under the circumstances."

"It never seems enough."

"Probably not. But you did more than most would have done with somebody tryin' to stop them at every turn. You never gave up. You never let them down."

"I'm afraid that's no longer going to be sufficient. Ferguson and that bunch have Nikki on their scope, and you know they'll use her to get to us. We'll have to move her. I saw you talking to her for some time. Think she'll fight it?"

"Tooth and nail. Hell, she's just like you. Remember when I told you it was no longer safe for you in the outside world?"

"I didn't give you such a bad time."

"The hell you didn't," Copeletti said.

Fetchenko smiled briefly. "She was more than a big sister, Tony. She was my mother, the only true parent I ever had."

"I know." Tony Copeletti thought for a moment. "But I wouldn't tell too many people that."

"Why not?"

"She's also your daughter's mother. They got a word for that — incest. The street has a name for it too — motherfucker."

Fetchenko flipped Copeletti off, then sat back and closed his eyes. His friend could be crude, but he had been a true friend forever, and he was the man whose opinion he valued above most others. "What did you think of her?"

"I think she's sharp, maybe sharper than you," Copeletti answered. "Better watch your back around her, Boss. She'll end up with your job."

Fetchenko smiled, his eyes still shut. "I don't think she likes me."

"She doesn't know you yet." Copeletti said. "But, what the hell? I didn't like you much when I first met you either."

* * *

Laura's funeral brought out thoughts in Arthur Fetchenko that he did not want to revisit, thoughts of the night he brought his daughter to her knowing she would be forever away from him. He hated Tony Copeletti that night. He hated everyone that night: Tony because he had insisted Nikki be left behind, and everyone else because his Maryann was gone. He knew she was dead at the first sight of the cop at his door. And there had been a boy — Little Tony. They called it an accident — a hit and run, but previous threats told him that was inaccurate. Nicole, an infant and only survivor would be declared dead for her safety at the insistence of Tony Copeletti. "They'll use her, Arthur, they will use her to get to you and you know it," is what he had said.

It was a fall evening in 1967: rainy, cold, threatening to snow. Arthur would be tied up in a meeting all night — a last minute thing — so Maryann and the kids had gone to see a friend. When Henry Tyler's father, Warren, finally gathered sufficient evidence to get Arthur Fetchenko sprung from the reform school and the promise of a life sentence that his grandfather stuck to him, he turned that evidence over to Arthur. Arthur used it wisely, or so he thought at the time. He traded for a career. Arthur gave the Party silence and in exchange the Party made him head of a new branch they named the Candidate Acceptance Group, or CAG, a unit with the mission of investigating and approving (or disapproving) anyone who wished to run for political office on the Party's ticket. The news, along with the warning that there were those in office who objected vigorously, had arrived less than a week before. Soon the first of many threats arrived. Arthur's meeting that night was with Tony Copeletti and Henry Tyler and concerned that threat, something they all felt would alarm Maryann, so sending her and the kids to a friend's seemed the prudent thing to do. Had any of them expected that threat to be carried out, especially against Maryann and the kids, they certainly wouldn't have been sent away. The attack was the first of many he would suffer, and the most devastating.

"Try and get some sleep, Boss," Copeletti said. "You look beat."

Fetchenko did not want sleep. Sleep would bring dreams and none of them good. But sleep would come and along with it — dreams.

* * *

Thaddeus Fetchenko had moved to the small mining town when Arthur was in his early teens. Upon learning of his grandfather's arrival, Arthur's excitement bounded to heights that paralleled nothing he had ever before experienced or even dared imagine. His plummet when he first met the elder Fetchenko was devastating. He had imagined someone who would intercede on his behalf against the tyranny that was his family, someone who would side with him, someone who would know his worth, and someone who would love him. That was, he imagined, what grandfathers were. He was wrong. Thaddeus Fetchenko, or as he now called himself, Thaddeus Malcolm Frank, was the master tyrant, a man without conscience, a man without scruples or moral fiber and he did not like Arthur or any of the family. He made that clear on his first and only visit to the Fetchenko home, a visit that lasted just ten minutes. The family was told he had returned to the area as a high ranking official of the union and not as a member of any family. He said he had no desire to renew relationships, to get to know grandchildren, or to make friends. He told them that he was a man of upper class, and them — lower. Stay clear of him, had been his order. And this unyielding position applied to the entire family, everyone except Arthur's oldest sibling, Joseph, who had already left the family in favor of the Party and the union. He was their man now, just like his grandfather. As for Arthur, he would see little of his grandfather after that visit and it suited him. In the end, though, Thaddeus Frank did find value in his youngest grandson, but only as a fall guy for the crimes he himself committed.

* * *

A pocket of turbulence woke Fetchenko. Sweat beads shone on his forehead and on his upper lip.

Tony Copeletti examined him surreptitiously, and then turned away. "Dreams?" he asked. "Maryann?"

"Maryann a bit. Thaddeus more."

"You know, Arthur, I'll never forgive myself for running out on you that night," Copeletti said, referring to evening Arthur took the fall for Thaddeus Frank.

"It wasn't your fault." Fetchenko insisted. "He was the union's boy, the Party's pick. They had too much invested in him and they had to protect that investment. They needed a fall guy. I was it. That's all. Nothing anyone could have done."

"Do ya think they knew it was the old man?" Copeletti asked.

"I know they did." Fetchenko said. "They told me they did, tried to smooth things over with me. They even promised they'd take care of me after it was all over with."

"Did they?" Copeletti asked. "Take care of you I mean," he added.

"Not intentionally."

"We're about to land," the pilot said. "Buckle in."

Chapter Eight

Jacob Rain hated assignments like this one. Night work was not his thing. Too quiet — hard to stay awake. And a babysitting assignment, had it not been Arthur Fetchenko's daughter he would have objected. But to object to Tony Copeletti, now... that wasn't wise anyway.

"Try not to be conspicuous," Copeletti had told him. Conspicuous — shit! Rain thought and rightfully so. Who wouldn't spot a six-foot-two, two-hundred-fifty pound, full-blooded Cherokee Indian in a nondescript four-door sedan, sitting all night in front of the girl's house?

Rain looked down at his watch, "2:37 a.m.". "Son-of-a-bitch!" he said. "This night's never going to end." He threw out the latest of his depleted cigarette butts. It landed in a pile — twenty in all — just outside the car door. He reached for a Styrofoam cup on the dash. It was three-quarters full of cold coffee. He'd drink it anyway, just to pass the time. The cup's bottom grazed the steering wheel, its contents spilling into his lap. "FUCK!" He quickly swung around to grab a dirty shirt from the back seat. He dabbed at the coffee. "I hate this shit. Drive all day, watch all night. Nothin's gonna happen." He wanted to close his eyes, just for a second — maybe two. He leaned back. Movement in the mirror caught his attention: a car, creeping, headlights off. He sank in the seat. The car moved past and pulled to the curb just ahead. It sat there, motor idling. Rain placed on hand on the door handle and pulled himself upright. He felt for his pistol, his holster — empty. What the...? Then he remembered. He had placed it on the seat for quick access. He grabbed for the gun. The passenger's door of the car in front swung open. His grip tightened, both on the wheel and on the gun. He watched. A young girl slid out of the car, stood, then leaned back into the car to kiss her boyfriend goodnight. She turned and ran between two houses and out of Rain's sight. "Goddamn teenagers," he said. But at least the thought of action had supplied him with adrenalin. Now he was awake.

Another hour brought daybreak, the toughest time for Jacob Rain. It seemed always to cause him to doze. Today was no exception. His heavy eyelids betrayed him. He fell into a pleasant sleep.

The loud tap-tap-tap on the window startled him awake. He reached for his gun just as his eyes focused on the pretty girl standing outside his car, coffee mug in hand. He rolled the window down. "Been here long?" she asked and she handed him the mug. She looked at the heap of butts on the pavement. "All night, I'd say. My father send you?"

"Tony Copeletti," Rain said.

"Same thing from what I understand."

She glanced at the collection of empty fast-food containers and coffee cups that cluttering the passenger's side of the car, then looked at Rain. "Had breakfast yet?"

"No."

She opened his door. "Come," she said and started toward the house.

Jacob Rain followed. Home cooking sounded great. A man would be a fool to turn it down. At the front door Rain said, "You shouldn't approach a stranger like that, Miss."

She stopped and looked at him over her shoulder. "What?" she asked.

"I said, you shouldn't approach a stranger like that."

"You're no stranger," she said. "You work for my father. I saw you at Mom's funeral — outside. Why didn't you come in and get something to eat that day?'

"I don't much like crowds, Miss." Rain said.

"My name's not Miss," she said, "it's Nicole, Nicole Carson." She reached her hand out. "What's yours?"

"Jacob Rain," he said and took the hand.

"Well, Mr. Rain, there's no crowd here now." She led him to the kitchen, sat him at the table, and topped off his mug. "How do you like your eggs, Mr. Rain?" she asked.

"Any way you fix them, Ma'am."

"Why are you here?" she asked and stirred potatoes in a pan.

"Watching out for you," he said.

"Why?"

"Your father wants me to," he said.

"Why?"

"To protect you."

She shot him a curious look and made her way to the table with the pan of potatoes. He missed it. She wore a thin pale-yellow t-shirt — no bra. Rain did not see past her small, firm breasts. He blushed slightly and looked away.

"Protect me from what?" she asked and shoveled a huge serving of fried potatoes onto his plate.

"Everything. Nothing. Whatever happens. I don't know, I'm just to watch over you," he said.

She returned to her stove for eggs and bacon. "Hope you're hungry."

"I am, Miss."

"Please don't call me miss."

"Yes, Ma-am."

"Don't call me ma-am either."

"What should I call you?"

"My name is Nicole, or Nikki if you prefer." *I wonder why I said that,* she thought. "And one more thing, Mr. Rain," she said. She could feel his eyes on her, checking her out.

"Jacob," he said.

"Okay, Jacob. One more thing, I assume since you've been sent to watch over me, you won't be leaving any time soon, so you'd better get used to the way I dress around the house. I have no intention of changing my ways. I'm going to be comfortable in my own home."

"Y-y-yes Ma'am, I mean, Nikki," he said.

She smiled but did not turn to face him until she could put on a sober face, then she brought their eggs and bacon to the table.

After breakfast, while they sipped coffee, Nikki Carson looked into Jacob Rain's eyes. Now was the time. The man was drifting in and out from exhaustion. "Exactly why are you here?" she asked.

"Your father has enemies. You might need protection from them."

"Why now?"

"They didn't know about you before."

"Before what?"

"Before your mother's funeral."

"And now these enemies know about me?"

"We think they might."

"Why do you think that?"

"There's evidence," Rain told her. He feared he might be saying too much.

"I'm not sure I like my father." She said bluntly. She took a long sip of her coffee.

"Can I smoke in here?" Rain asked.

Nikki got an ashtray and placed it in front of him.

"You don't know your father," Rain insisted.

"And you do?"

Jacob Rain did not answer. She sensed he was about to clam up. She gathered the dirty dishes and hauled them to the sink. It had been her experience that most men's tongues loosened if she let them ogle her for a time. It worked back in college. It worked in the courtroom. And it would work on Jacob Rain.

"I've known him for a long time," he offered, "since way back in high school."

"You didn't eat your bacon, Jacob." She said and scraped it into the trash.

"I never eat the sh... ah... stuff," he said.

"Why not?" she asked. "Don't tell me you're a vegetarian?"

"No! Nothing like that. An old truck driver," he said. "In a truck stop, you see, they never offer bacon or sausage or ham. They offer breakfast meat. The term turned me against eating any of it — always made me think road kill or mystery meat."

"Well... I assure you, mine is the real thing." She smiled. She turned to face him. She leaned against the counter. "You looked exhausted."

"I'm okay."

"So, who are these enemies that I'm to be protected from? Are they here, in Madison?"

Rain didn't answer immediately. She sensed another clam up. She turned her back and reached into an upper cabinet. Her shirt rode up. Her hip-hugger jeans showed dimples above her well-rounded bottom.

"Some here," Rain said, "and some elsewhere."

"How worried should I be?" she asked.

"You should just be cautious, and stick near me," he told her. "The ones around here aren't very threatening."

"Why not?" she asked.

"They're a paranoid bunch," he answered.

"What the hell does that have to do with anything?" she asked and turned to face him.

"Paranoids usually aren't so dangerous. They're more scared of us than we need to be of them, that is, with me here. They'll see me and move on."

"How would you know that?" she asked.

"My company does studies. We know pretty much where enemies are and what types they are, and we know pretty much what they'll do."

"So... what you're saying is that I shouldn't worry about my father's enemies around here."

"Not as long as you're with one of us."

"Where's the real danger then," she asked.

Jacob Rain did not answer. Nikki looked at him. His eyes were closed. "You need some sleep Mr. Rain," she said. "Why don't you stretch out on the sofa and take a little nap."

"Can't," he said. "Have to stay with you today. Someone else will be here tonight. I'll sleep then."

"You'll sleep now," she insisted, "I'll wake you if I need you. Should be safe enough. I'm not planning to go out."

"I was told you work."

His comment stirred an unpleasant memory, the memory of the day she resigned the DA's office over that case involving her two friends at social services...*what was that name? Rain!* "Ever live around here, Jacob?"

"Once. A long time ago."

She wanted to press further but his drooping eyelids told her it was useless. She could flash her tits and he'd miss it. She would bring the topic up later. "Really, Mr. Rain, lay down on the sofa for a while. I'm not planning on leaving the house this morning. I'll just be here cleaning and relaxing. I promise."

Jacob Rain agreed to nap. He moved to the living room, stretched out on the sofa, and did not feel her pull a blanket over him. His last conscious thought was a hope they didn't send that little, full of bullshit, simple son-of-a-bitch Eric Trumble to assist him. He hated that guy.

"Good night, Jacob Rain," Nicole Carson whispered as she covered him.

* * *

It was nearly eleven when Jacob Rain was startled awake by a loud crash. He sat bolt upright, a nine millimeter pistol appearing in his right hand like it came out of thin air. It seemed to aim itself at Nicole Carson like it had a mind of its own.

"DON'T SHOOT!" she screamed and squeezed her eyes shut.

Rain sighed, and then shoved the weapon back into his shoulder holster. "What the hell was that?"

"I... I knocked the lamp off the table." she said excitedly. "I was dusting, and I knocked... say, do you have to sleep with that gun?"

"I'm sorry, Miss Nikki," he apologized. "What time is it?"

"Half-past eleven."

He reached to the table looking for his cell-phone. It had fallen with the lamp.

"Looking for this?" she asked, picking it up from the floor and handing it to him.

He took it. "Thanks. I have to check in," he said. His gaze told her he needed privacy.

"I'll get us some coffee," she offered and left the room.

It surprised Jacob Rain to hear the voice of Elizabeth Harmon after just three rings. His calls always went directly to Copeletti's office, and were never picked up in three rings. Dead air followed.

"Is this Jacob Rain?" Liz asked.

"I... ah... did I dial wrong? I'm trying to reach Tony Copeletti."

"This is fine, Mr. Rain," she said. "Mr. Copeletti has been expecting your call. He's in Mr. Fetchenko's office. I'll connect you."

Shit! Rain thought. He hoped nobody knew he had been napping. He should have checked in hours ago.

"Jake. Everything ok?" It was Fetchenko's voice.

"Yes, Sir."

"What's the situation there? Any sign of trouble?"

"I doubt it. Pretty quiet so far." *Other than the fact I damn-near shot your daughter,* he added silently.

"Good. Let's keep it that way. Is she at work?"

"No, Sir. She don't work. Not anymore," Rain reported.

Fetchenko did not know what to think. Was this good news, or bad? It could be bad, too much freedom — tougher to keep an eye on. "Maybe it'll be easier to get her to leave there. Where are you now?"

Jacob Rain thought for a moment before answering. Should he be in Fetchenko's daughter's home? Would it bother Fetchenko? Should he say he's calling from the car? Then, just as he was about to answer, Nicole Carson came into the room with two cups of coffee.

"Oh. I'm sorry. I thought you would be off the phone by now. Is that my father you're talking to?" Rain nodded his head. "Let me say hello." She grabbed for the phone. Rain was glad to give it up. "I like your Mr. Rain," she said.

Silence.

"Are you there?"

"Yes. Yes. Nikki. How are you?" Fetchenko said.

"I'm fine. Listen. Is all of this necessary? I mean... I do like your Mr. Rain, but are you certain I need him here?"

"Probably not. But I'd feel better if you'd let him keep an eye on things for you, for me. Is that okay with you? He can put up at a motel near you," he said.

"He can stay here."

"You don't mind?" Jacob Rain at the house offered substantially more protection.

"I don't mind having Mr. Rain here. I'll put him back on the phone now. I'm sure you want to say more to him."

"I'm back, Arthur." Rain said.

"She's a smoking pistol, isn't she," Fetchenko said.

"You bet."

"I was going to send Trumble out to give you a hand but with you at the house? Not really necessary," Fetchenko said. "Unless...?"

"Absolutely not!" Rain answered.

Fetchenko chuckled and hung up the phone. He knew the mention of the name Eric Trumble made Jacob Rain's Cherokee blood curdle.

Jacob Rain sat silently sipping his coffee from a mug that read, 'LAWYERS ARE PEOPLE TOO'. Nikki Carson studied him: the lines in his face, the scar near his left eye, his thick black hair that looked like it belonged to a younger man, and his lack of expression as he read the words on the cup. He still looked tired and because he still looked tired she thought about letting him rest. But there were questions.

"Well... Mr. Rain," she began, "now that you've slept, are you going to tell me about my father?"

"What do you want to know?" He rubbed his eyes with his finger tips.

"How long have you known him? I mean, you told me it was since high school. I just don't know when that was."

"The late fifties or early sixties," he said. "I can't remember exactly. I always have trouble remembering dates. Anyway, I'd already been at the school for a couple years when he got there."

"What school was that?" Nicole asked.

"Reform school," he answered, "only I don't think that's what they call it now." He thought for a moment. "That's what they called it when I was a kid, reform school. They got a fancier name for it now though."

"Juvenile centers?" she suggested.

"That's it. Juvenile center. That's what they call it. Anyway, I'd been there about two years when, one day they threw this short kid into the yard. Right away these two bigger boys jumped him and started to beat the crap out of him. Initiation, you know?"

"No. I don't know."

"Thought you were a DA."

Sharp. Sharper than I thought, she admitted silently. "Go on."

"The little guy, the new kid, fought like a wild cat for the longest time, all the time keeping one eye on me. I think he wondered if I was going to join in and what side I would pick if I did. Then about the time he was going to lose the fight, he looked straight at me, looked right into my eyes, and nodded his head. I couldn't do anything but help him. You see, he was the first person to look at me, really look at me, since my grandfather. Most people looked past me, not at me, like I don't really exist or something — but not this kid. Not your father. He looked inside me." Rain stopped talking. He appeared in deep thought.

"Then what happened?" she asked.

Jacob Rain smiled. "We kicked their asses. Been friends ever since."

"What were you in the school for?" she asked. "I mean, what did you do?"

"Stealing," he said. "But mostly I was in the school for being Cherokee. You see, my parents died of some fever when I was four years old and my grandfather took me in and raised me. When I was thirteen he died, too. That left me on my own. I was too young to make a living and too old for anyone to want, so I had to fend for myself. I got caught stealing food out of a freezer on someone's back porch, and they sent me to the school for it. It was a good thing though."

"Why?" Nikki asked. "That doesn't sound like a good thing to me."

"I wasn't a very good thief. Probably would have starved to death."

She smiled. "What was my father's crime?"

"Rape. Murder," he said. He watched her face go pale. "But he didn't do it. He was set up. Some relative of his actually did it, I think it was his grandfather, and your dad took the fall for him. It all had to do with politics and unions or something. I really don't know that much about it, just that he didn't do it and that's enough for me."

Rain, after telling the girl that much and thinking he shouldn't have, went to the bay window to look outside.

Nikki knew there was more but her experience in the legal profession taught her to know when information was no longer going to flow freely, and that, if she wanted to get more later she would have to allow things it rest. She changed the subject. "Did you know my mother?"

"Yes. I was there the night you were born."

"I meant my aunt," she corrected, "I mean Laura."

"I knew her too. She was the only relative of your father's I ever met. I liked her the first time I saw her."

"Why?" she asked.

"She looked at me like your father did, not past me."

"That's a big thing with you, isn't it?

"Not so much anymore. But then? It was big — not all that long after the reform school."

Jacob Rain fascinated her. She liked him. The more they talked, the more she liked him. It was his honesty. "Well, I'd better see to that lunch meat." She smiled, picked up the coffee mugs, and left for the kitchen where she prepared cold-cut sandwiches and salads. Then she called Jacob Rain to the table. Together they sat quietly eating: her — lady like, him — like a wolf. "Slow down," she said.

"Sorry. Can I ask you something?"

"Ask away."

"It's personal," he warned.

"Not too, I hope."

"How come a pretty girl like you lives alone?"

Chapter Nine

J. Patrick Ferelli needed change. Today marked his forty-third and final year of public service and four of his closest friends would join him tonight, to celebrate, and to help him plan a big finale to his long and illustrious career. The final act he had in mind would set the political structure back on track and he would be written up in history books as the man who saved the Party.

His career would have ended with his last term had the Party come up with an appropriate successor to him. But this infamous office, this Candidate Acceptance Group, (whatever the fuck that's supposed to be, he thought when he first heard of it) had approved a woman for Christ sakes. No skirt would replace him — no sir. At least they hadn't done that for the coming election. The new guy on the Party ticket was actually a guy.

J. Patrick tipped his glass and downed the last of his brandy just as his wife, Martha, entered his study with a fresh one. "Getting anxious?" she asked.

"For what?"

"Your company."

"What time is it?" He laced his fingers behind his head and leaned back in his leather chair.

"Five-thirty," Martha told him. "Everyone's due to arrive any moment."

He hoped so. He hated long discussions with his wife. She would talk on now until the doorbell stops her.

"That colonel friend of yours, what's his name?"

"Ferguson."

"That's it, Colonel Ferguson. He seems nice."

He's a god-damned tyrant, Ferelli thought. "Yeah. He's nice," he said.

"It'll be good to see the Davidsons again," Martha said.

"Don't you have something to do, some little last minute detail to take care of?"

"No. It's all done, dear. Isn't it nice we have a few minutes for ourselves?"

"Peachy!" he said, and the doorbell rang. Just in time.

* * *

The Davidsons were the first to arrive. "Pat's in his study, Daniel. Go right in," Martha told him.

"What'd you think of the Freedom Hill meeting?" Ferelli asked, even before the doors to his study closed.

"Well... let me see. Mac MacArthur was squeamish, but agreeable. The colonel? Definitely not squeamish. Parker sees the need as do I. I guess, in the end, the new motto of The Veterans of Power could well be — 'When Fetchenko is gone, the world can move on'."

Ferelli smiled.

"I'm glad you could be there this time." J.P. Ferelli preferred to stay in the background on these things and often skipped out on those meetings that were more public. He wanted to stay out of Fetchenko's radar as much as possible.

"So am I!" Ferelli agreed.

"Starting without us?" McArthur asked as he entered, Victor Parker in tow.

"Gentlemen, you're late," J.P. said, as the doors closed behind them. Then they swung open. Colonel Ferguson filled them. "Fergie."

"J.P." Ferguson answered. He closed the doors.

"What's the good word?"

"For us? Or for Arthur Fetchenko?" Ferguson asked.

"Start with Fetchenko," J.P. said.

"There's no good word for Fetchenko."

"How about us?"

"There's no good word for Fetchenko," Colonel Ferguson said, and the room filled with laughter just as Martha Ferelli entered with a tray of fresh drinks.

"I see you boys are having a good time," she said and parked the tray on a table. "Yell out when these need refreshing."

"My guy in Wisconsin tells me Jacob Rain is in Madison," Ferguson said as soon as Martha Ferelli cleared the study doors. Ferelli watched the doors slowly close and shot Ferguson a look that said caution need be observed. "It'd sure be nice to take that Indian out of the picture," he added.

"Is that something we can do?" Mac Macarthur asked. He swept a hand across his balding head. He often did that when he questioned the wisdom of something, even in Congress he did it. It had become his trademark, his signal that a fight of sorts was about to begin.

"You got a problem with that?" Victor Parker asked.

"The girl's safety," he answered. But he knew as soon as the words cleared his lips, the objection was illogical. After all, wasn't the girl in hiding all these years for a reason? And wasn't that reason that these men, this very group, were after her the night her mother and baby brother were killed? It had always been a suspicion of theirs that the girl might have survived, so they've been looking for her ever since. Why would he think any of them would be the least bit squeamish about taking her out?

"That's right! The girl!" Ferelli said and wrung his hands excitedly. "Rain's with the girl. Imagine what damage it would do to Arthur Fetchenko if we could take both

Rain and the girl. Is that something your people can handle, Fergie?"

"I'll get them started," Colonel Ferguson said. He
had access, even though he was retired, to military force at
the drop of a hat, and, should that not get the job done,
he had access to mercenaries. He chewed on it. He would
hire mercs for this one.

* * *

As the hour turned late, talk had become more
brandy than logic and guests left for their homes to sleep
it off. Martha had heard enough — too much really. She
turned the evening of celebration and cloak and dagger
idiocy into serious conversation between her and her
husband as soon as her guests had all departed. "What
are you planning, Patrick?"

"What do you mean?"

"A politician's wife hears things, and politicians
choose wives who are smart enough to understand what
they hear. You're planning to go after Arthur Fetchenko."

"He needs taking down."

"Why?"

"This is government business, Martha. Stay out of
it."

"It isn't government. That's just the idea you sold to
your little following. It's what you're good at, Patrick. You
take anything, government, personal, it doesn't matter,
and turn it into an issue you can rally support behind and
damn the results. Arthur Fetchenko isn't hurting anything.
He's helping, and your crusade is personal and it always
has been."

"No! It's not! And just what is Arthur doing that's so
great?"

"He's getting people like you and that old colonel,
(her opinion of Ferguson had been drastically altered
from what she had overheard that evening) government

officials who want to rule, not lead and serve, and putting them out of business. That's what he's doing."

"You don't have the slightest idea, Martha. It's guys like me and Fergie, and the others who were here tonight who keep the world safe from the Arthur Fetchenkos of the world. You don't even know what he's about, so I'll tell you. He's the kind who will, without us in his way, put a green kid in the Oval Office, then do to the Republican Party what he's done to us, and soon, everyone in Washington will owe him. So... if that Albrecht kid gets the big office I'll give it ten years until Fetchenko runs the country single handedly. How dangerous is that? I can't let it happen. Not in all good conscience. And that's exactly what we must stop."

"You don't have a conscience, you and that bunch here tonight."

"You... get... the... hell... out ... of ... here! Now!" he screamed.

"You go after Arthur Fetchenko, Patrick, and that's exactly what I plan to do," Martha told him.

"That and a whole lot more," she added softly in the hallway outside his study.

J. Patrick Ferelli did not hear her.

* * *

The telephone on Arthur Fetchenko's nightstand rang at an unusually late hour.

"Who the hell could that be?" Fetchenko snapped.

"Pick it up. They'll tell you," Liz suggested.

"Yes." Arthur said into the phone.

"Arthur, this is Martha."

Chapter Ten

Copeletti filled his staff in on Arthur's late night call from Martha Ferelli. "It appears," he started, "Ferelli and that bunch are about to come at us."

"Ain't they always comin' at us?" Vinny Gotto asked.

"This is different," Copeletti said.

"How so?" Gotto asked. He was bolder than Tony's other men. They were cousins and Gotto thought that gave him rights above the others. Frankly, Vinny looked at himself as Tony's equal. Tony Copeletti did not.

"Because this time it's all the marbles. This time Fetchenko intends to put a man in the Oval Office."

"I don't see what difference that makes."

"Vinny! Shut the fuck up. This is a briefing. You don't have a say," Copeletti warned. "Now... it's important you guys know something," he went on. "We have a mole. Somebody leaked this information and they knew who to leak it to. And it ain't pillow-talk; one of us is dirty. So here's the way it goes on this one. Everybody partners up and nobody works alone. Watch your partner. Anybody fool enough to go against this outfit is fool enough to give himself up. Report anything you think suspicious — to me. Nobody else. I'll deal with the snitch myself." Tony already had his prime suspect picked out. Martha Ferelli had overheard a name. "Vinny, you're with me."

* * *

Henry Tyler stood in the courtyard of the Fetchenko headquarters with his assistant, Susan Burton, the ancient senator's chair once belonging to his uncle between them.

"You oil that thing?" Arthur Fetchenko asked as he approached.

Tyler gave the chair a twist. It let out a screech. "Arthur, you know Miss Burton."

"Of course. Tell me, Miss Burton..."

"Please, call me Susan," she said.

"Susan, then, how would you be as a campaign manager?" Fetchenko asked.

"You're kidding. This fast? How?" Henry asked excitedly.

"Didn't you read this morning's paper?"

"Not yet."

"You should. Senator Bloom died last night — car accident. Your name will be on the ballot," Fetchenko said. Bloom had held the seat from Henry's district back in Wisconsin. He was up for reelection.

"Sounds like you just found a use for me," Henry said.

"I sure did. So... Miss Burton, Susan, what do you think? Can you handle the job?" Arthur asked and smiled.

"I'll need coaching."

"We specialize in coaching around here, don't we, Henry?"

"That we do," Henry said and walked toward the door to Security.

"Where's Bess?" Fetchenko asked.

"Shit!" Tyler said. He ran back to the chopper. Soon he was back, urn tucked safely under an arm.

"Anything coming from home? Furniture? Anything?"

"Nah. I closed up the house with everything in it. Got someone checking on it now and then." Henry nodded to a man at the security station. He looked around. "This'll be like living in a goddamn cave."

"It'll grow on you," Fetchenko promised. "Besides, you won't be stuck here. You'll be on the campaign trail, you and Susan."

Tony Copeletti appeared. One look at Henry Tyler and a larger than life smile grew on his face. "Why, Henry Tyler. How the hell are you?" he asked as he threw his huge arms around him and lifted him cleanly off his feet. "And who is this lovely creature?"

"Put me down, you big oaf," Henry complained. And Tony opened his arms and dropped him. Arthur Fetchenko smiled and reached to steady Henry. "This is going to be great, Arthur," Henry said sarcastically.

"Hi. I'm Tony," Copeletti told Susan. "Henry had better manners when he was young. Now that he's old though... say... you aren't his girl are you? Because if you are, my hat is off to you. You marry him and you'll inherit in no time."

Susan Burton smiled and said, "No. I'm just his assistant."

"More than that," Arthur threw in, "she's his campaign manager."

"Oh, yeah. Senator Bloom's untimely death. What a pity. He was so young."

"Tony, I'll get Henry and Susan settled in," Arthur said. "Meet us in my office in an hour. We'll go over the game plan. We'll want security on them when they're out on the trail."

* * *

Going over the game plan, a statement which weighed heavy on Tony Copeletti as he neared Arthur Fetchenko's office. It's what they were doing in Madison so many years ago and it took the lives of Arthur's wife and son, and created the need for Arthur to give up his daughter in the process. Bad memories, those words. Tony Copeletti pushed the door open and walked in. He looked around the room. No one. He sat. That episode back then was a double whammy to him. He had let down Arthur Fetchenko having been the one who was responsible for security then. That was a certainty. It goes without saying. But he let down his uncle, Antonio Copeletti as well. You see, Maryann Danucci Fetchenko was the crime boss' niece and Tony's first cousin. So many years and Tony Copeletti still punished himself with those truths.

* * *

It was the early fall of 1967 and things couldn't be going better for Arthur Fetchenko, Tony Copeletti, and Henry Tyler. The three of them were together again, something they all thought would never happen. But here they were a team, just like the days of their youth in the little mining town on the edge of Minnesota's Mesabi Iron Range. Only this time they were the ones with the power. Henry's Father had seen to that when he freed Arthur from reform school and gave him irrefutable evidence as to the identity of the true perpetrator of the crimes he had been sent up for. And with that evidence Arthur could either see to it the perpetrator was punished, or he could trade his silence for a future and take the long road to total vengeance: a retaliation that would encompass all of the wrongdoers, not just the one. Tough choice. Get his grandfather or get them all. He had studied the evidence thoroughly. Yes, it did nail Thaddeus Frank, but so much more; it implicated high ranking party officials too. They were all at his mercy. He chose. So it was blackmail. So what! He would be their conscience and their guide and their thorn in the side, but they would never again, none of them, use children like they had used the three of them.

Thus the Candidate Acceptance Group was born.

Also born, unfortunately, were the threats and attacks on Arthur Fetchenko and his family. And it was on that night in 1967 when the three boys from iron country were celebrating their victory over their past and going over their game plan for the future that the first of those attacks was executed. To Tony Copeletti it was the biggest failure of his life and one he would never be able to atone for, not to Arthur, not to his uncle Antonio, not to Fetchenko's daughter Nikki, and certainly not to himself.

* * *

Copeletti stood. He walked to the window and looked out over the courtyard. "Where the hell are them guys?" he asked.

"We're right here," Fetchenko said as he entered the room, Tyler in tow. "Been waiting long?"

"Too long," Copeletti complained.

"Too bad," Fetchenko said. "Now let's get down to business. Who you sending with Henry here — on the campaign trail?"

"How about Phil Blackburn?"

"Hadn't thought of him," Fetchenko said. Blackburn was more of negotiator for the company. But he had come from the Secret Service, worked his way up through the ranks to a top level position before joining Arthur and the group. "You want him to select his own men, or do you want to do it."

"I wouldn't know who to send him."

"How about that cousin of yours? How about Vinny Gotto?" Fetchenko suggested.

"Not him!"

"Why not?" Arthur Fetchenko showed concern. He thought Tony and Vinny were close. Tony's tone and his look were disputing that right now.

"Let's just say I'll be keeping Vinny real close for a while."

"Listen, do you need me for this?" Henry asked. "I'm a little stiff from the ride in here. I'd like to stretch my legs."

"I guess not," Arthur said. "Take that pretty lady of yours on a tour. You know your way around."

"Boss," Tony said after Henry left, "back in '67, I should have stopped Maryann and the kids from going out."

"That again? C'mon, Tony. We've been over this. There's nothing you could have done. Even if I'd begged her to stay at home that night, Maryann was an independent woman. She would have gone. She chose her own paths. You always blame yourself thinking you should have stopped her. I don't think you could have. Let it go, man. It's time. Now who we putting on Albrecht? Blackburn will probably pull men from that detail." Jack Albrecht was the company's hopeful for the Oval Office.

"Think that's a good idea? Pulling men from Albrecht? Wouldn't want to open him up to Ferelli and his bunch," Tony cautioned.

"Ah! Jack's too high profile. J. P. wouldn't have the balls." Arthur stood and went to the door. He looked into the hallway — no Henry Tyler. He shut the door. "It's Henry they'll go after."

* * *

Vinny Gotto had been with Tony Copeletti for a very long time. What he was up to now, he hated himself for, but goddamn, it was a lot of money. And his little girl's treatments were draining him. What else could he do?

It was back in '67 he joined up. Tony called him at Uncle Antonio's house. He said he needed someone he could trust for an important job. That's all he would say on the phone. But it was Tony. And Vinny looked up to Tony. What else could he do?

Vinny Gotto began to have second thoughts as he drove up on the location Tony had given him directions to and saw flares outlining the twisted wreckage of an automobile. Bodies covered with blankets lined the sidewalk, one five foot, two small. Vinny could handle gunshot wounds and knuckle damage to faces, mob blood, but car wrecks? No! He spotted Tony and got out of his car. He saw an ambulance attendant nod at Tony Copeletti, then look toward the bodies. Tony went over and lifted the blanket, then nodded back. Vinny stayed back. "Take them to the morgue," Vinny heard Tony tell the attendant. Then Tony walked toward Vinny. "C'mon," he said.

"See that black Galaxy?" Tony asked and gestured toward a car half a block away.

"I see it," Vinny said.

"That's our doers. This ain't no hit-and-run accident. This is just a hit."

The black sedan pulled slowly from the curb, no lights. "That's our cue," Tony said and headed for his car.

Vinny followed. Tony got in on the passenger's side. "You drive," he said.

The sedan led them to the interstate and headed west.

"Follow?" Vinny asked.

"Follow."

Two and a half hours later they crossed the river into Minnesota. Thirty minutes more and they tailed the sedan to the rear entrance of the governor's mansion. That was enough for Copeletti. He may not have known the two thugs who got out of the sedan, but it was clear who sent them. "Time to go to work," he said and opened his door. Vinny followed his lead.

Tony Copeletti and his cousin, Vinny, both slid out of their car. They crept up behind the thugs from the sedan, and there, on the back steps of the governor's mansion, plugged them both in the back of the head. Then they walked, they did not run. To the car and headed back to Arthur's house. They would arrive before midnight, the job they set out to do, done.

* * *

"Get your goddamn feet off my desk," Copeletti said finding Vinny sitting in his chair, legs propped up, and eyes closed. "Get a limo ready. We got work to do."

"Where we going?" Vinny Gotto asked.

"You'll know when we get there. Oh, and Vinny, leave the cell-phone behind."

"What? Why?"

"Because it's not needed and it's annoying. That woman of yours must call twenty times a day."

"That's because of Lisa," Vinny explained. Lisa was the daughter with the illness. Tony Copeletti had checked and the illness, though serious, did not warrant constant communication. It was a condition she had acquired while playing in a sandbox, some sort of parasite that ate a hole in her colon. It required the use of steroids, expensive, and much extra attention. The whole thing was treatable but could take years.

"You leave the phone behind," Copeletti said again. "Now... get the car."

Gotto left the office to get a limo. Tony Copeletti called the garage as soon as his cousin was out of earshot. "Disable the phone in one of the limos and make sure Gotto gets that one," he told the head of the company's motor pool.

* * *

"You'll be meeting with J. P. and a couple of the boys this morning," Arthur Fetchenko told Henry Tyler. "Copeletti will take you."

"Right into the lion's den, eh? Do I get to know what the meeting is about?"

"That's up to you," Fetchenko said. "We got the meeting. You do what you can with it."

"I'm not sure I understand," Henry said.

"Sure you do. Why don't you begin with asking for their endorsement? You'll figure out what's next. Now go. Tony's waiting at the limo for you. And, Henry....."

"Yes?"

"Enjoy." And Fetchenko turned in his swivel chair, his back toward Tyler.

Chapter Eleven

The friendly reception Henry Tyler received from J. P. Ferelli surprised him. "Henry, it's been a long time. How the hell have you been?" Ferelli asked and sounded sincere.

"Can't complain," Henry said. "You?"

"I'm good."

"Where's Martha?" Henry asked. The last time he had occasion to visit, it had been Martha who greeted him. He had known her for years and was fond of her.

"Oh, she went back home for a visit. At times the old gal seems to want the lesser life." Ferelli referred to any existence outside Washington as the lesser life. It made most folks ask why he considered retirement. His generic answer was always that he didn't plan on leaving anything but work. "Listen, Henry, I have someone in my study you'll want to meet," he said and led Henry down a hallway. Inside the study, a wide man, his back to the door, hands grasped behind his him, looking out the window at the garden, seemed unconcerned. "Ferguson," Ferelli said, "this is Henry Tyler, the next Senator from Wisconsin. Henry, this is Randal Ferguson, a mighty important cog in the Washington political wheel, if you know what I mean."

Ferguson turned to face the new arrival. "How do you do, Mr. Ferguson," Henry said.

Ferguson grunted and nodded. "You'd be Fetchenko's boy," he said.

"Excuse me?" Henry said.

"He just means, well... that you got on the ticket through Arthur Fetchenko's organization, that Candidate... ah... whatever," Ferelli said.

"Candidate Acceptance Group." Henry finished for him. "That doesn't make me his boy, though. Nobody gets his name on a ballot as a Democrat without Arthur Fetchenko, do they?"

"Republicans, too, if Fetchenko gets his way." Ferguson said.

"Really. I hadn't heard that," Henry said.

"It's true," Ferelli said. "Blackburn's meeting with them early next week. Trouble is, the two parties are so far apart and so suspicious of one another, if the Dems tell them what they're up against, they won't believe it. They'll be sure it's something they need that we already have and are keeping from them like it was some treasure. Now... what's your take on the idea?"

"Dangerous," Henry said. It was the opening he had hoped for, the perfect opportunity to make these two feel that he, not necessarily the Fetchenko organization, he was on the level and had true politics, their kind of politics, on his agenda. But he must also protect against sounding disloyal. "It's no secret Arthur Fetchenko and I go way back, and I trust Arthur."

"So... you admit you'd be with Fetchenko on this one," Ferguson threw in.

"Not on your life. Like I said, Fetchenko, I trust. But side with one man or one little group of men to give them as much power as that would give them, hell, gentlemen, that's all the marbles. I couldn't support such a thing. Not in all good conscience."

"But you said you trust Arthur Fetchenko," Ferelli said.

"But he won't live forever. What then? Who takes over?"

"You goddamn right he won't live forever," Ferguson said. Ferelli shot him a look that told Henry Tyler the rumors were true. He had accomplished his mission.

Fetchenko had sent Tyler on this initial meeting with these two enemies for a dual purpose: to get in with them if at all possible and to find out if there was indeed a plan to hit Fetchenko. Mission accomplished as far as Henry Tyler was concerned. "Joseph, I must apologize and excuse myself. My campaign manager has me scheduled for speeches in the morning in Wisconsin. I really must go or I'll miss my flight."

* * *

After he watched Henry Tyler step into J. P. Ferelli's house, Tony Copeletti had an urge to get himself a coffee. They had passed a Caribou about block or two back. He walked to get himself a cup. Afterward, he stood on the sidewalk in front of the place straining his eyes to see who was leaned into the window of the limo talking to his driver. He thought of tossing the coffee and running for a closer look, but that would alert Vinny Gotto that he might be on to him. He didn't want that. Not yet. So he walked at a moderate pace. When he reached a half-block away, the visitor turned his back to Tony and shoved off down the street. Mob! Tony told himself. He was quite a student of body language. He knew the walk of soldier, of a bum, of a business man on top of his game, of an athlete or former athlete, and he certainly knew the carriage of a wise guy. He continued to the car and slid into the front seat. He handed Vinny a coffee and asked, "Who was your visitor?"

Vinny Gotto looked down and away. "Just some guy looking for directions," he said.

Tony Copeletti knew that look as well. It was the look of a lie.

* * *

Pauley Danucci picked at his lunch in the front window of the Royal Diner just a few blocks up the street from Ferelli's home. He sipped his beverage, the huge cup blocking all of his face but the eyes as the limo driven by Vinny Gotto and carrying Tony Copeletti and Henry Tyler passed by. He pitched a handful of bills on the table and abandoned his lunch. Moments later he entered the Ferelli home through the back door, the entrance used by the domestic staff.

"Get pictures?"

"Got my money?" Pauley Danucci wasn't in it for the money, not exactly. He was in it for revenge. He had been just ten years old when his big sister, Maryann, was run down by one of Arthur Fetchenko's arch enemies. It wasn't fair. Pauley had no mother. Maryann was it. And thanks to Arthur Fetchenko's greed for power, from that day forward he had no one; no one but a drunken father who left marks on him that would be there a lifetime. The money he would take, and he would piss it away like he always did. The revenge... now there was a sweet taste he would enjoy for the rest of his life.

J. P. Ferelli handed Pauley Danucci two envelopes. "Pass the one on to your cousin the photographer along with my concern for his little one with the viral thing."

"Parasite," Pauley corrected. "Vinny's little girl has a parasite."

"That's kind of funny."

"It is?" Pauley asked.

"Yeah! Don't you get it? A parasite with a parasite!" And he slammed the door on Pauley.

* * *

Colonel Ferguson sifted through photos for a full hour, studying, separating, scribbling notations on the backs of some while pitching others in the trash basket beside Ferelli's desk. "Pretty good," he finally said.

J. P. dug in the waste basket and looked at the discarded photos. "We don't need these?"

"I've been in the place before, back when it belonged to the military. What those photos show, I already know about."

Ferelli tucked them in a desk drawer anyway, despite the colonel's insistence that they weren't needed. "You say they're pretty good. They'd better be real good for the amount we paid those two."

"They'll do," Ferguson said.

"What now?"

"Now we map things out, chose our force, and decide how and when to hit them," Ferguson said. He studied a few of the photos over and over, and then said, "Should go like clockwork. What're your thoughts?"

"My thoughts? Well, as for the how, I leave that up to you. As for the when, now would please me, but, I suppose you'll need time to prepare, so... as soon as possible will have to do. Just keep one thing in mind as you plan, Randy."

"Randal," Ferguson corrected, "and what is it you want me to keep in mind."

"Arthur Fetchenko is no dummy. He probably already knows we're coming. Don't give him much time to prepare."

* * *

Tony Copeletti had the limo's door open and one foot on the concrete floor of the underground parking facility of the Fetchenko headquarters before Vinny Gotto brought the car to a complete stop. "See me in my office before you go home," he told Vinny.

Vinny did not respond. He finished his hurried parking job, then walked to his personal vehicle, got in, started it up, and headed out of the garage. He was going home. He had a bad feeling. He sensed that somehow his cousin, Tony, had gotten wind or otherwise figured out his involvement with Fetchenko's enemies. Sure he would report to Tony before the end of the day, but first, he would stop by his house, kiss his pretty wife and daughter, and hold them both for what could well be his last time — just in case. But he would know the one thing that would make all he had risked worth it. He knew that Pauley Danucci would be along with an envelope stuffed with enough money to take care of whatever his family could possibly need, including his little girl's medical expenses, for a very long time. To a man like Vinny Gotto, that was the closest he would ever come to dying a happy man.

* * *

Pauley Danucci felt absolutely victorious. It had been so long in the making, this vengeance of his that he had begun to think it would never come. He was a child when he first dreamed of it, this eye for an eye philosophy toward his former brother-in-law who should have been the one killed that night instead of his sister, Maryann. Maryann was everything to Pauley Danucci in those days. She was his only family. Arthur Fetchenko's enemies should have killed Arthur Fetchenko. That's what would have been fair, but no, instead they took Maryann. But alas, Ferelli and his people would see to it that the score was evened. They would see to it that the right party finally died. And it would be because of what he, Pauley Danucci, finally did that day. It was victory indeed. He strutted down the street. He felt the two envelopes, one in either jacket pocket, both of them stuffed with cash, and it dawned on him; heh, he didn't just get even; he got paid to get even.

* * *

"The boss is pissed, Vinny. He's been looking high and low for your sorry ass. Where the hell have you been?" asked one of the guards as Vinny Gotto drove his car back through the gate to the company's parking garage.

"Had to run an errand. I'm on my way to see Tony now."

* * *

"There's fifty G's in there," Tony Copeletti said and slid an envelope across his desk at Vinny Gotto. "Arthur wants your little girl's medical needs to be taken care of. If this don't cover to date, he'll give you more. Bring her future bills in and he'll take care of them as well."

Vinny Gotto wept. Tony Copeletti knew the gesture would stab his cousin in the heart. He was, after all, mob. Mob means loyalty; it is bred into them. The act would penetrate as cleanly as a knife. That would do for now. But when Tony Copeletti is able to verify his suspicions, a knife of steel will be used. But the little girl will be cared for anyway.

Chapter Twelve

The information Arthur Fetchenko received in his late-night phone call from Martha Ferelli had been good information, but not everything he needed. From it he knew he and his operation was about to be hit and by whom. What he needed now was the how and when. For the answers to those questions he needed intelligence. "Who can be bought?" he asked of Tony Copeletti as he entered the office.

"Excuse me?"

"J. P.'s camp. Who can be bought?"

"Can Martha get us more?" Copeletti suggested.

"She's disappeared," Fetchenko said.

"What do you mean disappeared?" Copeletti asked.

"I mean she's gone, history, maybe back home, maybe dead. No one seems to know."

"Should I send someone to find out?"

"Absolutely! Now, who can we bribe, Tony? We need info. They'll hit us. We know that. It'd be just super to know how and when."

"I'll dig into it," Copeletti promised.

"That would be nice," Fetchenko said. "I think we better alert Jacob Rain. Unless I missed my guess, they'll come at us from more than one direction."

"I'll call him. Anyone else?"

"That old colonel, he's a tactician. He'll try as many fronts at once as he can come up with. I'd bet on here and I'd bet on Nikki's. But he may go for anyone we're backing in the upcoming election as well. Most of them would be just collateral damage. It's Henry Tyler and Jack Albrecht we really need to watch. Those two end up on a slab and so will our plans for at least the next four years. We need to protect them."

"I thought you said they'd be too high profile," Tony Copeletti said. He specifically recalled Arthur telling Henry he was perfectly safe, and suggesting they take security from Albrecht to guard Henry, and... many other things which all added up to Arthur Fetchenko not being overly concerned for either of those candidates.

"I said that for Henry's benefit. You know how he is. And I've made similar comments around others I'm not sure I trust, just in case some of it would get back to Ferelli. He's likely to have Ferguson send less than his best if he figures we've pulled our best."

Tony Copeletti mentally kicked himself. He had been so wrapped up in his troubles, rather suspicions, about his cousin, Vinny Gotto, that he hadn't thought the real issues over. Rarely did Arthur Fetchenko come up with things Tony Copeletti wasn't already in tune to. But now he was lost. He found it unsettling. "What's our next move?"

"You can't think of anyone we can buy?"

"No! They've been on their game this time, Boss. We don't know anyone who's with them, at least none that I can think of."

"I think you might be wrong this time, my friend." Arthur Fetchenko turned on his laptop. He clicked to open an image Tony had sent him earlier, a photo taken by Tony's cellular phone of a man leaving Vinny Gotto's limo window. "Take a good look at this," he said and slid the laptop around to face Tony. "See if you don't recognize him." Copeletti studied it for a time, finally shaking his head in defeat. "That's that little shit of a brother-in-law of mine, Bonehead. That's your cousin, Pauley Danucci."

Copeletti stared harder at the image, and then flipped the laptop closed, almost violently. "Son-of-a-bitch," he mumbled.

"Yeah! Son-of-a-bitch," Fetchenko said.

Copeletti picked up the phone on Fetchenko's desk and pressed the extension for security. "Did Vinny Gotto leave yet?"

"We can't trust Vinny," Fetchenko commented.

"The ones you don't trust are usually the most useful at times like this," he told Fetchenko. Then, "Tell him I need to see him. Tell him to wait in my office." And he hung up the phone.

"What's your plan?" Fetchenko asked.

"We'll set the date. I'll plant the seed with Vinny and let him carry it to Pauley Danucci like a little bird. Vinny will go for the extra cash; I know him."

"And Pauley?"

"Pauley's obviously got a hard-on for you, Boss. Whatever we feed him, so long as he thinks it's legit, he'll bring right back to Joey Ferelli."

"So... how do we set the date?"

"Leave it to me. You just decide when you want these little wars. I'll make Vinny believe in an exact evening when we'll be vulnerable. You can bet your ass that's when we'll be attacked."

"Tony, you're a genius," Fetchenko said and smiled.

"Yeah! Who woulda thunk it?"

* * *

"Glad I caught you before you left for home," Tony Copeletti told Vinny Gotto when he found him with his feet on his desk. "Now... get your dumb ass outta my chair. We got work to see to."

"What kinda work?"

"What kinda work? Security work, you moron. That's what we do here," Tony said and slapped Vinny on the back of the head. It was how he had treated his cousin in the past, and to change now would let Vinny know for sure he was being watched. And... it would alert him that all of this was about using him. "I'm going to need you close for a bit. Jacob Rain is tied up in Wisconsin," Rain always served as Tony's second in command, "so I'm going to need you to help out on this one." He looked at Vinny to see what might show in his expression. It could be fear, question, pride, disbelief, or any number of other emotions. What he saw was cocky, the look of recognized opportunity. It was what he had hoped for. "You all right with this?"

"Yeah! Sure! Why not?"

"Good. We'll meet first thing in the morning. We need to go over the times that look most obvious for an attack and beef up security."

"How we gonna tell that?" Vinny asked.

"There's lots of ways. It'll be a moonless night, probably; maybe rainy, stuff like that. I'll go over things with Arthur; you and I will talk tomorrow."

* * *

"Well?" Arthur Fetchenko asked when Copeletti reported back to him after the meeting with Vinny Gotto.

"Well, what?"

"Well what'd you learn?"

"I think we can rule out an attack on a moonless night or a rainy night. I'll know more later. His cellular is tapped, his home phone, and I got a man tailing him," Copeletti said, then went silent for a time. "You really think that's Pauley Danucci Vinny's feeding info to?"

"I know it is. Look, is there any way we can find out what Vinny delivered so far?"

"Could be. My guys are checking on his cell phone records. If he used the phone to make contact, we'll soon know that. If he took pictures with it we'll pick up on that as well. I should have all the details before noon tomorrow."

"Should we wait to alert Blackburn?" Fetchenko asked. Phil Blackburn was head of the watch over Jack Albrecht's campaign trail. "And how about Henry? Should we call him?"

"Why don't we pull Blackburn and Albrecht in for a few days until we get a handle on this?" Copeletti suggested. "Jacob Rain is close to where Henry is now. He could check it out."

"Albrecht is safer where he is, so is Henry for the time being. We'll be the first target. No need placing Jack and Henry in harm's way. We'll bring them home after we kick ass on Ferelli and the boys. Touch base with Jacob. Keep him in the loop on this. Things get out of hand and we'll want him to move Nikki. Now get some rest. Come see me first thing tomorrow, but for now, I have a date."

"Damn right you do," Liz Harmon said as she entered the office. "Right on the other side of that door." Fetchenko's office backed up against his living quarters. Liz gestured impatiently at its entrance.

Tony Copeletti took the hint. He left the room.

* * *

Domestic living was beginning to appeal to Jacob Rain. Not since the early days, just after reform school when he found and married his former wife, had he been this laidback. And it was starting to concern him. Was he losing his edge? Was all of this making him soft? He was Security, just as much as Secret Service guarding the President was. This wasn't cool, this comfort that was falling all around him. Perhaps he should request a change. But... then... this girl was hot. And she seemed to like him — really like him. He watched her walk toward him, tight blue jeans, hip huggers so her pretty navel shone, sweatshirt cut off both on the sleeves just above the elbow and at the midsection just below the tits, no bra. What a sight.

He didn't notice the cell phone she carried. "It's Mr. Copeletti," she said softly as she handed it to him.

He placed it at his ear. "Rain?" Copeletti asked. "You got a new secretary?"

"No!"

"You lose track of your phone?"

"Just left it in the other room," Rain said.

"What room you in now?" Copeletti asked. Jacob Rain hesitated. Tony Copeletti chuckled. "Don't go gettin' soft on me now, Jacob."

"Don't you concern yourself with that, Tony," Rain said, his composure regained. He did, however, silently remind himself to keep a closer handle on the location of his phone. *What if it had been Arthur calling?* "What do you want, Tony?"

"Boss just wanted me to give you the heads-up. Ferelli's about to start something again."

"Joey? When isn't he up to something?"

"It's more serious this time. We got a leak in the unit, connected to a snitch on their side. We don't even know the extent of the information they have yet. Just be cautious, keep a sharp eye out, that's all."

"Who's the leak? You know yet?" Jacob asked.

"Not for sure. Got my suspect all picked out though."

"Who?"

"Vinny Gotto's my favorite pick," Copeletti said.

"Christ! Got a favorite for the snitch?"

"Arthur thinks it's Pauley Danucci."

"You must be proud, Tony," Rain said, mirth in his voice, "them two being your cousins."

"What about Arthur? Pauley is his brother-in-law," Copeletti said. "Anyway, keep on your toes. They'll probably try to pull something on the girl. At least that's what Arthur seems to think." And he hung up.

"What was that all about?" Nikki Carson asked as she straddled Jacob Rain on his kitchen chair, laced her fingers through his thick, black hair and pulled him toward her and kissed him hard on the mouth. The sweet taste of her hot tongue probing, searching for his, erased the contents of Tony's message if even just briefly.

"I'm not sure," he told her and kissed her again.

* * *

Arthur Fetchenko stood on his deck, twenty feet off the ground, cool night air surrounding him. He wore only boxers. He gripped the wrought iron rail and tried hard to come back from the clouds. Liz always did this to him, whenever they made love. At sixty years old after a life of hard work and little in the line of sensual pleasures he wondered if he'd ever adapt, not that he planned on giving it up if he didn't adapt. That was out of the question. This was too much like heaven on earth, a heightening within him he could never again see himself doing without. Tony and most of his close companions had tried over the years to convince him that this part of life was one he should not deny himself, but after losing Maryann like he had, then having Evelyn pass him up because of a fear of the same, he had settled on a life alone. Thank God he was no longer stuck with that decision.

He felt Liz's warm breasts on the bare skin of his back and shivered.

"Did that take some of the tension out of your hectic day?" she asked him.

"It left me like a rag-doll, all weak-kneed, barely able to walk."

"Want to go again?"

"I don't know that I can. I'm not a young man, you know?"

"Sure you are. You're the youngest sixty-two year old I know," she insisted.

That's right; he was sixty-two, not sixty. See what she does to you? He asked himself. "I don't know that I could handle any more."

"You can." She pulled him from the railing and swung him around so her back was to the rail and he was facing her. "I'll prove it to you." And she kissed him passionately and let her soft hand slide to his penis. She felt it harden. "See?"

"Out here?" he asked and smiled.

"See anybody in the courtyard?"

"Nope!" He kissed her on the mouth, then the neck, then nibbled at an earlobe, all the while working himself inside of her. "You're right," he whispered. "I'm not too old."

* * *

"Lucky bastard," Tony Copeletti said softly. He spat in the grass, looked up at the balcony just above him and smiled. He smashed his cigarette under his shoe and went back inside. It was enough night-air for him this time. Maybe he'd return later.

Chapter Thirteen

Pauley Danucci's text message the night before told him he was to meet Vinny Gotto for breakfast at the Royal Diner, just blocks from J. P. Ferelli's home. He sipped at a mug of coffee and watched Vinny circle the block several times. "Safety first, you shit," he whispered to himself on Vinny's third time past the window. "Park the fucking car. I ain't got all day."

"Them boys got any more money?" Vinny asked as he slid into the booth across from Pauley.

"I'd guess that'll depend on what you got for sale."

"Plenty. I got promoted to Copeletti's assistant on this one, at least until Jacob Rain gets back. And I been asked to help decide what our vulnerable times are and when we beef up the security."

A pretty waitress approached. Both Pauley and Vinny flirted. "Deloris," Pauley said, "I'd like you to meet my cousin, Vinny."

"Ain't there a movie about him? '*My Cousin Vinny*?" she asked and giggled a bit. The two men placed their orders and Pauley patted her on the ass as she left. She giggled again.

"So... what all you got?" Pauley Danucci asked once they were alone again.

"I tell you what I got for free. Tell your guys not to try an attack on a night with no moon, or on a rainy night. They'll be armed and ready for them. That's already been decided. Now... that's free. Everything else has a price."

"What're you lookin' for?" Pauley asked.

"I wanna retire," Vinny said. "Tell Ferelli five-hundred-grand gets him a time to attack when they all got

their pants down around their ankles, whackin' off."
Vinny pulled a handful of bills out of a pocket, tossed
them on the table, and headed for the door. "Call me,"
he added on his way out.

* * *

Tony Copeletti smiled sheepishly at Liz Harmon as
he passed her desk.

"Was that your cigarette I smelled last night?" she
asked.

He did not answer. He could think of nothing to say
so kept walking into Arthur Fetchenko's office and out of
her sight. He shut the door as he entered.

"Good morning," Fetchenko said. "Your people
learn anything from Gotto's phone records?"

"Pictures."

"Pictures?"

"Yeah. Vinny took pictures with his cell phone and
sent them to another cellular. Hell, I didn't even know
such a thing was possible," Copeletti said.

"You need to get one of your younger boys to teach
you, pull you into modern day. Where you been anyway,
Tony? Even I know that stuff is possible, and I don't have
a cell phone."

"You're probably right, Arthur. I probably do need a
few lessons in technology. But, at least, I've been smart
enough to keep some youngsters around who understand
it."

"So... who got the pictures?" Fetchenko asked.

"The number is listed to — you guessed it — Pauley
Danucci. You know, Boss, you've got a good eye. I never
would have identified Pauley from that picture. How'd
you do that?"

"The jacket. I sent it to him last Christmas," Arthur
admitted and smiled.

"You know what I find puzzling? You've done a lot for that kid over the years. Why would he turn on you?"

"He blames me for Maryann's death. Remember, Tony, he was just a kid, and Maryann was his only family. That accident, I should say 'hit'," he closed his eyes and shook his head for a moment, "put him in the foster system. I offered to take him but he hated me then. I guess he still does."

"Regardless, he has to be dealt with. You know that, don't you, Arthur?" Tony warned.

"I know, Tony. I know. I'll leave that all to you after this is done with. But it can't be easy for you, two cousins? Blood."

"That never is, but I'm family. These things happen within the family — greed usually — or revenge. Anyway, I've had to deal with it before," Tony said reassuringly. "Now, there was also a text message sent to Pauley this morning. Vinny made a breakfast date with him."

"What do you suppose he's telling Pauley?" Arthur asked.

"Probably very little. Pauley's not the one buying, and I doubt Vinny's doing this for anything other than money. No, he'll hold back. He'll have Pauley make the offer to Ferelli, then, if Ferelli's buying, he'll sell us out."

"Let's make sure the bastard doesn't get anything we don't want him to have, Tony."

"Will do, Boss," Tony assured him and left the office. His meeting with Vinny was to begin any moment. He would convince Vinny that security needs to pay closest attention to the parking garage. He would play down the idea of an attack by air, claiming that he (Tony) knew Colonel Ferguson, and he knew that Fergie preferred ground troops to paratroopers. It was a fact, and would be easy to sell to Ferelli since he knew the same about Ferguson. And he would convince Ferelli, through Vinny of course, that the upcoming Friday night, just five days in the future, would be his best time to make his play as the unit would be hosting their presidential hopeful, and all security would be concentrated on that event. Over the next four days, a special hand-picked team would meet after dark for training. Vinny would be at home while that training takes place.

* * *

"Are you sure?" J. P. Ferelli asked Pauley Danucci. "Five hundred thousand is a hell of a lot of money."

"I'm just the messenger," Pauley insisted.

"Oh, no! We're not playing that game. I hold you responsible for information you bring us. I don't give a shit where it comes from. I hold you responsible."

"Look! This guy's straight up honest," Pauley started.

"Ha! That's refreshing. An honest turncoat. How odd?"

"I'm serious, Senator. He's my cousin. I've known him all my life. He wouldn't betray anyone if he didn't need to, the sick kid and all."

"Yes, yes, I remember. The parasite with the parasite. Well... I sure hope this temporary loyalty shift lasts through Friday at least. For a half-million bucks, it had better, my friend," Ferelli said and handed Pauley an envelope. "There's an extra fifty grand in there for you." Ferelli never knew if he would have further need for Pauley Danucci, so decided fifty grand would be wise insurance. Besides, it was taxpayer's money anyway. "Now get the hell out of here."

J. P. closed the door and waited to hear Danucci's footsteps on the walk. "You get all of that?"

"I did. The information is correct at least about one thing."

"What's that, Fergie?"

"I am a ground pounder, not a sky diver," Colonel Ferguson admitted.

"Good thing you don't have to go then."

"There's more to it than that. I wouldn't even know who to pick. I have no expertise when it comes to assaults by air," Ferguson said. "I'd rather take my chances with a ground attack."

"It's by air, Colonel. On Friday night. Find somebody who can get you up to speed on such an attack. And do it quickly," Ferelli ordered. "Now... what about the girl?"

"We have a team in place, just waiting for word from us."

* * *

"Rain?" Nikki Carson sought Jacob Rain's attention.
"Yes?"

"After all of this is over with, what are you going to do?" she asked.

"I don't understand," Rain said.

"After I no longer need protecting, and the election is behind, and my father wins everything."

Rain smiled and said, "This never ends."

"You mean I'm going to need protection forever?" she asked and slid over his bare chest to grab one of his cigarettes and a match from the nightstand. She scooted up and leaned against the headboard. She smiled at the thought of having to be watched by Jacob Rain forever, and she lit the cigarette.

"I didn't know you smoked," Rain said.

"I don't, usually. But after a man like you, what's a woman to do?" She drew in a drag, then coughed, then snuffed the cigarette out in the ashtray. "Yuck!" she said.

Jacob Rain smiled at her in amusement. "We're going to a speech tomorrow," he told her.

"Who's speaking?"

"Henry Tyler."

* * *

Vinny Gotto, having told all there was to tell and having unknowingly set the date Tony Copeletti and Arthur Fetchenko had decided on for an attack by Ferelli and his people, was now of no more use to the company. Copeletti chose, however, instead of firing Vinny, or killing him, that he would reassign him. To do otherwise at the time would be an error. It would probably make Vinny suspicious.

"I'm sending you to Madison, to watch Henry Tyler's back. You'll move the family, all arrangements have been made and quarters have been secured, a place you guys can hold up until Jeannie finds (Jeannie being Vinny's wife) the perfect house," Copeletti told his turncoat cousin. He did so with a smile.

"So this is a permanent move?" Vinny asked.

"Yeah. It's permanent. You'll base out of Madison. You'll travel with Henry on the campaign trail until the election, and after Henry wins, you'll be liaison with Uncle Antonio."

Antonio Copeletti, head of the Chicago Copeletti crime family, uncle to Tony, Vinny, and Pauley Danucci, was very much a part of the Fetchenko organization, and in fact, was most of the reason Arthur Fetchenko had gotten his high level of power within the government. Well... maybe not the reason he got the power; that was accomplished through plain old blackmail. But definitely the reason he was able to hang on to it — all that muscle at his disposal at the drop of a hat.

"I do something wrong?" Vinny asked, hoping his indiscretion for cash hadn't been discovered.

"No. Not at all. We just thought, me and Arthur Fetchenko, that Madison was the perfect place for you. We did some checking. The university has a great outpatient program. They say they're having huge success dealing with what your little girl has," Copeletti said. He donned a huge smile, stood, and patted Vinny on the back. "Gonna miss you around here, Cousin." And he left the room. He went into his private office and closed the door behind him.

* * *

"Uncle Antonio," Copeletti said into the phone. "We have a problem." He went on to explain all that had happened with Vinny. "He has to be dealt with," he finished with. He waited while his uncle lectured on the value of family loyalty. Then, "I know. But Vinny Gotto has become a liability, a high risk liability." He listened in silence for a time, and then added, "He knows too much. We don't take care of this problem, Uncle, and he can undo everything Arthur has accomplished. Then we all lose out, you too." It always paid to appeal to his uncle's greedier side; after all, what crime lord backs anything for free? "No, Sir. Keep your people out of it. I'll send Jacob Rain to deal with Vinny." More silence, then, "Thank you, Don Copeletti." And he hung up. He wiped tiny beads of sweat from his brow and called Arthur Fetchenko's extension to fill him in.

* * *

"How should I dress for this thing?" Nicole Carson asked Jacob Rain.

"Not like that," He said, as he looked her over. Her hair was pulled up and piled on top of her head, long strands hanging sensually in ringlets falling onto her cheeks. She wore tight denim short-shorts which accentuated her tanned, slender legs making them seem even longer, a bright red low-cut sweater that exposed nearly half of her breasts then ended above the navel, and no undergarments — anywhere. "Henry wants you to stand onstage with him for a time."

She thought about objecting, Henry and her having fought over the last court case they were jointly involved in and over her decision to give up her position with the district attorney's office over losing that argument. But this was Uncle Henry. That one unpleasant encounter couldn't change the fact. She owed Henry Tyler more than that, much more. And now she was, although slowly and only through the need to be protected, becoming part of her father's, and Tony Copeletti's, and Henry Tyler's, and the Copeletti crime family's, and the Democratic Party's little consortium, like it or not. And she was finding herself enjoying it, mostly because of Jacob Rain, her personal protector who she had gone a long way past merely liking. "So I should put on something a little more... lawyerly?" she asked.

"Yeah," he told her. "But don't do too much with that hair. You'll look hot and lawyerly."

Chapter Fourteen

"Jack Albrecht's lead is insurmountable," Congressman McArthur told Victor Parker, Dan Davidson, and J. P. Ferelli in their evening meeting at Freedom Hill Speakeasy. "He holds nearly twenty points in front by most poles with only months to go."

"It's only money. It's clever advertising available only through spending big money," J. P. insisted.

"That may well be, but what are we going to do about it. In case you haven't noticed, our contender isn't exactly flush, and at this point in the game, Albrecht having that tremendous point spread over him, I'm afraid contributors aren't so willing to part with their money," Ohio's Senator Davidson said.

"There's another way," Ferelli insisted.

"Well, then, I'd sure be interested in knowing about it, J. P.," Victor Parker threw in.

"We stop Albrecht's cash-flow, that's how it's done," Ferelli said.

"And how do we do that?" Victor asked.

"We don't. We don't have to do anything. Colonel Ferguson's already on it. In just a few short days he'll be delivering, airmail if you get my drift, a very convincing message to Albrecht's money man. My guess is Jack Albrecht will fade into the sunset where he belongs once his cash is cut off." Ferelli held a glass in the air and donned a knowing smile. "Gentlemen, to Colonel Fergie Ferguson. May success knock on the door of his aircraft."

"Here, here," all said in unison and tapped their glasses together.

* * *

Randal Ferguson, dressed in civilian clothes, sat behind a gray steel office desk in a tiny room at Fort Meade. His long-time friend and confidant, Major Lee Palmer had completed preliminary interviews of twenty freshly trained warriors with jump school preparation, and was now ushering them in one at a time. Fergie would chose seven from the lot but would rely heavily on Palmer's judgment more than his own, because Palmer's expertise with this kind of operation and the kind of soldiers needed far outweighed his own. "They're a little green," he had commented to Palmer at one point during the process.

"An operation like yours, without clearance from higher up the ladder than the two of us, won't get you seasoned participants, Fergie. These are the best I can do, and you do understand, something goes wrong, these men don't come back in one piece, and I'll deny any of this took place," Parker had answered.

"What about a plane?" Ferguson asked.

"I can get you a chopper more easily. All of these men can rappel. That might be a better option for your mission: quicker, less chance of any of them missing the mark and ending up hung up in a tree someplace," Major Parker suggested.

Fergie milled it over for a moment. *Not a bad idea*, he thought. *I'll do it.* "A chopper will do nicely."

"When is all of this coming down?" Parker asked. "No way I can get you a bird or turn loose of these men without knowing," he added, seeing caution flash in Ferguson's eyes.

"Friday night, just after dark."

"They'll be ready," Palmer said.

* * *

Nicole Carson, stylishly adorned in Capri pants and matching waist-length jacket over a white close-knit sweater, soft ringlets still falling from her hair and dancing on her pretty cheeks, climbed the few steps to join Henry Tyler, already into his campaign speech. Jacob Rain had excused himself, declaring that he had some brief work to see to and that he would be back before she was done on the platform.

"Ladies and gentlemen," Henry interrupted his speech when he spotted the beauty out of the corner of his eye, "I'd like to introduce my very lovely niece, Nicole Carson, to all of you." He held his arms wide and, for his efforts, received an obviously meaningful hug. The audience ate it up.

Jacob Rain picked Vinny Gotto out of the small number of sunglass sporting men scattered around the stage and approached him. "Tony Copeletti is on the phone asking to speak to you," Rain told Vinny.

Vinny Gotto shot Jacob Rain a look, half curious, half fear-filled. "Tony?" he asked.

"Yeah. The phone over here," Rain gestured, "right through that door."

Inside the small building, a payphone hung from the wall, its receiver dangling from a metal encased cord. Vinny Gotto picked it up and held it to his ear. He knew it was over when all he heard was empty silence. He turned to face Jacob Rain — to accept his judgment. Rain placed a palm over Vinny's mouth, slid the sharp blade under his sternum and upward into his heart — clean — fast — humane. "Look into my eyes," he said and helped Vinny Gotto to the floor of the tiny room.

"And now... we have time for a few questions." Jacob Rain heard Henry Tyler inform his audience as he slid back into the crowd.

"Will Miss Carson be joining your staff if you win this election?" a gentleman in the third row asked.

"Nicole, would you like to take this one?" Henry asked.

Nikki stepped to the microphone, placed both hands around it, relaxed, comfortable, and said, "I haven't been asked."

"And if you are?"

"I will do whatever I can to help Henry Tyler, whatever he asks of me, and I sincerely hope all of you here today feel the same, because Henry Tyler is the right man for the job. He's who we need and have needed for a very long time."

"Does that mean you will join his staff if asked?" The question came again.

Nikki smiled. "That's all I have to say at this time. Thank you all very much." Then she kissed Henry on the cheek and left the stage to find Jacob Rain, hoping that his business, whatever it had been, was finished. She wanted to go home and get out of her semiformal attire and back into the comfort of her casual clothes. And she wanted it fast.

* * *

Tony Copeletti felt a deep sadness and he knew it was the moment of his cousin Vinny Gotto's death. Arthur Fetchenko walked into his office just as the phone rang. "Copeletti," he said when he picked up, then, "alright, thanks." And he hung up.

"Jacob?" Fetchenko asked.

"Yeah."

"Is it done?"

"Yeah."

"I'm sorry, Tony. I know this must be difficult for you," Arthur Fetchenko consoled.

"Just as hard as it is necessary, I'm afraid," Tony said and began shuffling through a stack of papers.

"Training tonight?" Fetchenko asked, trying to take his friend's mind off his troubles.

"Our first. I have the teams all picked out. We'll start just before dark." He looked around his desktop as though he had lost something. "Did I hear Phil Blackburn is coming home?"

"Yeah, I forgot to tell you. He's got Jack Albrecht all tucked away in a safe place. He wanted to be here for the Friday night war, says he's never seen one of those before," Fetchenko said and smiled. "He might just come in handy, too. That boy's got a lot of connections should we find ourselves in need."

Blackburn did have connections, many of them. He got them because he had been, over the years, Fetchenko's liaison between the Company and nearly everyone, a company schmoozer of sorts whenever anything seemed to get off track. Everyone liked Phil Blackburn, even those who despised Fetchenko and the rest of them liked Phil Blackburn. He was just that kind of guy, charismatic. "Phil could talk the skin off a snake," Fetchenko said.

The comment brought a smile to Tony Copeletti's otherwise emotionless face.

* * *

With Jack Albrecht safely tucked away in an obscure lodge in the Colorado Rockies for a much needed six-day rest and meetings with Henry Tyler and a couple other hopefuls — some Democrats and some Republicans but all supported by the Fetchenko organization — Phil Blackburn set out for home. He was anxious to meet the new challenges which lay before him. He had never taken part in any war, domestic like this one, or military like so many others. Weary of the campaign trail and its many pitfalls, he welcomed the call from Arthur Fetchenko. Arthur had suggested his services might be needed if he had the time. You bet your ass he had the time, and the timing was superbly on target. Jack needed rest. Philip Blackburn needed change. Tony Copeletti's little war, or, he guessed, Joey Ferelli's little war, couldn't have been more convenient if Phil himself had planned it. Only moments after he deposited Albrecht at his retreat quarters he was in a chopper headed for the airport in Denver. There he would catch a flight which, after whatever necessary changes came along the way, would put him in Cumberland, Maryland where he would chopper, once again, to the Fetchenko estate in New Creek. He should be home scrapping with Tony Copeletti not long after his nap in the air.

* * *

Randal Ferguson drilled his seven recruits long into the afternoon and then let them rest. The small remote camp, a one-time equine facility hidden deep in the Blue Ridge Mountains surrounding Front Royal, Virginia, was at his disposal for training purposes, courtesy of the same man who had gotten him troops, Major Parker. Parker also loaned him a master sergeant who had once been a drill sergeant for troops heading for Vietnam. At first sight, Ferguson nearly dismissed him as too elderly for the job, but now, after watching him run circles around the youngsters, was glad he hadn't. His name was Powell, and by evening mess he had the boys ready for naps while he looked full of piss and vinegar.

"Powell," Ferguson said over a meal they shared at a table away from the men, "how about leading this detail in battle?"

"Couldn't do that, Sir,"

"Had enough war in the Nam, eh?"

"No! It's not that, Colonel," the sergeant said. "The chopper's an old Huey — left over from Nam. Seven men with all their gear is a load."

"Then send one of them home." Ferguson knew the more experienced, more adaptable sergeant was worth more to this operation than all the rest of them combined. Powell was the kind of trooper he had in mind when he began planning this, not the bunch of green misfits he had been saddled with by his old friend, Major Parker. No wonder he was still a major. He lacked the know-how to put an effective team together, or he lacked the balls. "Pick the weakest and send him back. Then you can take his place on the chopper."

"Will you be going along?" Powell asked.

"On the ride over, I won't be rappelling, though." Fergie Ferguson was out of the military on a medical. He had been paratrooper-qualified and had made many jumps. On the last of them, though, he suffered a broken back. He had gotten himself tangled in the branches of a tree, and when he cut himself free from his chute, he fell nearly forty feet through thick branches, one of them smashing the lower five vertebrae. He healed, the injured vertebrae fusing of their own accord, but jumping, or most other military activities, became unachievable. "This old back won't take it. I could rappel, but I doubt I would make it to the landing. Too much."

"Who says we'll land?" the sergeant said. "My guess is this is a suicide mission. We'll be lucky to get off a few grenades or rocket launches at vital targets on the way down before they shoot us off the ropes."

"My intel says they'll be guarding against a ground attack, on the other side of the compound."

"Hope you're right, Colonel, but I think you're wrong. No... I think I'll stick with suicide mission."

"Then you'll do it?"

"Hell yes!" Sergeant Powell said and smiled. He had no family, only the military. And he had already been told his next enlistment would not be accepted. This was peacetime for the most part, and old soldiers were being retired to make room for younger recruits. Powell had no hankering to begin life again as a civilian. He just didn't see himself fitting in. Now... die in action? That, he found appealing. "Hell... yes, Colonel."

Chapter Fifteen

Two o'clock in the afternoon at the Fetchenko estate was uncomfortably quiet. Arthur chose to take the remainder of the day, not altogether sure what tomorrow would bring, and spend it alone with Liz. He called Tony's cellular, Tony was out taking care of last minute training of his men, and alerted him that the office would be locked and that he and Liz were going to get some rest since the night coming on them promised to be unusually long. "I wish you'd do as I asked," Copeletti complained. He wanted Arthur and Liz to board the chopper as soon as Phil Blackburn arrived in it, and he wanted them flown to his Uncle Antonio's secure South Bend estate until this was over.

"Liz will go, but I'm staying." It was the answer he gave when Tony first asked, and it hadn't changed.

Inside their lavish living quarters adjacent to the office, Liz Harmon ran water into a teakettle while Arthur settled onto a barstool at the island of their kitchen and watched her. At nearly fifty she was as lovely a woman as he had ever seen, sexier than most, never having given in to something as inconsequential as age when it came to desire and the flirtatious little things a woman could do with herself to let a man know his interest in her would not go unfulfilled. She stood there, back to him, subtle silk skirt cut to just above the knee and outlining her smooth, round bottom which seemed to sway enticingly at that very moment. "How tired are you?" he asked her.

"How thirsty are you?" she asked and placed a hand on her backside and stroked lightly, slowly. She let the skirt pull up a few more inches as she withdrew her hand.

She could hear his breathing, deeper, more rapid, and she smiled. She crossed her arms in front of her, her hands at the waistband of her sweater. She pulled up lifting the garment over her head. She shook the tangles from her hair and let the sweater fall to the kitchen floor. "Kind of warm in here, don't you think?" She scooped the hair from the back of her neck and piled it on top of her head and shifted her petite, flawless hips to one side. She wore no bra.

"Very warm," he said and slid off the stool. He came up behind her and kissed her bare neck, first on its center, then on each side. He slid his hands around and cupped her breasts. He kissed, time after time, as he let his face travel down her spine, quitting and heading back up only when he came to the band on her skirt. He let his hands slide over her smooth stomach and inside the waistband of her silk skirt, his fingertips gently stroking pubic hair. He bent his wrists, forcing her skirt and panties down a couple inches. He kissed more on her neck, and then nibbled on an earlobe. She shivered in excitement.

"Are we going in the bedroom?" she asked as she turned to face him.

His hands settled on her backside, the material of her skirt slipping down as he stroked. "Not on your life," he said.

"Right here?" she asked.

"Right here," he said and lifted her and let her skit and panties fall to the floor. He sat her on the counter. He kissed her on the breasts, gently closing his lips on each of her nipples and pressing his tongue to them, licking, sucking. Then he kissed between them and started to work his way down her stomach. She arched her back in anticipation. He worked his way down to her pubic hair. She kept it neatly trimmed in an inch-wide line so nothing unsightly would show when she wore a bikini. He licked its outline, and then kissed her thighs, one after the other, settling on what he knew to be a ticklish spot for her, and he licked gently with his tongue. The scream from the teapot whistle combined with tickling from his tongue on her thigh brought on an involuntary tightening of her muscles and locked his head between her legs with incredible force. His ears pinned, he could not hear himself yell out, "Turn it off!"

Things having calmed down, she suggested, "Maybe this is too dangerous for us."

He picked her up and carried her to the table. He sat her on the edge, slid his pants down, inserted himself into her, and they made love in that position for a time, then, without becoming disconnected, he sat on a kitchen chair, her straddling him, and they finished. They sat there, him still in her for a long time, enjoying each other until he became soft. Then they showered — together.

* * *

The ring of the telephone on the nightstand could barely be heard over the sound of Philip Blackburn's helicopter landing in the courtyard below Arthur and Liz's bedroom balcony. The afternoon sun, unusually warm, had caused them to leave their garden door open while they rested after their lovemaking and long, hot shower during which she wanted to go again. He had accommodated her, thus the need for a nap. Fetchenko picked up the phone, even though he already knew who was calling. It was Tony alerting him that Phil had arrived. "Are you packed?" he asked after hanging up.

"Do I really have to go?" she asked.

"Tony will have a shit-fit if you don't."

"Is that something we should fear?"

"It won't be a pretty sight. I can promise you that," Fetchenko said.

"Well then, I guess I'd better pack," she said. She sent him off to greet Blackburn while she threw some things in a bag. She wouldn't need much. Arthur had told her it would only be a day or two.

* * *

"I suppose you didn't think we could handle this without you," Tony Copeletti jokingly told Phil Blackburn as he got off the chopper.

"Let me ask you this," Blackburn started. "What do you two geniuses plan to do with the bodies?"

Tony looked at Arthur. Arthur looked at Tony. Both of them looked at Blackburn and shrugged their shoulders.

"That's what I thought," Blackburn said and reached for his suitcase. "That pretty young lady ready to go?"

"She'll be right along," Arthur said. The pilot nodded and idled the chopper's engine down. Fetchenko smiled at him knowingly. *He must have a wife*, Arthur thought.

* * *

It would be a quiet evening after Liz Harmon boarded the helicopter for Tony Copeletti's uncle's South Bend estate, an evening filled with solemn planning and tactical analysis. In a fight like the one about to take place the key is to never relax, never stop fine-tuning, not until the battle had been fought. And as darkness began to cloak the compound, everyone hoped that they had planed correctly.

Tony's guys were in position.

Arthur Fetchenko was safely tucked away in his quarters, Phil Blackburn with him to keep him there, out of harm's way.

A secondary crew of men had been placed strategically to guard against an intrusion through the tunnel and parking garage.

Two armed men stood guard outside Fetchenko's office.

Tony Copeletti watched from inside the security office doors and heard the first sounds of the approaching intrusion before anyone else. "I wish Jacob Rain was here," he said quietly. His thoughts turned to Vinny Gotto. Would this have been a better death for his cousin? Maybe, but death is death, no matter how it comes. Besides, it's too late.

* * *

Tony Copeletti, although not of military background, knew how to stage war. It had been his mobster upbringing which set his style; and that style was so dramatically different from standard military tactics, it would prove unbeatable to a bunch of kids fresh out of advanced infantry training. Colonel Randal Ferguson should have known better. Had he lost it? Was he getting too old for the game? He should have made wiser choices; he should have sent his best, perhaps Special Forces or Seals. But Ferguson picked seven of his average — even disposable — cock-sure that Copeletti had no best to throw back at him. And that was the least of his mistakes.

Had he taken a closer look at the photos he had written off as old information, Ferguson would have known that the cliff faces of the former military compound inside the mountain at New Creek, West Virginia had been altered. Bunkers had been added — six of them — midway to the top of the mountain and strategically placed. In the photos they were scarcely noticeable, but they could be seen. His failure to examine those few photos would come at a great cost.

Then there was Pauley Danucci, the man with an age-old grudge against Arthur Fetchenko. Fergie never once questioned his loyalty, for it was not loyalty at all, but something much stronger. It was revenge that drove Pauley Danucci. It was the mountain mover strength of pure hate that fueled him. A small thing like loyalty didn't enter into it. But Ferguson should have known Arthur Fetchenko would be on to Pauley Danucci early in the game. He should have guessed that. A life-long enemy, a man like Arthur Fetchenko always knows the whereabouts and activities of. It's how men like Arthur Fetchenko survive. Perhaps had Colonel Randal Ferguson been keeping an eye on Danucci's cousin, Vinny Gotto as well as Danucci himself he might have known more. But for his neglect, there would be defeat in his future.

All of these things began to cross Colonel Ferguson's mind as the Huey approached Fetchenko's mountain. Now he wished his old friend, Parker, had found him a better bird, not that the Huey wouldn't do the trick. But this one, this Huey had been decommissioned and was being made ready for scrap. Once an amiable gunship, having been stripped of her armament, she was now merely transportation for him and his men. Hell, if this old girl was what she was during Vietnam when Fergie was last aboard one, no one would need to rappel, at least not until the faces of the cliffs had been altered to an unrecognizable state by launched rockets and grenades and any glass in the compound had been pulverized by fifty caliber machinegun fire. What he wouldn't give for a fifty in each door right now. But that... they did not have. "You guys ready?" he asked. The sergeant was, the rest of them weren't but said they were.

Russian-made AK-47 assault rifles were Tony Copeletti's weapon of choice for his men. It wasn't that he thought them better than the M-16's his opposition would use; truthfully, he didn't know the difference. But he had heard both of them fire, and the Russian rifle just sounded more... frightening to him; and it was so distinctive, he would know where his men were without effort. Night-vision scopes would be added as their intelligence told Tony this altercation had been scheduled for after dark. It had also told him that it would come by air, and not through the tunnel which served the estate as the only access other than by air. To be on the safe side, however, the tunnel did have a system in place to gas any number of intruders into unconsciousness at the flip of a switch. And even if an enemy were to employ gasmasks, airlock solid steel doors would trap them in the tunnel. They would trigger along with the gas.

The whack, whack, whack of the approaching chopper's blades made adrenalin spike in each of Copeletti's men. Those in the blinds sat ready: safety off, round in the chamber, backup ammo accounted for, barrels leaning downward. Instructions were, no one was to fire until all of the intruders were beneath them. A two-man team with a mission, ex-military, hid out in thick underbrush atop the mountain. They were armed with a hand-held rocket launcher and their only job was to take out the Huey's rotor once all of her rappelling crew was well underway. Copeletti wanted them to fall, but hoped for one or two to survive that fall. Dead men don't talk and he might well need answers. Six well-armed men patrolled the courtyard — their job — stop anything that's moving, eliminate any threat, then wait for quiet and check the casualties and disarm any who were still capable of exacting damage to the compound or any of its occupants. Copeletti felt all would happen like clockwork: men would rappel, shots would ring out from above them before they could do much damage, the helicopter would be disabled, the ground crew would do cleanup, and the whole thing would be over in a matter of minutes. The only possible variable would be the chopper. No one seemed to be able to answer the question; what will the helicopter do once the rotor has been destroyed? Too much depended on the skill of the pilot.

The sound was coming closer.

The war was about to begin.

* * *

Ferguson looked back. He watched the sergeant pull an M-79 grenade launcher from a canvas bag. He smiled and nodded his head. Someone had thought ahead.

Chapter Sixteen

The helicopter hovered too long in the night sky to please Tony Copeletti. What the hell were they doing? Were they going to rappel or what? Then the whistle of armament being launched from the open door of the chopper rang out, then the explosion and the shower of glass. Fetchenko's quarters. They hit Fetchenko's quarters.

Phil Blackburn saw it coming. There was little he could do but throw himself on Arthur Fetchenko. He did not hear an explosion. He did not hear braking glass or feel it rain down on them. He did not feel anything.

Tony grabbed a gun. He began firing at the bird. A soldier toppled out and floated toward the ground. Ropes dropped from both sides of the helicopter, men rappelling before they hit full length a few feet from the ground, two, then two more, and then another two. Shots rang from the blinds and young soldiers died, one after another.

The first rocket went wide and high, missing the chopper's tail rotor by several feet. The pilot immediately employed evasion tactics. The second rocket flew under and exploded when it hit the cliff face, raining dirt and rock down on the still soldiers below. The third shot was a direct hit, not to the rotor, but to the tail section just ahead of the rotor. It brought the bird down where it landed hard in the center of the courtyard. An older soldier — was it Colonel Ferguson? No, it was a stranger — jumped from the chopper and darted into the shadows, under cover of the tree line at the edge of the courtyard. Shots were fired and bullets rained down, but no kill could be confirmed. Copeletti's ground crew dared not move out to check the casualties, to secure the area.

"Anybody see him?" Copeletti asked through his hand-held radio.

"I see rustling in the bushes," a voice came back.

"Then shoot for Christ sakes." And a long blast of automatic fire sounded.

"Get him?" Copeletti asked. A long pause followed, the shooter finally admitting he had no way of being sure. The only option, to send one of his ground crew in, was one he did not cherish, but... it was his only option. "I'm sending Beck in. Don't anybody shoot him." Beck shot Copeletti a curious look. "You heard me," Copeletti told him.

"Yes, Boss," Beck said and rushed off in the direction the assailant was thought to be, keeping low and in the shadows as much as possible. He came to a place where he had no choice. A patch of ground lay between him and the thicket he sought. It was open ground — no shelter — fairly well lit by a clear evening sky with a partial moon. He dashed in and as he came to the brush line, a shot rang. It came from the other side of the courtyard. Someone had survived the crash. Beck's arms flung high above his head, his back arching unnaturally, his AK-47 crashing to the ground at his side.

Gunfire peppered the position across the courtyard where the single shot came from. The scream of pain rang out. "Got him," Copeletti said softly. It wasn't softly enough. Another shot, and Copeletti felt a sting to his left shoulder, then the warm trickle of blood both front and back. He fell to his knees and grabbed his arm. Just then someone grabbed him from behind, pulled him to his feet and flung him around in the direction of the door to the security office. "Blackburn?" he asked. At least he thought it was Blackburn. Whoever it was had been splattered by blood so not so easily recognized.

"Yeah," Blackburn said.

"Is that yours or Arthur's?" Copeletti asked.

"The blood? Mine, primarily. Probably a little of Arthur's. They hit the balcony outside the bedroom. I saw the goddamn thing coming, so I tackled Arthur. Most of the blood's from window glass hitting us."

"Is Arthur alright?"

"Cut up a bit, but he seems alright. I left him in the office with the two guys you stationed there. You don't look so good though," he said and ripped a piece of cloth from the tail of Copeletti's shirt. He packed the cloth around the wound to stop the bleeding. "Can you hold this here?" He watched Copeletti's eyes roll back. "Tony? Tony?" He slapped him gently on the cheek. Tony opened his eyes. "Best you try to stay alert," Blackburn said. "I'll find Doc." The unit staffed an ex-military medic they called Doc, not a doctor but in most instances was all they needed. Even with the occasional gunshot wound, Doc's experience in a war zone seemed to qualify him.

"Look out there first," Copeletti said. "Is Beck dead?"

Phil Blackburn stood in the shadows inside the door and looked out onto the lawn of the courtyard for a moment. "He's not moving, Tony. But that doesn't mean he's dead." He spotted rustling in the bushes near Beck. "I think that soldier in the bushes is about to make a break for it. Who the hell is he, anyway?"

"No clue."

"I thought your intelligence was so good," Blackburn said, his concern genuine since Fetchenko's safety was everyone's concern.

"All I can say is, the guy must have been a last minute addition or a change in the roster. Hell, how do we know somebody didn't get killed or injured in training? Point is, Phil, my people do their best, but there's some things that are just not easily predicted," Copeletti defended. An onset of gunfire penetrated the silence outside. Copeletti scooted himself to join Blackburn in the shadows near the door. He watched. He listened, and as the noise of the AK's quieted and the dust cleared, he saw the figure dart from the cover of brush and storm toward the entrance where he and Phil Blackburn sat watching. He snatched Blackburn's shirt collar only to end up with it in his hand. He grabbed his forearm and pulled him to the wall. The intruder dashed through the open door and past Copeletti and Blackburn. Tony jumped to his feet. He began a pursuit. Too slow. Too much pain. The soldier jumped aboard the elevator. Blackburn ran to intercept but the elevator doors closed just as he got to them. Copeletti reached for his radio. Inoperable, and probably lucky for him. He had been using it when the bullet pierced his shoulder, and now that he looked at his handheld and saw a sizable chunk of it missing, he wondered where the round would have hit had it not gone through the radio on its way. He shot to a desk and grabbed for a phone. Gunfire rang from a story above. Too late to warn Fetchenko. What was done was done.

Copeletti looked at Blackburn. "You got two good men up there. I'm sure they did their job," Blackburn reassured him.

* * *

The phone on J. P. Ferelli's desk rang many times before he could reach it. Years prior, Martha had made him remove the one in their bedroom — far too many late night calls interrupting their sleep — and now as he stubbed a toe in the dark trying to reach his study, he cursed her for it.

"I'm trapped," the caller said.

"What do you mean, you're trapped?"

"I mean I'm on the ground, the chopper's been shot down, the pilot's dead, almost everyone else is dead or too injured to move," Colonel Ferguson explained.

"Christ, is there any good news?" Ferelli asked.

"Sergeant Powell, one of the troops Lee Palmer sent me, he's an old Vietnam vet.; he made his way to Fetchenko's office. I heard a lot of gunfire coming from there. With luck, the target may have been neutralized."

"With luck," Ferelli said. "Now... what about you? How you getting out of there?"

"I may not. I may end up a P. O. W."

"Well if you do you keep your goddamn mouth shut, you hear?" Ferelli demanded.

"What? You think Arthur Fetchenko don't know it's you after him, Joey?"

"It's J. P.," Ferelli corrected. He hated being called Joey. That's the name used by Arthur Fetchenko and his boys, and Ferelli's hate for the name ran nearly as deep as did his hate for Fetchenko."

"Someone's coming," Fergie said and clicked his cell phone closed. Its lighted face went dark. He reached for his forty-five he aimed at the oncoming sound. Click. Empty. A hand reached for him.

"You'll have to come with me, Colonel," his captor said. He was taken to an interrogation room behind Copeletti's office, his battle done with. As he was escorted by Copeletti's office he saw Doc patching up Copeletti's shoulder.

"Glad somebody got that son-of-a-bitch," he said and received a smack on the back of the head with an AK-47 rifle for his effort. He weakened, slumped to his knees, and was dragged back up and into the interrogation room where he was manhandled into a chair. His captor left him without a word and closed the door. No handle on the inside. No way to escape. He took out a handkerchief and dabbed at a trickle of blood running from the injury the AK had left on him.

Tony Copeletti watched the elevator doors open across the hall from him as Doc secured the field dressing over the hole in his shoulder. Sergeant Powell fell onto the hallway floor and the doors began to close, stopping when the hit Powell, then reopening, then closing until they ran into Powell again. "Somebody pull that guy outta there and make sure he's dead," Copeletti shouted out. "And did anyone clean up those corpses out by the helicopter?"

"We got 'em, Boss," one of his men shouted back.

Phil Blackburn entered the elevator on his way to check on Fetchenko. "Doc, if you're done with Tony, maybe you should come with me."

"I'm coming too," Copeletti said.

"He'll mellow in a bit," Doc whispered to Phil Blackburn. "I gave him something... you know... for the pain."

The elevator came to a stop and its doors slid open, a large patch of blood on the floor in front of them. Two men stood, rifles ready, in front of Copeletti, Blackburn, and Doc. Beyond them, sitting at Liz Harmon's reception desk, was Arthur Fetchenko, apparently unscathed. Copeletti drew a deep breath and let out a sigh of relief. "Is it over?" Fetchenko asked.

"It's over," Copeletti said.

"We lose anybody?"

"I'm not sure. I thought we'd check on you before sending Doc out. Are you alright?"

"I'm fine. Doc, see to the others. Call and let us know," Fetchenko said. "Now... Tony, how many did they send?"

"Nine. The pilot, he's dead, Colonel Ferguson, he's in lockup waiting for questioning, and that sergeant whose body came down in the elevator — nice shootin', by the way," Copeletti said to his two soldiers.

"Thanks," Fetchenko said.

"You had to shoot him? What the hell were you two doing?" Tony asked his guys.

"They froze," Fetchenko said. Tony ran them off, assuring them that he would deal with them later. After they left, Arthur said, "Don't be too hard on them. I'm just a lot quicker than them. They would have got him if I hadn't. Now... finish telling me about the attackers."

"Well... there were six more of them, all kids. I'm pretty sure Doc's going to find them all dead.

Fetchenko got up and examined the bandage on Copeletti's shoulder. A sizable spot of blood had leaked through but didn't seem to spread. "You okay?"

Copeletti put a hand to his wound. He winced a bit. "It's fine. Bullet went clean through. Missed the bones. Doc says I'll be sore, but I'll make it."

"Joey Ferelli needs to be dealt with, you know," Fetchenko said.

"I know, Arthur. I'm going to make Ferguson admit Joey's in charge. That'll break that little group down, one of them squealing. Let me deal with this, and then I'll figure out a surprise for Ferelli that he'll never forget." And he stepped over Sergeant Powell's blood and into the elevator.

"Tony," Phil Blackburn called before the doors could close. Tony pushed a button to hold them. "Call me and let me know how many bodies I need to make arrangements for."

"Nine," Tony said.

"Nine?"

"Nine, Philip. Plan on nine stiffs," Copeletti said.

Chapter Seventeen

Tony Copeletti sat across the table from Colonel Ferguson in the interrogation room. Two of his men leaned against the wall behind Ferguson, cracking knuckles.

"Is that supposed to frighten me? Because I'll tell you punks something..." the colonel began, mirth in his voice.

Tony Copeletti nodded and a fist shot into Ferguson's neck from the back. He tipped forward, his chin smashing down on the table.

"Who was in charge?" Tony asked.

"Me."

Another nod. Another hit. Another smash into the table.

"Who was in charge of this operation? Whose idea was it?" Copeletti waited a few seconds. "No? Not yet?" he asked and nodded. A slam came to the colonel's ribcage on his left side. Ferguson bent at an awkward angle and gasped hard, trying to take in air. "Who?" A moment passed, then came the nod.

"J. P.," Ferguson called out before the punch landed. The punch came anyway.

Tony Copeletti got to his feet, slowly, painfully. He tapped three times on the door and a buzzer sounded. He pushed the door open, and then turned to face Ferguson. He glanced at his two men, then back at Ferguson. "Kill him," he ordered.

* * *

Phil Blackburn placed his order to General Monroe Garrison over the telephone in Fetchenko's private quarters while Fetchenko surveyed the damages to his bedroom. "Monroe," he said when he got the general on the phone, "Phil Blackburn here. How's that little war of yours coming along?" Garrison was leading a small, covert operation in a remote and tiny corner of a Middle-East country. Few knew which country, or what part of it was involved, just that it was one of those necessary little squalls that needed put-down before it got out of hand and caused the whole area to heat up and oil prices to skyrocket out of sight. "Got a hot spot?"

"Always. Why?"

"I have nine men who need to perish in the heat of battle. Can you help?" Blackburn asked.

"I can," the general said. "How will they get here?"

"In a limo. I'll need a C-130."

"When?"

"Noon tomorrow," Blackburn said and looked at Fetchenko for confirmation. Fetchenko nodded. "That little airstrip north of Cumberland, Maryland, if that's possible."

"It'll be there," Garrison said. "Anything else?"

"Yeah. Keep the limo, Monroe," he said and hung up.

* * *

Tony Copeletti, when he put Vinny Gotto on an airplane bound for Madison, snatched Vinny's cell phone from his jacket pocket and had one of his staff trace all recent calls. He had Pauley Danucci's cell number. He text messaged Pauley that he (Vinny) had more for Ferelli in the way of information that he was certain the Senator would want, and asked to meet up at the same little café they had met at before. Copeletti even promised Danucci breakfast.

"Now what?" he asked Phil Blackburn.

"We're set," Blackburn said. "While you've been playing around with Vinny's phone, I've been busy hacking into J. P. Ferelli's personal schedule and guess what I learned."

"What?"

"J. P. has an early meeting with a committee he serves and a limousine will be dispatched to bring him to that meeting."

"Now there's a stroke of luck," Copeletti said. "That just kinda shoves everything in place. That is, if you can intercept that limo."

Blackburn smiled. Of course he could intercept that limo.

* * *

Pauley Danucci glanced out the front window of the café. Aside from the stretch-limo across the street, all was quiet. But it was still early. He glanced at his watch and hoped Vinny Gotto would show soon. Vinny Gotto was always late and it always pissed him off and left him wondering. Had something happened? He saw the limo's driver get out and head toward the café, a familiar man he had seen around. Probably picking up Ferelli or something. He focused on his coffee — empty. "Darlene," he called out and held his cup high.

"Mind if I join you?" the strange voice asked.

Pauley's subconscious began kicking his ass. *You should know better. You never sit with your back to the door. Can't see who's coming that way. Didn't you learn anything from Uncle Antonio?* He shook his head and motioned toward the seat across the booth from him invitingly. "Help yourself."

"We gotta talk."

"Who the hell are you?" Pauley asked.

The stranger remained silent while Darlene filled Pauley's cup and placed a fresh one in front of him. Then, "Don't matter who I am. It's enough for you to know I work for your brother-in-law."

"Arthur? You work for Arthur Fetchenko?" Pauley asked.

"I do."

"Well... what you want with me? What's Arthur want?" Pauley tipped his coffee cup, stared over its rim at the stranger, eyes narrowed to show no fear.

"I'm to take you with me."

"Like hell you will," Pauley said and took another sip.

The stranger looked toward the back of the café, then at the walk out front, both being guarded. "C'mon, tough guy. There's no way outta this." And he stood. He reached for Pauley's arm. Pauley tried to jerk away but the stranger's grip was too solid. The man at the back of the café began to advance and the man out front opened the door. Pauley gave in. He was in no real danger anyway; after all, Arthur Fetchenko was his brother-in-law.

Fear struck deep when Pauley Danucci was stuffed into the limo. The ride to Ferelli's house, just blocks away, would be one of the longest of his life.

* * *

J.P. Ferelli hadn't heard from Colonel Ferguson since last evening's phone call. And from the tone of things, Fergie hanging up so suddenly and all, there was cause for worry. Had the colonel gotten away? Or... did he get captured? And if he had been captured, did he spill his guts? No... Fergie was a soldier; an old one, grant you, but still — a soldier. Ferelli thought he had heard once that Fergie had been a POW during Vietnam for a time. He could handle an interrogation if it came to it. Ferelli looked out the sidelight of his front door and

watched the limo pull to the curb. No more time to ago-
nize over his lost colonel now. Time to go.

The limo's driver was at the side of the car long before Ferelli arrived, his handle on the door, ready for his
passenger. "You're not my driver," Ferelli said.

"Get in," the driver said and pulled the door open.

"Where's my driver?"

"Sick. Get in." He placed a palm between Ferelli's
shoulder blades and shoved him in. On the two facing
seats of the Limousine sat the dead from last night's battle, packed like sardines, each one wedging the next in
place, Pauley Danucci sitting on the floor next to the body
of Colonel Ferguson. Ferelli landed on the floor facing
Pauley and the colonel. Pauley's eyes were big as cat-eye
shooters, his skin pale as milk.

"What is this?" Ferelli cried out. "Where you taking
me?"

"For a ride, Senator. Compliments of Arthur
Fetchenko," the driver said, pitched his hat in the back
and slammed the door.

Pauley Danucci was wrong. The ride from the café
to Ferelli's would not be the longest of his life. This ride,
to a remote airstrip two and a half hours away, the smell
of death surrounding him and joining with the odor of
urine and vomit from both himself and Senator Ferelli
filling his nostrils, this ride would be the long one. And
what would come next was the question that traveled with
him. And if nothing came next, the scent of this, the feel
of this, now that would be with him always. He wanted to
die.

J.P. Ferelli, frightened as he was, filled himself with
hate for Arthur Fetchenko, something he had done so
long now that it came easily and could be called up at will.
It made the journey bearable. He did not fear death.
What he feared was that death would prevent him from
taking his revenge.

Alterations to the car, interior door handles re-moved, power windows disabled, windows themselves painted black so no one could see out, prevented both captives from knowing where they were as the car turned into the airstrip. Only the sound of the props of a C-130 transport plane chopping air told them where they were. They were at an airport. Nothing more could they tell. Ferelli stood and banged on the glass which separated them from the driver. "Open up, you son-of-a-bitch," he shouted and banged again. The window lowered an inch. "Stop this goddamn thing and let me out of here."

"Soon enough, Senator," the driver said and closed the window. A metallic sound followed, that of wheels hitting the steel ramp of the transport plane. Then the slam of a door, then another. Mumbled voices made both Ferelli and Danucci wonder if they would be set free, or if they were to take a plane ride and maybe be dropped like a giant rock from the sky to their deaths.

The door opens. "Out," the driver said and waited a moment. "No?" And he began to shut the door.

Ferelli stuck his arm out and cried out with pain when it was caught between door and post. He wiggled his way out, Pauley Danucci close behind him.

"You know what to do," the limo driver said to one of the airplane's crewmen.

"What about us?" Pauley Danucci asked.

"You," The driver pointed at Pauley, "get your ass on that plane." He gestured toward a Cessna on the other side of the C-130. "You're going to your uncle's." He looked at the Senator. "I don't give a shit where you go, but wherever it is, you are walking."

"Wait a minute," Ferelli begged as the driver walked away. "Where am I?"

"A long goddamn way from your meeting, Senator." He did not look back. He boarded a Jeep on the runway. "Might want to clean yourself up along the way. You smell like piss." And he drove off.

* * *

Tony Copeletti woke up in a hospital bed, two of his men in chairs outside his door, a top-heavy nurse with missing blouse buttons leaning over him. He smiled.

"It's good to see you awake," the nurse said and let go of his wrist. She removed the blood-pressure cuff with a rip of Velcro.

"It's good to see you," Copeletti said and smiled. Then he let out a small groan as he tried to lift his head from the pillow for a closer look.

"A Mister Fetchenko has been calling all morning. He asked that you call him as soon as you feel up to it."

Copeletti tried to reach for the pone beside his bed. Another groan. "Here," the nurse said. "Let me get it." And she handed him the receiver. "What's the number? I'll dial it for you."

Bad idea. Arthur finds out his private number is in the hands of a busty nurse and there'll be hell to pay. "Just get me my cell phone, Darlin'. It's in my pants pocket."

A doctor walked in and stood at the foot of his bed reading a chart. "When can I go home?" Tony asked.

"Well... I sewed you up, no problem there, but I also pumped you full of antibiotics and pain killers. I doubt you could even stand, Mr. Kangas."

Copeletti frowned, and then looked at the plastic band on his wrist. **Albert A. Kangas,** it read. *Clever, these men of mine.*

* * *

Arthur Fetchenko surveyed the damages to his balcony and bedroom. Glass everywhere. Blackburn was seeing to repairs. It still worried him though. He picked up the phone and called Liz at the Copeletti South Bend estate. "No," he told her to jumping a chopper back right away. "Not yet. You vacation there a few days. I want to carpet the bedroom before you come home." And when he hung up he called his daughter in Madison.

"Everything quiet there?" he asked.

"Nice and peaceful," she told him.

"You get to Henry's rally?"

"Sure did," Nicole said. "Jacob Rain took me."

"Is he there, Nikki? I need to talk to him."

"I'll get him," she said and laid the phone on the counter.

Fetchenko filled Jacob Rain in on the last evening's activities.

"I know," Rain said. "It was all over the radio, the tragic ambush on Colonel Fergie Ferguson and his small band of observers. Car bombing? In a limo? I figured that had to be you, and say, I also heard a blurb about some missing Senator, Ferelli I believe the name was." Rain chuckled in amusement.

"Seen anything around there?" Fetchenko asked.

"Nope. Am I about to?"

"I think you can count on it. Joey Ferelli hasn't given up his pursuit of me in forty years, no matter what we do to the guy. I don't imagine he'll stop now."

"What'd you guys do to him this time?" Rain asked.

"We made him and Pauley Danucci ride with all those stiffs to Cumberland. Then we turned him out, afoot, after taking his cell phone and wallet away from him of course."

"So, should I just be on the lookout? Or should I make some sort of move here, Arthur?" Rain asked.

"You think Nikki can be convinced to leave there, move back here where we can keep her safe?"

"Maybe better to keep her out of it completely."

"That's just it. I don't think she's out of it anymore. The blow we dealt them last night, well... that leaves Ferelli with only her safety to use against us," Fetchenko said. "Last night will slow him, but still... it's only a matter of time."

"How much time?"

"That's a tough one. We've never had things go this far. Just be extra careful and get her out of there as fast as she'll let you" Fetchenko said.

"I understand, Boss," Rain said. "I'll talk to her."

"One more thing, Jacob. We stuffed Danucci on a plane headed for Antonio Copeletti's Madison place. Antonio will hold him, but he won't take care of the problem. He will, however, let us deal with Pauley there. I want you to see to it."

"What you want done?"

"Use your judgment. He's been as much an issue over the years as Vinny Gotto. Maybe more," Fetchenko said not wanting to be specific over the phone.

"I'll see to it," Rain said. He hung up and looked into Nikki's eyes.

"We'll have to move to the compound," he told her.

"Orders from my father?"

"Yes."

Chapter Eighteen

Tony Copeletti swung his legs over the edge of his hospital bed. If it was rest he needed, he'd get it at home. He called out for one of his guards to assist his escape from the confines of the hospital. He had work to do. But the doctor had been correct; he couldn't stand, not on his own. A young man who joined the Fetchenko organization six months prior and came highly recommended by Antonio Copeletti himself, a twenty-six year old named Bernie Jade, came to his rescue. His technique, somewhat unique, brought Tony to his feet through a series of rapid jerks. Tony had often wondered why most of his crew referred to the kid as Bobber, and now he knew. Whenever excited, Bernie Jade tended to bob up and down, like the red and white ball on a fishing line when a fish would take the bait. The unique habit, comical as it was to those in the organization, seemed somehow intimidating to strangers. Too difficult to predict what might come next. But Tony Copeletti, grateful that he was for Bobber's assistance, did not see the chore of putting on his pants as something he wanted Bobber's help with. He asked for his other guard.

* * *

J. Patrick Ferelli spent a chilly night in a cardboard bin behind a market, tired, pants wet and smelling, hungry, and without his cellular phone with which he could have called for help. He woke up shivering, weak, and disoriented. It would be a long walk home if he didn't get some help.

The girl at the checkout looked as though she was going for the phone as she watched Ferelli walk into the market. And who could blame her? There he was, a full day's growth covering his soiled face, hair looking as though he hadn't combed it in weeks, suite jacket, expensive that it was, looking like it had been fished out of a dumpster, tossed aside by the Good Will. This was not a United States Senator despite the many times she had seen his face on television. "Is your manager in, Miss?" he asked her and she was happy to page him so that she would not have to deal with the bum herself.

"Good morning. I'm Erick Lazear. I'm the store manager. How can I help you?" Lazear was pleasant enough, but Ferelli could tell by the way he looked at him, the store manager thought he was dealing with an undesirable.

"I'm Senator J. P. Ferelli," J. P. told him.

Lazear focused. He studied; he even shifted both to the left then to the right to catch a glimpse of Ferelli's profile. Although television required strait on shots for public speaking, Ferelli preferred to be seen in profile, so that's how most folks saw him. He turned his head. "I believe you are," Lazear finally said. "What happened to you?"

"I got mugged, and then stuffed in the trunk of a car." He did not feel it prudent to bring politics and Fetchenko into the light for common citizens. One might get the sense there was more going on in Washington than the public was told about. From a personal standpoint, everyone should know about Fetchenko and his band of blackmailers, but some things, after all, were sacred where public office was concerned. So... from a professional standpoint, he was required to implement confidentiality. "I was driven out here, robbed, and thrown into the woods."

Lazear glanced at the Rolex on the senator's wrist. "Funny they didn't take the watch," he said.

Ferelli thought quickly. "I slid it up — like this." he pushed the watch up his arm to the elbow. "Then I pulled the sleeve down to cover it," he explained.

To Lazear though, the watch being there and being expensive seemed to prove the senator's identity. "Melissa," he said to the cashier, "get Sheriff Brady on the phone. I assume you want to report this, Senator."

"No! Please. Mr. Lazear, may I have a word in private?" he asked and stepped a few feet away from Melissa. "Look, Mr. Lazear, I'm sure you understand. I don't care to have folks see me like this. You'd be doing me a great service if you could just let me get a hold of my people in Washington. They can send someone to retrieve me from all of this, and then see to reporting it."

"I understand, Senator. Come with me. I'll put you up in my office. No one will see you and there's a telephone you can use in private. Meanwhile, why don't I send out for an egg sandwich for you? There's a little café just up the street. I'll send Melissa."

"She won't say anything, will she?" Ferelli asked as he sat in a chair at Lazear's desk and reached for the telephone.

"I'll go myself if you prefer."

"I'd appreciate that, Mr. Lazear."

Eric Lazear started to leave the office, then at the doorway, turned. "Senator Ferelli, it's an honor to be able to help you. That bill you sponsored to cut taxes for independent stores like mine was a godsend. It helps men like me compete with the chains."

Ferelli picked up the phone as the office door closed. He called Victor Parker. "Send a car for me," he said. He dug through a stack of invoices on Eric Lazear's desk. "Cumberland, Maryland. Lazear Country Market. And bring me something to change into."

"What are you doing in Maryland?" Parker asked.

"Never mind that. Just call my housekeeper and have her get some clothes together, and Parker, that thing with the girl, it's a go. See to it."

"I'll call Ferguson," Victor Parker said.

"Fergie's dead. Call our man in Madison." Ferelli had learned nothing. Fear did not pile up on him as Tony Copeletti had hoped, just anger.

* * *

Jacob Rain pulled through the gate of Antonio Copeletti's estate, Nicole Carson in the car with him. The gate guards knew Rain, but questioned his having the girl with him. Nikki became uncomfortable.

"I don't like this, Jacob," she said.

Rain didn't expect her to, but sooner or later, to be part of the Fetchenko organization, something that had become much more than a choice for her, she would need to accept a reality. Her father's whole existence required connections with people like the Copeletti family, and that was all there was to it. So... since he could not leave her alone while he took care of this little problem with Pauley Danucci, she needed to adapt. The time for that need had come. "You're going to be just fine, Nikki," he told her. "You'll like Antonio. I promise you."

"He's a crime lord, Jacob. I'm an attorney. How is it you think I'll like him?"

"Look around you, Nikki. Look what's become of your world. You can't be an attorney. You're Arthur Fetchenko's daughter."

"I've always been that, haven't I?"

"The difference is, now people know it, dangerous people, people who would kill you in a heartbeat just to get at your father. And people like this, Antonio Copeletti and his, they're your new best friends, like it or not, Nikki." Jacob Rain was getting frustrated. He had never thought of himself as convincing. He was an enforcer, a protector, that's all. Diplomacy, that was for others. Not him. "Look. We gotta be here," he told her as he pulled to a stop in the circle drive at the front door of the Copeletti estate. He got out and opened her door for her and escorted her inside where he left her in Antonio Copeletti's company. And he would be proven right. Copeletti would charm her, attorney or not.

Rain was shown to a boathouse at the shoreline of the lake the estate bordered. Pauley Danucci sat in a chair, his back to the door, discussing some inconsequential matter or event with one of his Uncle Antonio's guys and suspecting nothing in the way of repercussions over his recent acts against Arthur Fetchenko. To him, he hadn't done anything wrong. He had only exacted justice. Or more correctly, saw to it justice was exacted. Jacob Rain approached unnoticed from behind. He leaned close to Pauley's ear and quietly whispered, "Do you know who I am?"

Pauley Danucci cocked his head and looked at Rain. "No," he said.

"Do you know Vinny Gotto?"

"Yeah. I know Vinny. He's my cousin."

"He's nobody's cousin," Rain said.

"What you mean?"

"He's dead. I know that. You know how I know that?"

"No. How?" Pauley asked, his voice now showing tension.

"What do you know about Arthur Fetchenko?"

"I don't know who that is," Pauley said. He didn't know why he said that. Hell... everyone, at least everyone who'd be around Uncle Antonio's would know he and Arthur Fetchenko were brothers-in-law. Jacob rain reached out and smacked Pauley Danucci on the back of the head. "Okay! Yeah! I know Arthur. He's my brother-in-law."

"And what did you do to your brother-in-law?" Rain asked. He got no answer, just sweat and tears. "Look, kid, I know that Gotto's dead because I killed him. And lucky for him, he's Tony Copeletti's cousin, and because of that he got to die quick, almost painless."

"I'm Tony Copeletti's cousin too," Pauley Danucci cried out, hoping for mercy.

"Yeah, but you don't get to die painlessly because you're Tony's cousin, Pauley," Rain said and pulled out his gun. "You get to die quick because you're Arthur Fetchenko's brother-in-law." And Jacob Rain put a bullet in his head.

Chapter Nineteen

Arthur Fetchenko was furious with Tony Copeletti for leaving the hospital. What if Tony suffered complications, a stroke, a heart attack — what if he died? And all because he left the care of a real doctor.

"I'm alright," Tony defended his actions.

"Yeah, you look it," Blackburn threw his sarcasm in.

"You're going to bed, Tony. I'll send Doc to see to it you stay there," Fetchenko said.

"That's all I wanted, Arthur. I want to be here in case I'm needed."

* * *

Nikki Carson had remained silent for the car ride from Copeletti's estate to her home. Jacob Rain thought it might spell trouble, especially when it came down to convincing her that she had to be moved to a safer location — orders from her father. "Are you alright?" he asked as he pulled into a Seven-Eleven a few blocks from her house to pick up a pack of smokes.

"I'm fine. Why?"

"You're more quiet than usual, that's all," Rain said.

"I liked him. You said I would like Antonio Copeletti, and I did."

"And that's a problem because?"

"Pride," she said. "I assured you I would not like the man, and I was wrong. He's hospitable. He's charming. If he weren't a crime boss, I'd want him for an uncle. I just have this internal struggle going on, that's all."

Jacob Rain pulled the car to a stop. He walked around to open her door. "I think I'll wait here for you," she said.

Inside the convenience store, as Rain paid for his cigarettes, he caught a glimpse of a car tucked in an alley across the street. It seemed out of place. Dark color. Deeply tinted windows. Out of state plates. He left his change on the counter and walked out of the store and to the car. He got in and adjusted his mirror so he could see the dark sedan in the alley across the street. He started his engine, lowered his window, and listened as the sedan's engine started. "Hold on!" he said and threw the shift lever into reverse. Seconds later and he was on the street and moving at breakneck speed away from Nicole's home and toward the interstate, the sedan from the alley tailing more than a block behind.

"What's going on?" Nikki demanded.

"They've found us."

"Who's found us?"

"Your father's enemies," Rain told her. He pulled a hard right, tires squealing and smoking, and shot down a ramp to the interstate. He spotted their tail hitting the ramp just as he edged into traffic. The next exit, maybe a quarter-mile ahead, he could see clearly in both directions for several hundred feet. He would risk it. He looked in the mirror. Still there, gaining, but not fast. He shot up the off ramp without slowing. "Hold on," he shouted. He shot over the crossroad, wheels clearing the road and landing on the onramp across the street. He poured back onto the freeway and checked his mirror. His tail sat at the top of the ramp, trying to guess which way he had gone. "Lost them," he said.

"Them and my lunch," Nicole said. "Now what?"

"We make our way back to your house and pack," he said. "You'll have to guide me. I'm lost."

"There's something I need to ask you, Jacob," she said as he pulled his car into her garage. "Where my father lives, it's called a compound, isn't it?"

"Yeah, that's what most call it."

"Why?"

"Because that's what it is. It's an old military compound that was built during the cold war of the sixties. It was set up to launch return missiles and to house diplomats if there was ever an attack on Washington. The government had abandoned the place years ago, so your father talked them out of it. Now it's our headquarters and living quarters, that's all, but we still call it the compound."

"He talked them out of it?" she questioned. "I'll bet he talked them out of it. I'll bet he's trying to talk that Senator out of something too, the one who's gone missing."

"So... you heard the news too," Rain said.

"I did," she said. "And this Senator, he wouldn't have anything to do with that car you just outran, would he?"

"More than likely," Rain told her. "Look, Nikki. That's a time-honored war, Senator Ferelli and your dad. Been going forever. Probably never end — one of those deals. Now... let's pack a few things. We'll head out at daybreak." Dusk was upon them and Rain wanted rest and daylight should he need to do battle. Well... daylight anyway. Rest would be replaced with vigilance this night.

Nicole Carson did as he asked, pack, but in light of the little time they had, she packed light. Soon she was cooking what would be her last meal in her mother's house and it saddened her, although not as much as she would have thought. Jacob Rain sat in the dark in the living room, curtains drawn so he could see the dimly lit street which ran in front of Nikki's house. "Will you be eating in the dark?" she asked, not sure if she should set a table.

"Yes." He sat on the sofa.

"Then I'll join you." She handed him a plate and sat beside him. "You think they'll find us, don't you." It was not a question; it was a statement.

"Too soon," he said. These were not fools. His temporarily losing them on the interstate was just that — temporary. He doubted he would see daylight before he saw the dark sedan again. But it was his hope they would watch for the night and not act.

It was past midnight when Rain spotted a car on the street outside. He had dozed if only for a moment, and focus did not seem to come as quickly as usual. Perhaps he had slept longer than he imagined. He looked at his watch, pushed a button on the side which made the face light up — mistake. A shot penetrated the glass of the picture window and whizzed by his ear. Nikki sat upright on the sofa. He snatched her shirtsleeve and pulled her to the floor. "Lay still," he said. Another shot, this one through the wall. They were good. They guessed accurately where he might be. He felt a sting to his thigh. A hit. "Let's go!" he said. "Back door. Stay low." And they crawled from the living room through the kitchen, to the back of the house and opened a steel door which led to the attached garage.

As he opened a car door for her, Nikki spotted the leg of his jeans — blood soaked. "My God, look at you."

"It's a scratch," he said but knew it wasn't.

Nikki pulled the tie string from her hooded sweatshirt. She tied it around Jacob Rains thigh, above the bullet wound. "We have to get you to a hospital," she said.

"No," he said. "They'll follow us and they'll finish us off. We must get to South Bend. You know where that is?"

"Sure. I've been there many times. I have a good friend there, Victoria Partanna."

Rain smiled at her.

"What?" she asked.

"You know the Partannas?"

"Yeah, why?" she asked.

"Vickie Partanna's husband, Carlos, is Antonio Copeletti's right-hand-man at the South Bend estate. You're a friend of the mob. I find that amusing." A bullet whizzed through the wall of the garage, ricocheted off Rain's car fender, and broke a glass jar on a shelf. "Time to go," he said. "Can you drive?" He jumped in the passenger's door, reached and started the car, and waited for her to get in. Then he saw her in her car, fumbling for the automatic door opener control. "C'mon. Just drive through it. You open it first and all you'll find is them."

Nicole did as he said, jumped behind the wheel, put the car in reverse, and put her foot to the floor. Rain's big sedan went through the overhead door like it was made of paper and crashed into the attacker's car beyond it, plowing it into her neighbors back yard, two enemies pinned between their car and a fence. One of them shot, missing widely.

"Ram it again," Rain shouted. And Nikki pulled forward ten feet, threw it in reverse, and rammed into the car again. "One more time," Rain said, and she did. The car died. It would not start. "Keys in yours?"

"Yes." Both of them hit the alley running. Seconds later they were pulling away in Nikki Carson's small, quick sports car, sparks flying behind them as she jumped the entire street, undercarriage scraping pavement in the alley beyond. She checked her mirror and saw Jacob Rain's car burst into flames. She headed for the freeway, South Bend, Indiana her destination.

As Nikki reached the onramp to the interstate she had a sudden change in plans. She looked at Jacob Rain. His eyes were shut, his head leaning awkwardly to one side and she wondered, *Asleep? Alive? Dead?* and she took the onramp west, rather than east like Rain had instructed her to do. She would find help. She would not lose Jacob Rain. Two exits, dark, no businesses, then she came to one with a convenience store atop the ramp. She pulled behind, in the far corner of a deserted truck parking area. She looked Jacob over under the brightness of a street lamp. Even though he had lost blood, and she had no real sense of how much, the bleeding appeared to have stopped. Perhaps there was much she could do to keep it that way.

In the convenience store she purchased a roll of paper toweling, a large bottle of alcohol, a gallon of purified drinking water, a pair of scissors, all the gauze and surgical tape that the store stocked, and two large cups of strong coffee. She wanted to keep Jacob awake if she could.

"Starting your own clinic?" the clerk asked.

"Boyfriend cut himself," she said and dug for cash. She had seen enough television. Using a credit card was a bad idea. "Just a scratch. I could probably patch him and ten more like him up with all of this, but heh, he's such a baby. You know how men are when they get a little injury."

"Not all of us," the clerk said and smiled. He wouldn't be calling the cops to report suspicious activity.

At the car, Nikki opened Jacob's door and cut his pants leg from cuff to crotch. She began cleaning blood from his skin. That done, and things didn't look so bad. It had been a clean wound, the bullet passing all the way through, no artery hit, bleeding slowed to minimal. She swung him so that his wounded thigh could be doused with alcohol, most of it spilling outside the car, then wrapped and taped the wound and swung him back into the seat. She handed him the coffee. "Drink this. I need you to stay awake," she said. She went around the car and got in behind the wheel. His head nodded forward as she began to drive off. "I mean it, Jacob. You have to stay awake. I don't know where we're going."

"I thought you knew where South Bend is."

"I do. But once we're there, I don't know where to go," she told him. But he had already fallen off. She decided to let him sleep. She'd check on him now and then, and wake him when they got to South Bend. If she couldn't wake him, there was always her friend, Vicky Partanna. If Jacob Rain was right about Vicky's husband, they'd know where to take them.

Rain began to snore. It comforted her. *The dead don't snore.*

* * *

"Any word from Madison?" J.P. Ferelli asked entering his study after he had washed the filth of Cumberland off of himself. It had been too long a day following an unpleasant night. And the night they were well into now was faring poorly as well. His people — Mac McArthur, Victor Parker, and Daniel Davidson — all waited in the study and all were anxious for this meeting. Fergie was dead, the attack on Fetchenko, they had been told, was far less than successful, and they all thought they had lost J.P in the mix. They hoped for an upturn in events now that J.P. was safely back at home and, they hoped, had a plan.

"The last report we received came shortly before midnight. They had Rain's car blocked in the girl's garage and were about to begin blasting them out of there. We haven't heard since," Victor Parker began filling him in.

"Haven't heard? Well... I certainly hope they didn't take an ass kicking like Ferguson and his boys did," Ferelli said.

"J.P., there were six of them, and only one Jacob Rain. How could they lose?" McArthur argued.

"I hope your right, Mac," J.P. said. "Because if you're not, the next step we need to take to defeat Arthur Fetchenko, well... it'll be a risky one."

"And what would that step be, J.P.?" Davidson asked.

"Henry Tyler and Jack Albrecht," Ferelli said.

"Why, for God sakes?" Parker asked.

"Because if either of them gets into office this election, it's all over. The Republicans might be considering him now, more like teetering I would imagine, but let him get Henry in there, remember, Henry replaces one of us, and then give them the White House, and they'll believe they need Fetchenko. He gets the Republicans, well... the Fetchenko people will be the future, and we'll be so much forgotten history. You do realize, Victor, that there are only a handful of us left who don't owe Arthur Fetchenko. We need to make our numbers larger — his smaller. Keep that in mind."

"I just wonder, J.P., all the gunplay already, and nothing any of us can really call progress... "

"Now don't you go getting skittish on me, Victor, or any of you. I'll die if I have to, if that's what it takes to stop that son-of-a-bitch. Why the hell would I care if one of them dies as well? And you remember one thing. Just in case you come up with some foolish thought of turning me in. You're in this all the way up to your ears, all of you. I go down, so do you. Keeping all of that in mind, I didn't call you here to ask permission, I called you in to plan this, now let's get to planning. Everyone clear on that?"

* * *

"Tony," Arthur Fetchenko said and shook Copeletti until he awakened. "I need you."

Copeletti struggled to sit up in his bed, still groggy from all the medication, more than just a bit stiff and sore. "What is it, Arthur?"

"I can't get through to Nikki."

"You try Jacob's cellular?"

"No answer there either." Fetchenko pushed his hair back with a hand. "I called Elaine. She said there were a lot of sirens — police, fire, ambulance — in the neighborhood."

"Want me to call Antonio and have him send someone to look in on them?"

"I'd appreciate it. Say, you feeling better?"

"Not too bad," Copeletti said.

"Come up after you reach your uncle. We'll have a nightcap." Fetchenko left for his quarters. He always felt more tranquil once he turned problems over to Tony Copeletti. Tony had the touch. If an answer was needed, he knew how to get it.

The telephone in his apartment was ringing as Arthur entered. It was Liz.

"When can I come home? I miss you," she said.

"Soon, I promise. Just as soon as the carpenters get done. You're getting a new garden door, new carpet and paint in the bedroom, and a bit of refurbishing to the deck. Shouldn't take more than another day or two." Copeletti nudged the door open. Fetchenko motioned for him to enter. "I'll call you in the morning and let you know how much longer. You get some rest now. I'm going to do the same." But he wouldn't. It would be a long night.

"My uncle's man thinks they got away from the looks of the scene. Rain's car was destroyed, burned to cinders. It apparently rammed the car blocking it in the garage and pushed it into the neighbor's fence. The only bodies found, two of them, were trapped between the other car and a fence — burned to death from the look of things. Neither one matched Nikki or Jacob. They got out, Boss."

"How? Rain's car was destroyed."

"Apparently her car was in the garage. Antonio's man reported a second set of black marks coming from the garage." Tony looked at the worry on Arthur's face. "They got out, Boss," he assured him. "My guess is Rain will stop at my uncle's place in South Bend and regroup. Want me to have them keep an eye out?"

"Yeah. Do that. Now... let's have that nightcap."

"Where's Blackburn? I thought he'd be here," Copeletti asked.

"I sent him to check on our competition. Maybe he can uncover their next plan."

"Think they'll try again?"

"Shit, you know Joey. He'll quit when I'm dead or he's dead."

Chapter Twenty

Nikki Carson traveled the Indiana toll road whenever she visited her friend, Vicki, in South Bend. It was the route she knew. And after the long journey in silence aside from Jacob Rains snoring, interrupted only by the nerve-racking pauses when he seemed to not breath at all, she was at her exit for 31 South, the lower bypass to the city. And on that long journey, an old piece of information surfaced. She did in fact know where the Copeletti estate was. Her friends had shown it to her years ago; it was near their place. It was on the south side of US 20 just past where 31 turned south.

She hadn't given thought to the car parked on the shoulder near the off-ramp toll booth as she paid, didn't pay it any mind. Cars were often deserted, broke-down, out of gas, driver hauled off for DWI and the car awaiting a tow ride to the impound. Whatever. They were common. But this one, she should have been watching. It pulled onto the road as soon as her rear bumper cleared it, headlights off. She watched it in her mirror as she traveled 31 south. It seemed to stay back, more following than chasing, lights still off.

"Wake up," she told Jacob Rain and nudged him. He did not move, just snored louder. "Jacob, Wake up," she said, her volume raised, her nudge more aggressive. He still did not. She sped up, 60mph, 65mph, then seventy. The car kept with her. "Shit," she said aloud. What now?" But it would not be long before that question would be answered.

The car pulled into the passing lane and came up beside her, its passenger motioning for her to pull over.

Nikki looked ahead — an off ramp. She sped up. The car beside her sped up. She steered at the last possible moment onto the off ramp leaving her pursuer no time to join her escape. She screeched to a stop at the bottom and searched for Jacob Rain's handgun. Then she waited. They would be back.

The tailing sedan, after finding it impossible to take the off ramp, sped ahead and flew down the on ramp from the wrong direction. Soon it was nose to nose with Nikki's sports car. The driver got out. He walked purposefully yet cautiously toward her. She sat there, window down, Rain's gun in her lap, safety off. "That's far enough," she said when he reached her front fender. She watched another man get out of the passenger's side and begin making his way back to her. She pulled the gun up and rested it on the window opening, aimed at the first man. "Tell him to stand in front of the car." He did. "Who else is in the car?"

"Nobody," the man answered. She pulled back the hammer. "Antonio Copeletti warned us you'd be a tough one," he said.

"How would he know?"

"You were with him this afternoon. He sizes people up quickly and he's never wrong."

"Anyone could come up with a statement like that," she said. The other man moved. "Tell him to stand still," she demanded.

"Stand still for Christ sakes. She's Arthur Fetchenko's daughter. She will shoot. Even if she doesn't shoot us, something goes wrong here, and he will."

Nikki began to believe these men were on her side. She eased the hammer back. "What do you want?" she asked.

"We've been called by Tony Copeletti and your father. We're to lead you to the estate and make sure you get there safe and sound. Has Jacob been injured?" the man asked.

"Shot."

"Maybe we better look at him."

Nikki Carson opened her door and got out of the car. She stepped off several yards, holding a steady hand on Jacob Rain's gun, keeping her aim on the man. "You stand still. Your friend can look at Jacob."

"Fair enough, Ms. Fetchenko," he said and motioned for his partner to check out Rain.

"Ms. Carson," she corrected. She pulled something from her pocket and threw it to her captive. "If you're who you say you are, you'll know how to reach my father, won't you? That's my cell-phone. Call him."

"I don't have his number."

She pulled the hammer back.

"I can call Tony Copeletti," he said.

"Do it," she ordered she let the hammer forward again. And soon he had Tony Copeletti on the phone. She instructed him to step back and to leave the phone on the fender. She told his partner to join him. Then she answered the phone.

"Did you disarm them, Dear?" Copeletti asked her.

"No," she said.

"Well... you got guts. Probably lucky those are my guys or you'd be dead by now. Next time, take the time to get their weapons, and just in case it comes up again, most of the time they have more than one. Now, here's what I need you to do, Nikki..."

"It's Nicole. Nicole Carson."

"It's Nikki Fetchenko, Dear. Now you get used to that because there are far too many people looking for Nicole Carson... to do her harm. Now you follow my men to the estate. There's a doctor waiting for Jacob, and your father's lady, Liz Harmon, will see to your needs. You'll like her. She's spunky like you. Do me a favor, Nikki. Get Jacob Rain to safety. We'll talk later." He hung up.

* * *

Milton Courte, a fifth generation driller and head of the multi-billion dollar Texas based Texamera Oil Company, got the call from J.P. Ferelli just past seven in the morning. "I wondered when I'd hear from you." Milt knew of J.P.'s Fetchenko problem. This new kid, this Albrecht, was anti-oil as anti-oil could be. He was the enemy — U.S. oil and foreign alike hated him. That is until recently. Albrecht's ideas had changed. He had done a three-sixty and now supported the use of fossil fuels. But he had issued a statement in a news interview which suggested objectionable limits be placed on the use of domestic oil, an effort to maintain the country's levels, and an open door for import oil. Texamera and other stateside producers were now up in arms. Previously, they all agreed Albrecht's end would come soon enough, at the hands of OPEC nations. "I heard about Colonel Ferguson's failure. He kinda underestimated his opposition, didn't he?"

"Who cares? He's gone," Ferelli said. "Trouble is, Fetchenko isn't. Any suggestions?"

"I think we should meet face to face, J.P. You want to come down here?" Courte asked.

"I'd rather you come here. I shouldn't be away right now. We're up to our elbows trying to prevent Fetchenko from expanding into the Republican Party. Besides, I'd like all of us to meet, not just you and me."

"I'll have Brandy fire up the jet," Courte said. Brandy Bradford, a pretty and busty young redheaded pilot, flew Milton Courte wherever he went, and served as his social assistant when they got there. "We'll be there this afternoon, late. That lovely woman of yours cooking dinner?"

"Martha? She left me. But I have a fine Portuguese girl who'll come in. Man, can she cook, or so I'm told."

"I look forward to it," Courte said and hung up.

* * *

"Good morning," a pretty lady said. Nikki rubbed her eyes. It was one hell of a night. The whole day, actually. She wondered if this one would be the same.

"What time is it?" she asked.

"Nine-thirty."

"Shit!" she sat up quickly — too quickly. The room began to twirl.

"Easy. Not too fast. The doc gave you a sedative when you got in last night," the woman told her and sat on the edge of her bed. "I'm Liz," she added.

"My father's girlfriend?"

"That's me."

"How is Jacob Rain?" Nikki asked.

She looked into Nikki's eyes. "You're quite fond of him, aren't you," she suggested.

"Is he alright?"

"Not yet, but I'm told he will be."

Nikki pushed herself back and leaned on her pillow. "Well... where do I go from here?"

"Home," Liz told her.

"Home? Where the hell is that? I'm lost."

"I know. It wasn't all that long ago I was in your shoes, Dear. I didn't know where home is either. But I found it and so will you."

"With my father?"

"Yes," Liz said.

"Jacob Rain has told me much about my father's estate. He makes it sound nice."

"It is nice."

"But nice or not, no going outside the place without an escort, no having friends in for a visit without Tony Copeletti's scrutinizing eye all over them, it sounds a bit like a prison doesn't it?"

"It could at first, I suppose. But then you look at the other inmates. Make some logical comparisons. Maybe take in a movie on prison life. You'll see the difference."

"I don't know, Miss Harmon," Nikki said.

"It's Liz," she insisted. "I tell you what; let's go check in on Jacob Rain. Then we'll get a breakfast into you before we talk more. Things are bound to look better."

"And what made things look better for you?" Nikki asked.

Liz chose to postpone her answer.

* * *

Arthur Fetchenko had moved well past his fear for the safety of his daughter and on to a concern over her ability to adapt to the inevitable. A life, after all, confined to the protection available only at the price of seclusion is a pill that can be hard to swallow, especially for someone with an adventurous spirit like Nicole Carson, now to be known as Nikki Fetchenko. This was a mess of sorts, but a mess that had to be cleaned up. Fetchenko's cleaner of choice? His lady — Liz Harmon. "What are your thoughts," he asked her.

"She's tough like you."

"I adapted."

"From what I know of it, Arthur, you adapted, but you fought it tooth and nail," Liz said. "Tony Copeletti told me that much, and so far as I know, Tony Copeletti is no liar, so don't try to deny it."

"I'll have to talk to Copeletti. So... what you're telling me is that she'll not be an easy sale."

"Subject to change," Liz said.

"Change? How so?" Fetchenko sensed optimism in her words.

"I'm taking her to see Jacob Rain as soon as she's dressed. If what I hear from the guys who found her last night are true, our job may get a whole lot easier."

"Why? What was said?"

"Nothing precise, really," Liz told him. "They just indicated that she and Jacob might have a deeper connection than normal. I guess she was as protective over him as a she-bear over a cub. Might be nothing — might be something."

Her comment startled Fetchenko. Jacob Rain was a friend, it's true. But more than a protector and the protected relationship between him and Nikki? How could that have happened? Did it happen? And if it did, what should he do about it? Something? Nothing? He was too old for her, by more than a few years, same as Fetchenko and Liz Harmon. *Woops!* "Let me know what you think after you see them together, okay?"

"I will," she said. "Arthur?"

"Yes?"

"Can I come home?"

"Not yet."

"Why? When?"

A question asked that should not be answered was always tricky. "We'll get you home real soon, I promise," Arthur Fetchenko said and hung up. Maybe he should have told her there was more trouble brewing, but for now, since he really didn't know if trouble was coming to him, or going elsewhere — to Henry Tyler and Jack Albrecht for instance — he would remain silent about it. He would have the answer to that and many other questions by morning.

Chapter Twenty-One

Milton Courte generally sat in the cockpit as Brandy Bradford's copilot even though he had no idea how to fly his private jet. He simply liked to look as though he did. But this trip he would spend in the cabin, devising a plan and then refining it. When they took off from Dallas he had no clear idea how to help J.P. Ferelli win his war with Arthur Fetchenko, only that he could help him — he had the resources. By the time they landed in DC however, Milton Courte not only knew exactly what needed to be done, he knew how it must be done.

"Why, Milton Courte. As I live and breathe," Phil Blackburn called out passing Courte in the airport.

"Blackburn?" Courte questioned. "What the hell are you doing here?"

"I was about to ask you the same."

"You first," Courte insisted.

"I have to catch a junket to Colorado to meet with Henry Tyler and Jack Albrecht," Phil Blackburn said. "You?"

"Got a meeting with J.P.," Milt said without meaning to. Blackburn was that way. His calm and unobtrusive manner caused people to blurt out the truth most of the time. It was his utmost quality and the one that kept him on staff with Arthur Fetchenko.

"Well, it was great bumping into you," Blackburn said, allowing Courte to think his blunder had gone unnoticed. "Gotta run. Have a blast in DC, Milt." And he was gone. Around a corner and out of sight, Phil Blackburn called Arthur Fetchenko from his cellular and confirmed that the oil concerns were indeed meeting with Ferelli just as had been anticipated. "Lucky for us, it'll be our gal serving him dinner tonight," he told Fetchenko. Blackburn had also arranged when Martha Ferelli had gone missing and J.P. found himself in need of a cook, for someone from Fetchenko's personal staff to step in — enter the Portuguese chef, Marta Azevedo. "Marta will keep her ears tuned in. And she'll hear plenty too."

"How's that?" Fetchenko asked.

"Ferelli thinks she speaks only Portuguese."

* * *

Nikki Fetchenko, after her chaotic and treacherous night on the road with the wounded Jacob Rain, as much as she wished to be by his side, hadn't the strength to join Liz Harmon in looking in on him, not first thing in the morning at least. She fell off into the deepest sleep in recent memory for her, and stayed that way well into the afternoon. Three p.m. had come and gone before Liz was able to wake her.

"Wow," Liz said. "You didn't sleep. You passed out."

"What time is it?"

"Almost four," Liz told her.

She sat up in the bed, panicked. "How is Jacob?" she asked.

"He's awake. Want to go see him?"

"Yes."

"I'll give you a moment to dress, only, don't fall asleep like you did this morning," Liz said and smiled to let Nikki know she was kidding. She left the room. When she returned, Nikki was ready to go.

Jacob Rain moaned when a nurse adjusted his hospital bed so he could see his visitors better. Nikki rushed to his side. She took his hand and kissed it gently, and then she kissed him on the forehead. Liz Harmon took it all in. "I'll leave you two alone for a time. Need coffee, Nikki? I'm going for a cup myself, be happy to bring one back for you."

"That'd be nice. Thank you."

"Jacob, how about you?" Liz offered, but Jacob Rain declined.

When Liz returned a half-hour later, she found Nikki sitting on the edge of the bed and Jacob Rain smiling. She also found a rather insistent nurse determined to run Nikki off so that Jacob could get some needed rest. Liz was able to convince Nikki that the demanding nurse had Rain's best interest at heart and the girls left. In the hallway Liz spoke. "Earlier you asked what made my staying with your father more than a prisoner's life. Do you recall?"

"I don't recall making it sound that harsh, but yes, that was the general question," Nikki told her.

"Some men are worth that. Your father is one of them. I've watched you with Jacob Rain. I'd say you think he's one of them too. Am I right?"

"I've grown fond of him," Nikki admitted.

"As fond as to say you'd maybe share a deserted island with him?"

"I suppose you could say that, no matter how unlikely the situation would arise."

"Look around you, Dear. That situation has arisen. And the Fetchenko estate is your deserted island to share with your Jacob Rain," Liz said and smiled. "Now, let's do something about that growling stomach of yours."

* * *

Milton Courte despised public transportation, especially taxicabs. In this neck of the woods they were always driven by Niggers or Iraqis so far as he was concerned, and he'd rather walk than ride with either of those breeds. "You get me a car over here, Ferelli, or my ass is back in the plane, headed for Texas," he told J.P. by telephone.

"Sit tight, Milt. My driver's on the way. I'd have had him there but you never told me what time to expect you," Ferelli said, his way of apologizing, at least as much of an apology as he'd give any man. He was, after all, a United States Senator.

"He'd better be. Listen, you contact your man. Have him find me in the bar. I'm parched." Milt hung up the phone, tipped his cowboy hat back, winked at Brandy Bradford, slapped her on the ass, and said, "Told that son-of-a-bitch now didn't I?"

"You sure did," Brandy said and poked her arm through his. "Why don't we go get us a hotel room while we wait?"

"You're a handful now aren't you?" He couldn't perform and he knew it. So did she, for that matter. After all, she nailed him, auto-pilot engaged, not more than two hours ago, at 5500 feet. "That'll have to keep till after my meeting." He wondered if he could perform then. He pulled a stool away from the airport bar and ordered them drinks for the wait.

* * *

Marta Azevedo preferred to work alone on these away assignments. It was much easier to gain information without someone, a stranger usually, looking over her shoulder. Alone it was a cinch. Her nationality made it that way. Most thought of her as a really great cook who spoke and understood little English, and often things were said in her presence that would not be said if the talker thought she understood. Reality was, she was a Smith grad. Spoke English, her native tongue, and a half-dozen other languages, handy if someone suspected she might be catching some or all of what was being said and switched to some other language, say Russian. Today though, her unwanted partner in the kitchen would turn out to be an asset. She would be Brandy Bradford, Milton

Courte's pilot and confidant who found herself unwel-
come at J.P. Ferelli's meeting and highly insulted and
more than a little disgruntled as a result. She would prove
to be useful. But Marta would need to open herself up to
avail herself of this new turn of events. Or would she?
Brandy Bradford was an educated woman as well. She
began cussing out her host, J. Patrick Ferelli — in French,
one of the languages Marta spoke. And as she listened to
Courte's pilot and companion, she knew she could use
her. "Malpropre solopard!" Brandy said and Marta
smiled at her French for dirty bastard.

"You speak French," Brandy commented — in
French.

"Oui," Marta said. And the remainder of their evening, the disgruntled pilot using her French on Marta who
was thought by all not to comprehend anything that was
said in English. She would double her intake of information. She would pick up on conversations between
Ferelli and Courte and the two other guests, Mac McArthur and David Danielson, and as a bonus, would be told
in French many useful tidbits about the newest threat to
Fetchenko, Milton Courte.

Meal and meeting done, cleanup by Marta Azevedo
and Brandy Bradford ended in a, "It was so nice to work
with you, Brandy," in perfect English by Marta who threw
in a sinful smile along with the comment, and she was off
to report to Arthur Fetchenko and Tony Copeletti.

"Anyone catch on that you were listening in?"
Fetchenko asked.

"Not until it was too late." She went on to explain
about her parting words. "I couldn't stop myself. The
woman was so... so... anti Ferelli; it seemed the right thing
to do."

Copeletti began to jump on her about it, but Arthur
stepped in. "Don't mind him," he told Marta. "He's on
medication — gunshot wound you know. I'm sure we
won't have further need to send you out anyway." Arthur

Fetchenko knew things were coming to a head with Ferelli, and he sensed that end would only come with the death of himself or Joey Ferelli. That scenario had been developing for too many years, since before Fetchenko began his involvement with Ferelli's political party, and the hate between them had grown past containment. It would happen. Fetchenko could feel it. "So... Marta, what do you have for us?"

"Two men are on their way to pay Henry Tyler and Jack Albrecht a visit, one of them Milton Courte called Knuckles Moran and the other, Jimmy the Blade. Courte himself, according to the ravings in French by his pissed-off pilot and playmate, has many more to send if those two disappoint. And as for Courte's word to Ferelli and his general disposition, again per the discontented girl-friend, he will never give up. I'm afraid Henry and Jack are in for it."

"Tony," Fetchenko said, "you know either of those two thugs?"

"I know both of them — Jimmy personally. He's slick, accurate, deadly. I wish we had Jacob Rain to send after him. Jimmy's better than most, but Rain would stop him."

"Well, that's not possible. Who's your second choice?"

"Bobber," Copeletti said.

"Bernie Jade?" Fetchenko smiled. "Animated Bernie with the head bouncing up and down every time he gets excited? That Bobber? He don't seem right for the job."

"He's a surprise, Boss. They won't even guess him a danger — won't see it coming; he'll make a performance of it. But he'll get the job done."

"What about the other guy? What about this Knuckles character?"

"I only know him by reputation. He's said to be smart and tough — more of a shooter than a knife man. I got guys we can send with Bobber," Copeletti said. "But if Marta's on target, or her French speaking friend, Courte's gonna send more. What'll we do about that?"

"Take out Courte. That's our only choice." Fetchenko looked at Marta Azevedo. "Good work, Marta, he told her. Tony," he redirected his attention, "call Henry and warn him, then get your guys on it."

* * *

Henry Tyler was pissed. "You told me no harm could come to me, that I was too high profile for that. Remember that, Arthur?" he said when Fetchenko and Copeletti conference called to warn him to be on the lookout for Courte's two goons. "All you got out here protecting us is a couple of armatures, Copeletti."

"More men are on the way, Henry. Pros," Tony assured him.

"Who?"

"Bernie Jade and a couple others."

"Bobber? What's he going to do? Entertain us while we wait to die? Where the hell is Jacob Rain?" Henry wanted to know.

"Jacob took a bullet. He's recovering at Antonio's South Bend place. Bobber will get the job done alright. Don't you worry about that. He just looks funny doing it, that's all. Look, Henry, you tell those guys there with you now to keep a vigilant eye out. Bobber and the boys will be there in a few hours. And don't mention any of this to Jack Albrecht. He'll panic." Albrecht was no brave man. Frankly, he was a puppet, a pawn for Fetchenko to use once he got into office. His qualifications, his background, all of it manufactured and protected from the real truth.

Henry started to object, thinking Jack Albrecht had a right to know, but Fetchenko threw in his two cents. "The right? Yes. The need? No. Tony's right. He'll panic, probably disappear on us. Leave him out of the loop."

Jack Albrecht was a pretty face who would draw the women's vote and the younger generation's vote easily away from the opposition in extreme bad times for that opposition due to eight years of leadership that all but ruined the nation's economy and grew government to an outrageous size. And for all of it, Fetchenko was pleased. It would be his crowning jewel to get a man in the Oval Office at a time when government itself was larger than it ever had been, or was likely to become. That was real power. But it was also dangerous. Those who would endeavor to slow or stop him in the past would be much more diligent now. Milton Courte was one of them. "There's far too much at stake to let Jack do something extreme out of fear or panic. You keep this to yourself. Alert your staff, but not Jack, and make sure none of them tells him. Good night, Henry."

"Good night, he says," Tyler said, mirth in his voice. "Easy for him. He gets to sleep." And he hung up.

Chapter Twenty-Two

For a second night Nikki Fetchenko, God how she labored with thinking of herself as Nikki Fetchenko rather than Nicole Carson who she had been for as long as she could recall, slept far past her usual wake-up hour. But when she did finally awaken, she was pleased to find Jacob Rain standing at the foot of her bed. "They all told me you were tough," she said.

He walked to her side, then bent and kissed her on the forehead. "Good morning," he said and pushed her hair back from her face. He studied her swollen eye for a moment. She had received it on their escape from her mother's house.

"It's nothing," she said and pulled away.

"Did you have the doc look at it?"

"No."

"You should."

"Like I said, it's nothing."

Rain gave up. Nikki was a headstrong woman, proud, thought of herself as tough and probably was. He changed the subject. "Feel up to traveling?"

"Today?" she asked. "Are you strong enough?"

"He'll be in a chopper," Liz Harmon said from the open door to Nikki's room. "Four hours by air. He should handle that alright."

"What about me?" Nikki asked.

"You'll fly with him. So will I."

"What about my car?"

"Someone will see to it your car gets there safely. Don't you worry about that," Liz said.

"I'd rather drive it."

"I'm afraid that's not possible. I just talked to your father. Seems there's still somebody hunting the two of you. Copeletti's guys will have it cleared up in no time, but for now, it'll be safer if we fly and let somebody else do the driving," Liz said.

Nikki looked at Jacob. He nodded his agreement with Liz and added, "You drive, I drive. And it'll probably kill me." She did not argue further.

* * *

"What the hell happened to you?" Jack Albrecht asked. Henry Tyler's hair, what little of it was left atop his head, seemed to stand out at the sides; bags under his eyes indicated a definite lack of sleep. Despite all of that, he was oddly alert, not stumbling around the kitchen groping for a coffee cup and missing it by inches like Jack had seen him do nearly every morning since Henry arrived at the Rocky Mountain rest site. Fetchenko's men had set them up with it to get them a much needed break from the rigors of life on the campaign trail. This morning Henry didn't look as though it had been beneficial.

Bernie Jade (Bobber) entered.

"Who are you?" Albrecht asked.

"This is Bobber. Arthur sent him," Henry said.

"Bobber? What kind of name is Bobber?" And Bobber's head started to dance in excitement while Jack Albrecht looked on in amazement. "Why did Arthur send him?" he asked, more to keep himself from laughing than from a need to know.

"He's here to..." Henry started. He was interrupted by the ring of distant gunfire and the quiet whistle of a bullet breaking through the glass of a garden door and landing in thick wood of a table leg in front of Jack Albrecht's knee. The second shot was higher. It took Albrecht in the neck, severing an artery. He fell from the chair, grasping instinctively at the wound, blood spurting in all directions as he rolled from side to side. It would not take long for him to bleed out and lay silent, looking up at Henry as though to ask, "What was that?"

Bobber sprung from his chair, knowing he was about to face Milton Courte's two strong-arms, Knuckles Moran and Jimmy the Blade. He flew out the door, ducking and dodging as he ran toward the sound of more shots. The two men who had accompanied him on this mission remained with Henry Tyler and Jack Albrecht, one of them trying CPR on Jack while the other covered Henry, and for his efforts took a round to the back. He died slowly, painfully, while able to do nothing to defend himself or his charge. His partner, after seeing Henry escape the kitchen into another room safe from outside visibility, and knowing he could do nothing for Albrecht or his partner, darted into the yard to lend a hand to Bobber. Bobber made his way almost to the tree line before taking a bullet to the calf of his leg. It hurt like hell but did not stop him. He circled around. He came up on Knuckles Moran, tapped him on the shoulder, then stood face to face with Moran, his head bouncing like a bobble head doll while he slid a long knife blade under Moran's rib cage. Moran smiled, and then slumped to the ground in a convulsion. He died seconds later, about the same time Bobber Jade felt the sting of his second bullet, this one from Jimmy the Blade's gun. He felt the air escape his lung. He turned to see Jimmy coming at him — rapid pace. He felt his lung fill with blood. Jimmy advanced. Bobber raised his gun. It happened spontaneously. Bobber's guy shot Jimmy in the back, Jimmy the Blade stumbled and fell dead to the ground, Bobber fired, his bullet just grazing Jimmy's head and landing between the eyes of his own man. Then Bernie (Bobber) Jade fell to the earth — dead.

Henry Tyler waited. It seemed hours before he decided it was safe to leave his hiding space. He cautiously looked through the entire house, room by room, until he felt secure in the knowledge that he was the only one left

alive in the building. His security, those who had originally been assigned to protect him and Jack Albrecht Henry
supposed had all perished from having their throats cut or
worse before any gunshots were fired. He waited a while
longer. He summoned up courage. He ventured out toward the tree line where the shots all seemed to come
from. Bobber was dead. Bobber's assistant was dead.
Two bodies that he did not recognize, obviously assail-
ants, lay dead in the brush. He returned to the building to
call Fetchenko. Dead phones, all of them. Cellular was no
good, no bars here in the mountains. He would drive. He
would hope an ambush did not await him down the road.

* * *

Tony Copeletti, despite his ongoing pain from his
recent gunshot wound, had the right answer when Arthur
Fetchenko asked, "Did you take care of our friend, Milton Courte?"

"Done."

"Done, as in I'll take care of it? Or done, done?"

"Mr. Courte's private jet crashed on landing early
this morning. No survivors. Alcohol showed up in the
blood stream of that big-titted foxy pilot of his. FAA's
blaming drugs and alcohol."

"What about Henry? Anybody raise him? Or Jack?"

"Not a word out of either of them since we talked to
Henry and told him Bobber was on his way."

"You try this morning?" Fetchenko asked.

"We get no answer," Copeletti said. "Tried his cell
too, no service. You know how those mountains can be
on cell phone signal."

"Well... keep trying."

* * *

Waking up in unfamiliar surroundings was becoming altogether too common to Nikki Fetchenko. Yes, she knew it was her father's estate this time around, but really, enough is enough. But then, according to the long talks with Liz Harmon over the past few days, this was the end of the line for her anyway. Anything else was simply not safe. And there was Jacob Rain. She really liked him, probably loved him, so where he would be, well... that wouldn't be a bad place for her, and that was right where she was, at her father's estate. "It won't be so bad, Nikki," she told herself aloud. "Look at this; I'm even calling myself Nikki."

"Who you talking to, Dear?" It was Liz, come to see if she was awake yet, see if she wanted breakfast.

"Is it lonely?" she asked.

"Not at all. At first I missed my friends, and what little family I have left, a couple of cousins. But that passed. Did you have close friends? I know you didn't have family left back home."

"No. I've always been a bit of a loner," Nikki admitted.

"Like your father."

"Worse. He has Copeletti, and Henry Tyler, and you."

"So do you, Nikki. But you also have Jacob Rain, and from the look of it, will have him forever."

"That obvious?"

"That obvious. Even your father sees it," Liz said.

"Will that be a problem?" she asked, not knowing how Arthur Fetchenko would be as a father, not really knowing Arthur Fetchenko at all. So far as she was concerned, he was a likable stranger with personal politics, Liz had been filling her in, which seemed unorthodox yet somehow agreed with her own.

"He promised me something. He promised me he'd keep his opinions to himself where your personal life is concerned, not your professional life, mind you, your personal life."

"What professional life?" Nikki asked. She didn't know she had one.

"This election, you know it's all about getting a Fetchenko-sponsored President in place. I already told you that."

"Yes."

"Well, win or lose, after the elections, he wants to retire. And he wants you to take over," Liz said.

"Me? Why me? I don't know anything about any of this."

"You will. That is if you agree to take on the job. You're about to be slam-dunked with a rigorous training program. Actually it's already begun."

"How? When?" Nikki asked her.

"From the beginning. Your mother, Gloria that is, began it. She followed Arthur's instruction on raising you. That's why you went to law school, and that's why your ideas closely match your dad's. Then there was Henry Tyler. Ever wonder why he showed up and played the role of an uncle and a mentor? Even Jacob Rain."

"What about Jacob Rain?" Nikki asked. She did not want to hear he had been planted with her as part of some master plan.

Liz sensed oncoming trouble. She decided to head it off. "You and Jacob weren't part of any plan, if that's what you're thinking. Stuff just happens sometimes. But Jacob was sent because he was the best for the job. He's tough. He's dedicated. He's loyal and your father and Tony Copeletti knew he'd lay down his own life before he'd let anything happen to you. But he's also smart, onboard with Fetchenko politics, and persuasive. And he has that animal magnetism that you can see in the eyes of young girls and old women alike from coast to coast. One more thing, Nikki. He's yours. That can be seen in his eyes. Get dressed. Let's go find some breakfast. I'm starved."

And she left the room, indicating she would return for her shortly.

* * *

"I want you at Milton Courte's funeral," Arthur Fetchenko was telling Phil Blackburn as Liz walked into the office.

"I thought you didn't like Milton Courte," Liz said.

"I don't, but Mac McArthur and Victor Parker, and probably Davidson will be there. Hell... maybe Joey Ferelli himself will show. Won't hurt any of them to see Phil there. It'll give them the sense we're still paying attention to all of their shenanigans," Fetchenko said. "Take off, Philip. Go to Texas. And pick a nice wreath out for the guy, will you?"

Fetchenko waited for the door to close behind Blackburn before speaking again. Then, "How's she doing this morning?"

"She'll come around just fine. Fast, too, I expect," Liz told him and pushed a folded newspaper at him. "You're not going to like this."

Arthur Fetchenko unfolded the paper, glanced briefly, folded it back, sat back in his chair and closed his eyes. "Oh, no," he whispered.

"I'm sorry, Arthur," Liz said. "I know you were fond of her.

"He opened the paper once more. '**Martha Ferelli, wife of Senator Joseph Patrick Ferelli, victim of hit and run driver**', the headlines read.

"That evil son-of-a-bitch," he uttered.

Chapter Twenty-Three

Henry Tyler nearly threw his neck out whipping his head around to see the car pull out of the rest area halfway down the mountain. It seemed in an awful hurry. But when it passed him on a corner, and he saw its occupants, kids with beers in their hands, he relaxed. They weren't there for him. At the worst, he'd have to stop for the accident they were likely to have as a result of their recklessness. He thought back to his college days. He drove like that. He drank like that. It was a wonder he even graduated, let alone aced law school. He looked ahead at the taillights as they disappeared around another corner. Who knows? Maybe there goes a future senator or congressman — maybe even a president. He had himself so tied in his thoughts he did not see the truck approach from behind. And when he looked in his rearview mirror, it was too late. The truck rammed Henry's rear bumper at the precise moment it needed to for Henry's car to skid out of control and dive over an embankment where it came to a stop a hundred feet below after rolling over several times. The truck screeched to a halt; its two occupants got out and ran to the shoulder. "Let's go. He's a goner," one of them said as he watched smoke bellow out from under Henry's car.

"What if he got out?"

"He didn't. Look. The top's caved in on him. He's trapped."

* * *

Phil Blackburn's cellular vibrated in his pocket just as the priest sprinkled holy water on Milton Courte's casket at graveside. He slid back from the crowd to answer.

"Where are you?"

"At the cemetery," Blackburn said.

"Who's there with you? Fetchenko asked.

"The gang's all here."

"Ferelli?"

"Not ten feet from me."

"Hand your phone to him."

"Hello?" J.P. said into Blackburn's phone, curious look filling his face.

"Joey, this is Arthur."

"What the hell do you want?"

"You did it, didn't you? You son-of-a-bitch," Fetchenko said and hung up. Moments later he called Phil back. He sent him to Minnesota — to attend another funeral — Martha Ferelli's.

* * *

Nikki Fetchenko took Jacob Rain for a walk in the courtyard. Exercise would do neither of them harm on a sunny but mild afternoon. Jacob's strength was building, his limp less than Nikki would have thought. She wished she were that tough. Her movements seemed more labored from their experience than his, and she hadn't been shot. "It is peaceful here," she said.

"I like the quiet," Jacob said. "I like the action, but I like the quiet."

Everyone had been filling her in, working on her. It began at the Copeletti place in South Bend with Liz Harmon. Liz had done a sales job on her, subtly, and even Nikki had to admit, effectively. Either she was good at it or Arthur Fetchenko was one of the good guys and his efforts really were noble. She did see flaws in his thinking as presented to her by Liz, just understandable flaws when added to the stories of his background. And the close Liz used on her, the story of the tragic loss of her real mother and the brother she had never been told she had, pushed a button in her, a button that caused her to swing to her father's side of things — right or wrong. "If I decide to stay on here and do the work my father has in mind for me, will you stay with me?" she asked Jacob Rain.

"Is that your plan?"

"Not totally. I'm entertaining the idea."

"I have it in my mind," Rain told her, "that I go where you go." He knew when he said it that it might not be how Arthur Fetchenko would want him to answer the question. Fetchenko would have had him indicate that he would stay by her side only if she stuck around. But Jacob Rain loved Nikki Fetchenko, unconditionally like a puppy, and he did not want to place restrictions on that love. That's what seemed right to him, and, honestly, no one counted on the two of them falling for each other. It changed the rules.

"Then I still have thinking to do."

"I guess."

"Jacob, what would you have me do?"

"I would have you stay here. I can protect you better here. And I believe in your father and what he does and I can see you taking over for him."

"Do you think I can do that?"

"I do. You think like him. The two of you share the same values. Really, we all think you can do the job, probably better than your old man."

"How can that be?" Nikki thought of her father's long years of experience and wondered if she could match the ability he had gained throughout those long years with just education. That's all she felt she had to offer that her father lacked, law school.

"He carries baggage that you don't, and it sometimes clouds his vision. You won't be so hindered." Jacob Rain studied her expression. If he was convincing, it would show. And when he saw it did, he added, "You probably don't feel qualified because he hasn't trained you yet." It was what Arthur had instructed him to say should the occasion present itself.

"Come," she said. "I think we best take you back in. That's enough exercise for now." She tucked an arm through his and guided him towards the doors. "It's back to the bat-cave for you, my friend."

* * *

"Milton Courte might be dead," J.P. Ferelli whispered to Victor Parker who had accompanied him to his wife, Martha's funeral, "but so are Jack Albrecht and Henry Tyler. This close to the election, well... I'd say it's time for you to start shopping for a running mate."

Phil Blackburn eavesdropped on the conversation. He pulled back out of the crowd. He reached into a pocket for his cell-phone. "Arthur, please," he told Liz Harmon. Then, "Have you heard anything from the boys in Colorado?"

"Nothing. Tony's been trying to reach them, but no signal on Henry's cell, and the lines are out due to some storm out there."

"Rumor is Courte's thugs got to them. Ferelli's telling Parker both Jack and Henry are dead." A long silence followed. "Arthur? You still there?"

"Yeah. I'm here. Are you sure?"

"I was pretty damn close to them. I'm pretty sure that's what J.P. said."

"Try to dig a little further. Maybe you can pick up more. Call me with whatever you pick up on. Meanwhile, I'll have Tony look into it for confirmation." He hung up and asked Liz to have Tony Copeletti report to his office.

"I just got off the phone with Blackburn," Fetchenko told Copeletti. He explained what Phil overheard at Martha's funeral. "If this is true, we may not be finished, but it's sure a big step on the wrong direction for us."

Liz Harmon, in the office in case Arthur needed her to find someone from his staff, or make a call, or just needed information from this file or that, saw deeper into Arthur's meaning. She knew that Henry had been part of Arthur, just as Tony Copeletti had been since they were boys and that the thought of any of this threesome dying would be a deeply felt loss for any of them. And Arthur had sent Henry to Colorado. She knew the man sufficiently to know that he would think he had sent Henry to his death. "There is someone out there I can call." she said. It was a boy she dated in high school — almost married. But she would not tell Arthur Fetchenko this. "He's a guy I knew in school. He's a deputy sheriff from out in that country." She knew this because just before she came to work for Fetchenko she attended a class reunion — likely her last — and had spent much of the evening, both of them having come stag, catching up on old times and the days since. Had there not been the great physical distance in their way, they maybe would have taken up their romance again after that night. But the case being what it is, that didn't happen. "Should I call him?"

"Yes."

"What would you like him to do?"

"Give him the address of the retreat. Ask him to drive up there and check it out. And, Liz... how well do you know this guy?"

"Pretty well," she said.

"Well enough to ask him for discretion?"

"I don't understand."

"If everything's gone wrong, and I think it has, I don't want to read about it in some paper. Any mess, we clean," Fetchenko insisted.

"I'll see what I can do," Liz agreed and rose to walk out of the room. She would make the call from the privacy of her own office. "Anything else you want him to do?"

"Check hospitals," Fetchenko said. He had a feeling.

* * *

Mel Toby's squad car rounded a sharp turn on the mountain trail to come nose to nose with a wrecker. Someone had gone over. He skidded to a stop, dust from the unpaved road rising like a cloud around both vehicles. He slapped his car in reverse and turned his flashing emergency lights on. He backed around the corner and set up to serve as a warning to anyone coming up the mountain. He opened his trunk and dug for an orange emergency vest. He would set out on foot to guard against traffic from above.

When Deputy Toby passed the wrecker he saw the ambulance beyond, lights flashing. Attendants were hauling someone on a stretcher up a steep embankment. Mel looked down, the victim was not completely covered; apparently he or she was still alive. He looked down at the car. It was a miracle. "Somebody survive that?" he asked the wrecker operator.

"Not even hurt bad. A few broken bones. Lucky he was thrown clear."

"Anyone get an ID?"

"Some guy named Tyler. Harry or Henry. Something like that. Wanna stand back, Sheriff? Wouldn't want the cable to snap and take your head off. Never quite know what to expect on these mountain accidents."

Mel Toby went to the ambulance to check on the victim's identity. It was Henry. He was coherent. Toby was able to interview him on the spot. Then he called Liz Harmon as he had promised to do. He reported all that had happened. And Liz took the information to Arthur and Tony. Nikki Fetchenko joined her.

* * *

J.P. Ferelli wasted no time. Before the end of services and a lunch which had been served to mourners after their trip to the cemetery to say farewell to Martha Ferelli, he had made a call to party officials. "Jack Albrecht is dead," he told them.

"How do you know that?"

"I know it; I have it on good authority. And so is Henry Tyler." So was Milton Courte, but he was only financial support and of little interest to the party other than his contributions. No sense in clouding the issue with unneeded information. "I think we need to throw Victor Parker's hat in the ring... fast."

"Can he win?" It was the main concern. It was always the main concern among party officials. "You know, J.P., once Jack Albrecht came on the scene, his Democrat ties and Republican principals, the whole country fell in behind him. Can Victor shine through that smoke cloud Albrecht and Fetchenko created?"

"I think he can, especially if we concentrate on the fact that he and Jack were friends. Hell, the sympathy vote alone should do it."

"Well... there is a plus. Parker doesn't owe Fetchenko."

"Exactly," Ferelli said. "All Victor needs to do is play like he's going to continue with his old friend's policies. Meanwhile, we do our best to lay blame for Albrecht's death on Fetchenko and his new-found Republican friends. If this whole thing doesn't put him out of business, it'll sure slow down his momentum."

"So, you're convinced that by the party's backing Victor Parker and following the rest of your plan, Victor's a shoe-in and Fetchenko's finished. Is that what I'm hearing?"

"That's it," J.P. Ferelli answered.

"If you're that certain, throw Victor's hat in. We'll support the move."

* * *

Arthur Fetchenko had an alternant plan. No Ferelli or anyone else would turn the tables on him. What none of them seemed to realize was that nothing depended on Jack Albrecht... or Henry Tyler for that matter. And in this unfortunate turn of events, he would, as always, adapt. He placed a call to Republican HQ. "Look for the Dems to blame you," he told them. "Call me when they do. I can make it go away."

Chapter Twenty-Four

A broken clavicle, contusions and lacerations on his cheeks and forehead, three cracked ribs and a knee in excruciating pain from being popped back in its socket by a clumsy EMT, and still, Henry Tyler chose to hop an airplane rather than check into a hospital. He was going home. He had had enough. And what he saw awaiting him at a local hospital was another attack. Whoever did this meant to kill — and he wasn't dead.

"Henry's alive," Tony Copeletti told Arthur Fetchenko, his security office having received the call. "He's busted up a bit — they run him over the side of the mountain — but he's still alive. He's on his way home."

"No hospital?"

"He thought they might still be after him, probably right too. I told him to land in Cincinnati. Nobody will think to look for him there. I sent a chopper to fetch him."

"Good thinking." Fetchenko picked up the phone and placed a second call to Republican HQ. "We'll be backing your man running against Henry Tyler. Henry died in a car accident this morning. Do me a favor though, will you? Put out an ad by your guy, one of those 'My heart goes out to Henry's friends and family' sort of things. We'd be grateful for it, and so will the voters come election day." He hung up and turned to those around him, Tony Copeletti, Liz Harmon, and Nikki Fetchenko. "Nobody lets it out that Henry isn't dead."

"Why are you pulling him from the race? Couldn't he win?" Nikki asked. She had a soft spot for her Uncle

Henry. Blood or not, she felt protective over him. She owed him.

"He could win. I just feel something coming, and if I'm right about what I feel, you're going to need Henry here with you," Fetchenko explained.

"I don't understand," Nikki said.

"You will."

* * *

Jacob Rain wasn't certain of his future now that he had let things go so far with his boss' daughter, a somewhat younger girl than he should be letting himself fall for. He was even less certain when she came in, forlorn look on her pretty face, after spending most of the afternoon working with her dad, beginning to learn the ropes. "Something happen?" he asked. "Arthur say something about us?"

"He did."

"Well... what did he say?"

"He told me that you would be my Tony Copeletti when I take over for him."

"Why?"

"Because Tony Copeletti will be taking over for his aging and ailing uncle. I didn't know Antonio was sick. He seemed healthy when we were at his place. Didn't he seem healthy to you?"

"He's had two heart attacks and a stroke," Jacob said. "Now back to what Arthur told you. What did he mean? Is he planning to retire?"

"He might be. But I got the sense that he expects something bad to happen to him — not just retirement," Nikki answered as best she could, not really in tune yet to the way Arthur Fetchenko stated things. Her opinion came more from how she interpreted his words than what was said. Training from law school — read your opponent. "Jacob," she said and sat beside him on his bed. She slid close and pushed his hair from his eyes with her fingers.

"Yes?"

"Is this really a good place for me?"

"It's the only place for you. Sins of the father; that sort of thing. But in your case, it's really the sins of the grandfather."

* * *

An abnormally smug J.P. Ferelli stared across the bare wood floor of the turn of the century northland pub in the town he grew up in and his wife had just been buried in. He looked at Phil Blackburn. He nudged his glass in a toast-like gesture and grinned. It was an "I told you so grin." Uncharacteristic for a man in mourning. It made Blackburn's skin crawl. Ferelli's actions were to Blackburn, unthinkable. He wanted to tell him. He wanted to reveal all he knew of Fetchenko's plan for him. But he didn't. He couldn't.

Ferelli slapped his glass on the bar, ordered another, and then headed toward Blackburn. "Nice of Arthur to send you." It was a backdoor slam. What he was really saying was, "Why didn't Arthur come himself?" Phil wanted to answer him. He wanted to tell the son-of-a-bitch Fetchenko didn't come because he was way ahead of him. Arthur Fetchenko knew Ferelli would have someone waiting at the funeral, dead wife or not. This would be opportunity, a chance for a kill.

"Arthur sends his sympathy. He wanted to be here for you, Joey. He couldn't. He had commitments he couldn't get out of," Blackburn explained.

"Don't call me Joey," Ferelli snapped, to which Blackburn raised his glass and donned a smug smile reminiscent of the one Ferelli had used on him from across the room. *Touché!*

Ferelli tipped his glass back and emptied it. "Heard from your hopefuls in Colorado lately?" he asked, referring to Albrecht and Tyler.

Blackburn tipped his glass up. He drained it. "Heard from Milton Courte or his two henchmen lately?" *Touché once more.*

"Well listen... as fun as all of this is, I really must mingle. Good to see you again, Blackburn. Give my best to that boss of yours."

Blackburn wanted to tell him his best was not good enough for Arthur Fetchenko, but didn't. He, too, had had enough fun for now. He pulled out his cellular and called in. "How long do you want me to stay here, Arthur?" he asked.

"Come on home. I have a special project for you."

"Have anything to do with this prick?"

"Everything."

"I'm on my way. See you in the morning."

* * *

Victor Parker celebrated. He could not help himself, President of the United States? Ferelli had to be kidding. But he had never known J.P. to kid, not about a thing like this. To celebrate at a funeral though, that was bad taste, would be inexcusable if Ferelli wasn't right there beside him celebrating. It was his wife they had buried that afternoon after all. What the hell. If J.P. could cut loose so could Victor Parker.

"Having a little trouble wrapping your mind around the concept, Victor?" J.P. asked and held a glass high.

Parker stuck his glass in the air and tapped J.P.'s with it. "Never thought I'd see the day. I thought old Arthur Fetchenko had things all sewed up, and us old-timers were near to finished."

"Never say that. And never give Arthur that much credit. That little son-of-a-bitch is going down," Ferelli said and lost his footing and went down himself, as if by some paranormal act from Fetchenko. Victor Parker laughed, but only briefly once he caught Ferelli's glare.

"You know what I'd like, J.P., as a way of really turning up the heat on this celebration? I'd like a go-round with that feisty little red-headed pilot of Milton Courte's. Wasn't she something?"

"That she was. But the operative word there, Victor, is was. She's dead, died in a plane crash with Milt."

"Pity. Know any other big-breasted redheads?"

"I do. But I think we better get you off to bed. In your condition, I'm afraid you wouldn't know what to do with a big-breasted anything. Besides, we have to get you to Party headquarters first thing in the morning. Might pay to have control of some of your senses when you get there." Ferelli hooked an arm through Victor Parker's and guided him toward the saloon door. He'd tuck his candidate in personally. Victory was at hand and J.P. intended to see that it did not go south on him.

* * *

Oliver Trap did not think he heard Phil Blackburn correctly. "You're going to get a good share of the Democrats to do what?" Oliver was, at present, leader of the Republican Party, and in the race against Jack Albrecht. He hadn't as yet heard the news.

"We're going to get them to back you."

"How the hell are you planning to do that? And why? What about Albrecht?"

"Haven't your people filled you in, Senator?" Phil Blackburn asked.

"Filled me in on what?"

"Jack Albrecht is dead."

"Well... Well... I don't know what to say." Trap expressed legitimate concern.

"You will know what to say. Your staff is preparing it as we speak."

"But won't you be backing his replacement?" Trap had Fetchenko and his people as Democrats exclusively. To his recollection, they had never backed anyone from his side of the isle.

"No. Not if you want our support," Blackburn said.

"I'm not sure I understand. I thought you guys were Democrats."

"A common misconception. We're independent. Think of us as a union."

"A union?"

"Yes. A union. An independent organization who looks out for the politician and the political system, protects it, advances it even. We'll back you simply because you're the better choice."

"And what do I have to do for this backing?" Trap asked, cynical now.

Phil Blackburn pulled a document from his inside jacket pocket, placed it on the table, and pushed it to Oliver Trap sitting across from him. "Just sign this, Mr. President. It's the authority for the Fetchenko organization to do for your party what we've been doing for your opposition for years, getting you the best of the best, winning elections. No promise for this term, Sir, but for your second four years, we can make sure the right party gets in to help you." Phil pulled out a pen and handed it to Oliver Trap. "President Oliver Trap," he said. "Has a nice ring to it. Panache." He knew he had him. Trap had been running behind by fifteen points in all the poles.

An aide entered as Trap signed, and handed him another paper. "Your speech, Sir. You have a press conference on the hour." And he left.

Phil Blackburn stood, reached out for the already signed agreement, and said, "I'd wish you luck, Oliver, but now...," he held the document up, "you really won't need it." He smiled and excused himself.

* * *

After Phil Blackburn left Arthur Fetchenko's office, Nikki picked up the paper he had presented to her father. She read it, slowly, carefully. Then she read it again. Her eyes hung up on the signature — Oliver Trap. Maybe he wasn't the frontrunner, but she knew who he was. Hell... everybody did.

"Well. What do you think?" Fetchenko asked her.

She placed the paper back on his desk. "What is it?"

"It's all the marbles, my dear. All the marbles."

Chapter Twenty-Five

An ear-to-ear smile nearly preceded J.P. Ferelli into the office of the Party leadership when he brought them Victor Parker. "Gentlemen," he said in his 'addressing the full Senate' voice. "I give you Victor Parker, the next President of the United States." But his smile would not last. Oh, they approved of Victor Parker alright, unanimously. He had been this group's choice long before Arthur Fetchenko shoved Jack Albrecht at them. It was J.P. they shied from. Following his introduction of Victor, almost part of the same speech, he announced his decision to seek another term himself. It was that decision that lacked support among Party leaders. "What the hell is this?" he asked, his anger elevated, his face red.

"There seems to be some suspicion brewing," the chairman said.

"Over what?" Ferelli asked.

"Over your wife's cause of death. There are those out there who think you may have had an involvement."

"That's outrageous."

"Maybe. But damaging, don't you think?" the chairman said. Then, "Victor, where do you stand?"

"I wouldn't be here without the support of J.P. Ferelli. Don't make me stand against him. It wouldn't be right."

"So... your stand would not be with him?"

"Please, don't."

"Victor," said the chairman, "if you're going to be President, you have no choice but to take a stand, on this and many other things. Now... what say you?"

"J.P.," Victor Parker said while he studied his shoes, "you were going to retire anyway." And J.P. Ferelli cursed and stormed out of the room.

He was still cursing when he pushed his driver aside, opened his own door to the limo, and slid in shouting, "HOME!" Then he grumbled, "Goddamn Arthur. I'll get your skinny ass for this. Wait and see."

The driver shook his head, walked around the car, and got in behind the wheel. He tossed his official government limo driver's hat onto the seat beside him. He hated those goofy hats, but even more he knew how Ferelli hated for his driver not to wear one. Let him bitch, was the driver's motto.

"Get over to my house," Ferelli said into his cellular.

"I don't think so," Mac McArthur told him. "I don't think Davidson will either, J.P."

"Why not?"

"Party HQ. We've been told. We shy from you or we're out. J.P., I think we've lost the war," McArthur said and hung up.

J.P. Ferelli threw his phone at the windshield of the limo, shattering it and the glass into tiny pieces, one of which, a large chunk of sharp plastic, ricocheted into the driver's eye and caused him to veer over the center line and smash head-on into an oncoming vehicle. The driver died instantly. Ferelli survived. And now, the policeman waiting at Ferelli's home to question him about the uncertain circumstances surrounding his wife's demise would have to wait for another time.

* * *

Midnight had come and gone. Nikki Fetchenko had not slept. *Coffee, coffee was the culprit,* she reasoned. Or maybe it was her father, and all that he was involving her in. She did have an interest in politics, it's true. But she had no practical experience or reason to take him at his word when he said she would learn. Quick study? Certainly where the law was concerned. But what she had discovered over her short time as Arthur Fetchenko's understudy was that politics had little to do with law. What she really needed right now, was a diversion from it all — a way to clear her head. Perhaps a good piece of ass would do the trick. She made her way quietly down a dark hallway and entered Jacob Rain's bedroom.

"What the...?" Rain slurred, waking from a sound sleep and feeling the bed sheets being pulled back.

"It's only me," Nikki whispered and slid her naked body into his bed and close to him. She knew from experience and from the one conversation with him about it, that he would be naked as well. And she knew that he would be erect, maybe not at first, but shortly. For an older man, he was considerably older than she, he was quick to rise. "I thought you might like some company."

"Daddy ain't gonna come in here and shoot me, is he?"

"Don't worry about that. My father won't. Maybe Copeletti, but not my father." She snuggled close and nibbled on his neck, then on his earlobe. She slid a leg over him, held it there briefly, and then slid the rest of the way on top of him. "Tell me if I hurt you," she said.

"Not on your life," he said. He grabbed a handful of her hair and pulled her face to his. He kissed her hard on the mouth, passionately, both of their tongues probing as she helped him into her. Their perspiration lubricated them both as she slid up and down his body until he sensed a scream coming. He clamped a hand over her mouth and shushed her quietly, gently, until her climax tapered and she regained control. "Wow!" he said.

"Is that all you got to say?"

"It's all I had left in me."

She rolled off of him, kissed him on the cheek, and began getting out of the bed. "Wait a minute," he said. "Where you going?"

"I think I can sleep now." She pulled her nightshirt over her head and she was gone.

* * *

Liz Harmon let out a screech when she rounded a corner in the hallway and ran into Nikki Fetchenko.

"Busted," Jacob Rain whispered, then smiled to himself.

"What are you doing up?" Liz asked.

"Couldn't sleep."

"Me neither. Care to take a walk?"

"Sure." Nikki did not pass on an opportunity to spend time alone with Liz Harmon. Liz knew many things, being so close to Arthur Fetchenko and being a fairly big cog in the wheel of the organization. And she was not so tight lipped as most around the estate. "Where to?"

"I like to spend time in the garage when I can't sleep."

"Garage? I didn't know there was one," Nikki said although she really didn't know why. She had simply never given it a thought. But where would they keep the limos if they didn't have one. "What do you do in the garage?"

"Clean cars sometimes. Sometimes I just sit in them."

"Cars, you mean limos?"

"Heavens no. The drivers see to them. I like your father's cars. He has a few vintage automobiles. He still has the one he drove when you were born. It's his favorite. Come. I'll show it to you." And they took an elevator at the end of the hall that took them to the garage on level one.

Inside the large garage facility at the Fetchenko headquarters Nikki Fetchenko found herself in awe: floors so clean one could eat off of them, vehicles lined up like soldiers at the ready, limos shining like mirrors, and a half-dozen classic cars in showroom condition, none of which she could name.

"This one is a 1946 Chevrolet Fleetline. He keeps it around because that's the year he was born." She pointed to the next car in line. "Chevy BelAir, '55," she explained.

"What's the little one over there?" Nikki asked pointing out a small red convertible across the room.

"That one is a Chevy Corvair. Not sure of the year."

"My dad likes Chevy's, eh?"

"It seems. Although that one over there is a Ford, a '56 Crown Victoria.

"What's that old one over there?" Nikki asked pointing out what appeared to her to be from prohibition times.

"I don't know what it is, just that it had been owned by a gangster first, and then it was owned by a President. I don't even know which one," Liz said. "It's supposed to be bulletproof." She led Nikki to the last car before the collection of limos used by Fetchenko's people. "This is the car Arthur drove when you were a baby."

Nikki looked it over. She could see why her father was fond of it: sleek, black with a shine a foot deep, sporty. "What is it?"

"It's a 1956 Studebaker Hawk. Your father claims if he ever retires, this will be his only car. I don't know how he'll pull that one off. It's not very inconspicuous, is it?" She opened the driver's door and slid in behind the wheel. She motioned for Nikki to get in on the other side. They sat there, windows down, dead silence surrounding them for a time, and then Liz spoke again. "I'm comfortable here," she said.

"You look natural." Nikki reached to the dash and flipped the keys hanging from the ignition. "Does it run?"

"Like brand new," Liz said and fired up the engine. The mellow tone of its dual exhaust put a smile of both women's faces. Liz gunned it a bit, and then shut it off.

"Is my father really going to retire?" Time to pump for information.

"He is, I think. I never used to believe it until lately. I wonder, was he waiting for you?"

"For me?"

"Yes. Since his sister died, the woman who raised you, all he's talked about when he wasn't up to his ears in company affairs, was you getting here and him leaving the business to you. I think he's tired."

"Tired of what?" Nikki asked.

"Tired of politicians. Tired of threats and attacks, not that they'll go away in retirement. Mostly though, he's tired of Pat Ferelli, sick of having to deal with him."

"Pat Ferelli?"

"J.P. Ferelli," Liz said.

"Oh, you mean Senator Ferelli." Nikki knew who that was. His name came up in nearly every conversation in the office beginning with her first day here and ending, well... never ending. "What is he, like an archenemy of my father's?"

"You could say that."

"So... will this conflict, the one between Ferelli and my father, end when he retires?" Nikki asked.

"No. That'll end when one of them dies." Liz stretched her arms back over her head brushing the head-liner with her hands. She yawned. "Finally," she said. "I think I can sleep." And she opened her door and got out of the Hawk. She rubbed a smudge from the paint with a corner of her nightgown and headed toward the elevator. Nikki Fetchenko followed.

In the hallway outside the door to Nikki's room, Liz Harmon stopped for a moment. She brushed Nikki's cheek lightly with the back of her hand and bade her a goodnight. From a few feet away she turned and said, "Kiss Jacob goodnight for me."

* * *

Liz Harmon pushed her nightgown from her shoulders and let it drop to the floor beside the bed where she and Arthur slept. She crawled in beside him.

"Car still run?"

"Like new. When do we go?" she asked.

"When do you think she'll be ready?" Arthur asked.

"I think she's ready now, she just doesn't know it. She's got your smarts and guts. She's got Henry Tyler to guide her. She's got Jacob Rain to protect and love her. She has Phil Blackburn to smooth over any rough spots. What more could a girl need?" She turned her back to him and pushed her bare backside to his stomach.

"Christ," he said and flinched. "Your ass is like ice."

She pushed against him harder. "So, when can we go?"

"After the elections. After Henry gets back here and heals up a bit. Maybe after I kill J.P. Ferelli so he can never come for her." He kissed her on the back of the neck. He kissed her again. "Wouldn't happen to be feeling frisky, would you?"

"Frisky or animalistic?" she asked.

"What's the difference?"

"Frisky... I take the top. Animalistic... I tie you to the headboard, spread body lotion all over both of us, then I take the top."

"You got anything in between?"

"I'll see what I can come up with," she said and rolled to face him.

Chapter Twenty-Six

Antonio Copeletti rolled down an entire flight of stairs. Two of his house staff, his cook and a maid, rushed to him. In his eyes — a blank stare. His heartbeat — pounding and irregular. Drool running down the side of his face. "Call an ambulance!" the maid shouted.

"No! We call Mister Fontaine." Freddy Fontaine had been the Copeletti family's head of security for longer than either the maid or the cook had been around, and it was well known that the first person called in any incident whatsoever, was Fontaine, not an ambulance. The cook ran from the room. Fontaine showed in only moments.

Freddy took one look at his boss, determined that he was still alive, then ordered the maid to get Billy G. He had been a medic in Viet Nam, and had come to work for the Copelettis right after the war. His name had been so long and hard to pronounce that he went by an initial rather than encumber others with having to learn it. It had been so long since anyone in the family had heard it, no one even knew what it was nowadays. But Billy, last name or no last name, was always the one who took care of medical emergencies, and was soon enough giving CPR to Antonio Copeletti on the landing at the bottom of his stairs. "Will he make it?" Fontaine asked.

Billy G. breathed air into Antonio Copeletti and pumped his chest a number of times. "I think so," he said and repeated the process.

"Should I call an ambulance?"

"No," Billy said and pushed on his patient's chest a few more times. "Call Doc Wilkins. Tell him to bring ICU equipment. Don Copeletti already made arrangements with him, just in case." Their concern was for privacy, for secrecy. Should word get out to other factions in the area, opposition gangs, trouble would erupt. Takeovers would be planned. War would come. "He told me to tell you to call his nephew in, Tony Copeletti."

"He did, did he?" Fontaine was angered. He thought he would be next up. After all, he had been at the old man's side, his second in command, for years. Why would anyone be called in? "What for?"

"I don't know, Freddy. I just know what he told me. Gonna call him?"

"Yeah. Yeah. I'll make the call. Soon as I call Wilkins." Maybe he was reacting to something that didn't exist. Maybe it was simply a courtesy that Antonio's nephew be called, and not a changing of the power. Time would tell.

* * *

J.P. Ferelli waited until after dark, and then took a cab home. He had received word that the police were hunting him, full of questions about his wife's death. Questions he did not care to address at the moment. He had enough for one day: the Party turning its back on him, his two remaining friends deserting him for no reason, his cell phone junk, and oh... yes, having to squeeze himself out of a wrecked limo after the inept driver veered off and crashed into oncoming traffic like that. Perhaps if he had kept his hat on, the sun wouldn't have gotten in his eyes and caused him to have the accident. He made the cabbie stop up the block. He sat. He watched. He waited. And when he saw no movement around the place, nothing out of the ordinary, no cars parked out front, no pedestrians lingering, he paid the cabbie and got out. He pulled the mail from the box at his door as he unlocked. Inside, he looked at the mail. One letter caught his attention. It was from a lawyer back home, Martha's lawyer. He opened it. He read. It was an overload. He wrinkled it up and threw it on the floor and stomped on it like a child throwing a tantrum. Many years in the past, a relative had given him a valuable piece of property. Concerned that his constituency would think less of him, the relative had some trouble and a questionable political reputation building that he did not wish to be attached to, he transferred title to his wife. It had been an election year. He didn't need voters making a connection. He picked up the paper and reread it. It was true. Martha had executed a will. That valuable property now belonged to Arthur Fetchenko. "God damn it!" he shouted at the top of his lungs. He threw it back down and stomped it again. He would not sleep tonight. He would plan.

"Arthur Fetchenko," he told himself softly as he settled into his desk chair, "must be put down like a rabid dog." He pulled a black book from a drawer and thumbed through it. He settled on a name. He picked up his phone and dialed the number. "Vernon," he said. "J.P. Ferelli here. You seen Pauley Danucci?"

"Pauley Danucci's dead."

"Really? How? When?"

"Some say Tony Copeletti himself killed him, some say it was Jacob Rain. Happened several weeks back. That's all I know." Ferelli didn't know what to do. Danucci was his connection. Who should he trust now? Vernon Pratt? He hardly knew the guy. He knew he worked for Fetchenko and that he had been a friend to Pauley Danucci and the guy he contacted Pauley through. But aside from that, he didn't know much about the Pratt. And now may not be the time to take chances. "What about that cousin of his, Vinny what's his face? Know where he's at?"

"He's with Pauley." Silence followed, then, "Somethin' I can do for you, Senator?"

"Well... I don't know. Is there?"

"I can do anything them guys could do," Pratt said.

"Like what?"

"Name it."

"How much?"

"Depends on what you want."

"What's your job with Fetchenko?" Ferelli asked.

"Security."

"Can you get me in to the place?"

"Fifty G's. When you want in."

"I'll let you know," Ferelli said and hung up.

Vernon Pratt smiled across the table at Tony Copeletti. Tony rose, walked around the table, patted Vernon on the shoulder, and said, "Good work. Keep me posted."

"I'll do that, Boss," Vernon said.

* * *

"Will you need me with you, Tony?" Jacob Rain asked.

The call about his uncle's sudden illness did not come until almost two days after the heart attack occurred. Copeletti feared that the Don's second, Freddy Fontaine, was holding out, that he might have been waiting for the old man to die, and Fontaine himself to grab the reins before Tony got there to take up his uncle's business as he had promised to do. He would sort this out when he got there. But at least he could be certain of one thing; his uncle would not die — not yet anyway, or Fontaine would delay further. "I need you here, Jacob." He went on to explain about Ferelli's phone call to Vernon Pratt the evening before. "He's planning to come here. I don't know what his reasoning is, if he plans on killing Arthur or what. Probably. He sure ain't coming to kiss and make up, not after all these years. Anyway, as much as I appreciate the offer, it'd be best if you look after Arthur while I'm gone."

"Will do. The chopper's ready whenever you are. You be careful out there. Last time I was at Antonio's, I got me a feeling about that Fontaine. There's something not right there, can't put a finger on it. You just be cautious," Rain said, grabbed his walking stick, and hobbled from the room. He needed to meet with Vernon Pratt. He needed to be brought up to speed.

Tony Copeletti packed the remainder of his things in a suitcase and rolled Jacob Rain's warning over in his mind. It wasn't just him. Rain had picked up on it too. There is something amiss with Freddy Fontaine.

* * *

"Will my name ever be Fetchenko?" Liz asked Arthur as she placed a cup of coffee on his desk.

"Is that a proposal?"

"One of us has to."

"Why now?"

"Oh... I don't know. Maybe it was being in the garage with Nikki last night. I sat behind the wheel of the Studebaker and it made me wish for the road, for freedom."

"That right?" he asked and opened an envelope.

"That's right. So?"

"So? What?" he read the letter.

"So... will my last name ever be Fetchenko?" she asked and smiled.

"Unlikely," he said and handed her the paper.

"Why not?" she asked and began to read. "What is this?"

"That's two questions. Which would you like answered first?"

"You choose," she said, now paying more attention to the paper than to him.

"That's Martha Ferelli's will. She's left me a lake home, a mansion really."

"Really? Why?"

"I don't know. I guess she liked me more than J.P."

"What about the other question?"

"You won't become a Fetchenko because we are going to skip out of here, move into Martha's mansion, and when we do, neither of us will be a Fetchenko."

"What will we be?"

"Free. But as for a last name, we'll come up with one that suits us."

"Is this your way of avoiding marriage?"

"Absolutely not."

Jacob Rain had overheard portions of their conversation on his way through Liz's office. "Shouldn't she be on her knees?" he asked, walking into Arthur's office and finding Liz straddling him on his office chair.

"This is nice too," Fetchenko said. Liz rose and left the office, red-faced.

* * *

The helicopter, the one waiting for Tony Copeletti to board, sat running in the courtyard, its pilot walking its perimeter, checking to see that all was safe for yet another flight. He had just arrived from Cincinnati where he had picked up Henry Tyler. Tyler and Copeletti met in the yard. Henry limped. "You okay?" Tony asked.

"Bruised and battered a bit." Henry looked at the sling on Tony's arm. "How about you?"

"It'll take time, but I'll heal." His shoulder was recovering nicely from his recent gunshot wound but, as Doc said, the sling was necessary if he wanted full movement out of it later. Tony did, so wore the sling religiously. "You best have the doc look you over."

"Where you headed?" Henry asked.

"Home. Antonio's had a heart attack."

"Oh, no. I hope he recovers. Is he going to be alright?"

"Time will answer that one too."

"Give him my best. I'm fond of that old man, you know."

"I'll tell him you asked after him. Listen, Henry, after you see the doc, check in with Arthur. He's worried as a she-bear with a lost cub over you. And Blackburn needs you too. He should be in his office. See ya," he said and boarded the chopper.

* * *

Blackburn's office was one of the few with a window looking out onto the grounds. It had always been an issue with Tony Copeletti — a possible weak spot which might be used in an attack. It puzzled all of them when it was not shot out by Ferguson's band earlier. But since it wasn't and Arthur Fetchenko's garden door to his private balcony had been, when Tony had workmen replace it, he had them replace Blackburn's as well. Now, both of them have bulletproof glass. And at the moment, Phil Blackburn watched Henry Tyler's slow progress toward the entry door through it. "Poor son-of-a-bitch," he said quietly. He had the unpleasant duty of informing Henry that he would not take his ancestor, Senator Alvin Beckworth's chair back to the Senate. Maybe what he really meant to say was, "Poor me." Tyler would not be happy. After all, he had put up with Joey Ferelli and his cronies, dodged bullets, watched his entire party die in the mountains, and had been forced off the side of a mountain to get there.

Chapter Twenty-Seven

Lights out, blinds closed, and Ferelli could still see the flashing red and blue of the squad car parked in front of his home. He thought for a moment of confronting the police, demanding that they show respect. He was a United States Senator for Christ sake, not some commoner. He parted the blind a fraction of an inch and peeked out. Two uniforms were coming up his walk. He let go of the blind. He wished he hadn't told the detective to fuck off when he called earlier; he wished he had invited him over — maybe hashed this whole thing out over a brandy or a cup of coffee. But no! Not him! Not the great J.P. Ferelli. He couldn't bring himself to be cordial, not after all that's gone south on him. But what a cost. They were going to bang down his door in a moment. And the closer they came to that door, the less he felt like J.P. and the more he felt like the little Joey of his youth. He wiped the sweat from his brow and gathered his senses. They weren't going to bust the door down. They would take him in for questioning if they found him, that's for certain, but for now, all he had to do was remain silent for a time — until they give up and go away. But then... he'd best get the hell out. He stifled a sneeze and peeked out the blinds again. They were leaving, too slowly he thought, but they were going. Probably radioed in for a brown-wrapper car to park in front and watch for him. Who were they trying to kid. He was no fool. He'd know a cop car, any government car, markings or not.

He watched. He was right. A tan Ford — minimal trim, small hubcaps — pulled to the curb in front. No one got out.

Ferelli dug for inconspicuous clothing — blue jeans, sweatshirt, a tan windbreaker — by the light of a penlight, changed and slipped out the back before it, too, was being watched. He walked the alleys to the Royal Diner. He arrived just as the place was about to close for the night. "I just need to call a cab," he told Deloris, the waitress that evening.

"Say... ain't you Senator Ferelli?"

"I am," he said, then thought it a mistake. A United States Senator afoot was bound to bring out a question or two.

Deloris looked out the window and saw no car. "You walking?"

"A little night air," he said. "Can I still get a cup of coffee?"

"I recon so. I'll have to make you some though. I just threw out the last of it. Want decaf?"

"No. The hard stuff. I need to be up for a time yet." Ferelli looked around the place. No one in sight. Phone hanging on the wall near the door. "Got some change? I need to make that call."

"Pay phone's out of order. Come. You can use the one behind the counter."

Ferelli almost thanked her. For a second he forgot his station in life, or more correctly, hers. He followed her to the counter, entitled to this courtesy — no thanks necessary. He called a cab while Deloris made a fresh pot of coffee. He examined Deloris' enticing figure and mid thigh hemline. He told the cabbie to give him forty-five minutes. Deloris might be just the thing to take the troubles from his mind. "You alone here?" he asked her.

"Yeah. Everyone skipped out early, slow night, dates, that sort of thing."

"No date for you?"

"Nope."

"Pity. A fine woman like you deserves a date every night. No boyfriend?"

"Used to have one. He disappeared though, couple weeks back. Pauley Danucci. You know him?"

"Afraid not."

"That's interesting. He talked of you often... like he knew you or something." Deloris turned to face him, coffee brewing behind her. She placed two cups on the counter. "Mind if I join you, Senator?"

"I'd enjoy the company. And call me J.P."

"Okay, J.P." And she slid onto a stool beside him. She heard the front door open, turned, and said, "We're closed."

"I just need the phone," the newcomer said and made his way to the payphone.

"It's out of order," Deloris said and rose to usher him out. She locked the door behind him, turned down the lights, and pulled the blinds covering the front windows. "You don't mind it a little darker in here, do you, J.P.?" She knew other girls who screwed politicians in this town, many of them, and for the most part, all of them benefited. Politicians could be discreet, appreciative, generous, and this one, although older than she saw herself with, wasn't bad looking. And now she found herself halfway there, midway into the process of seduction — the place alone and the lights dimmed. Might as well go for it. It wasn't as if Pauley Danucci would walk in and catch them, was it? Pauley's gone — history. And even if he did return, she no longer owed him. "It'll keep us from being interrupted," she said and poured them both a cup of Coffee. She sat beside him again, legs crossed.

"Interrupted from what?"

"Our coffee," she said and took a sip. Then she looked over at him, batted her pretty eyes, donned a flirtatious smile, and added, "Or whatever."

J.P. placed a hand on her thigh. She made no attempt to stop him. She uncrossed her legs. She pushed a thigh against him and hooked an arm through his. His hand traveled up as he leaned and nibbled on her neck, sending a chill of excitement down her spine. Then she was on the counter, facing him, her skirt around her waist and her panties hanging from one ankle. She tugged at his belt, then the buttons on the fly of his jeans. Soon they were rocking back and forth, perspiring, her blouse open and her bra snatched from her revealing round firm breasts with nipples that stood up in response to the touch of his lips. Only moments, and their climaxes came in unison, leaving them both weak — breathless. "Wow!" she whispered.

"Jesus!" he said.

* * *

The four A.M. phone call Daniel Davidson received was one he knew would come, but wished wouldn't. "I need your help," Ferelli said. "I need transportation — and cash."

"I suppose you do." Davidson was in the loop. He knew all about Ferelli's troubles, that he was thought to have had involvement in Martha's death. Hell... Davidson suspected it all along, from the way Ferelli talked and how he reacted when news of her passing came. A man of grief acts a certain way, not like it's business as usual like Ferelli had accepted the news. "I'm up for the VP, running on the ticket with Vic Parker. I can't afford to get involved with you."

"Do you honestly think Arthur Fetchenko will allow that?"

"Why wouldn't he?"

"Why? Because you're one of the Veterans of Power. Arthur may not be able to stop Victor from taking the Oval Office, but he will see to it that Victor's successor, should something happen to him and it will, is a man of his choosing."

"But Victor has already chosen me. And the Party has backed that choice," Davidson said.

"That'll change by morning. But if I'm wrong, if Fetchenko doesn't get your name removed, know one thing, old friend. Know that he will remove you — permanently."

"What do you mean, permanently?" Davidson asked.

Ferelli was losing patients. "Let me spell it out for you," he said. "Arthur Fetchenko will have you put down like a broken-legged racehorse. Now I want you to send a limo and a driver, and a couple thousand in cash, to..." And he gave Davidson the address of the Royal Diner. "By nine in the morning."

"Are you coming back to bed?" Deloris asked J.P.

"Where are you?" Davidson asked. "Who's there with you?"

"Just have the limo and money where I told you. Nine sharp." He hung up.

"Darlin', I need to ask something of you. I'm tired and I have some things to take care of that can't be taken care of from my home or my office. I wonder could I stay with you for a few days?"

Deloris saw no reason to refuse. He seemed nice enough, and he was a Senator, trustworthy and all of that. And he was a pretty damn good piece of ass to boot. "Sure. Stay as long as you like. Just come to bed now. I have an early morning."

* * *

Tony Copeletti napped most of the chopper ride to his uncle's estate in Madison, awake only long enough for his mind to sort things out a bit, time to evaluate events of late and come to a plan of action for the future. That future, the immediate, concerned his uncle's second in command, Freddie Fontaine. With rest and clear thinking, Copeletti realized that his first suspicion had been correct; Freddy was planning to slide into position one if the old man died. Dangerous. What's to stop him from putting a pillow over his head in the dark of night? It wouldn't be the first such activity, even within his own family. So Copeletti chose something he never chose. He chose a covert approach. He ordered the pilot land at a nearby airport rather than at Antonio's estate. And he rented a car. Then... when he drove up to the estate, he relieved the guards of all communication devices so they could not warn Fontaine.

Tony Copeletti entered the front door of Antonio's mansion, and came face to face with Freddy Fontaine. Freddy turned white.

"What?" Tony Copeletti asked. "Not happy to see me?" He watched Freddy's posture for a moment. It seemed to hold, but his eyes did not agree. Freddy's demeanor said loyalty while his eyes indicated a take-over plan. But loyalty was what Copeletti sought. Freddy Fontaine was mob through and through. Power and ladder climbing came with the territory, especially in the higher ranking. It wasn't necessarily a bad sign. After all, a ranking member of a Mafia family who did not aspire to greatness, like a politician who only wanted to do his job, wasn't worth a shit. That climb to the top of the heap is the natural order of things.

"Well... like it or not, here I am." And he moved in and embraced Freddy Fontaine, a standard greeting among mobsters — close or distant.

"He's awake, Tony. He waits up for you."

Chapter Twenty-Eight

Susan Burton cried uncontrollably. Her violent sobs as tears washed the makeup from her eyes produced convulsion-like tremors that caused a pounding in her ears loud enough to mask the rings of the telephone. She had felt it. She had felt Henry Tyler's fear as his automobile skidded off the side of the mountain. True, she was only his assistant and that's all she had ever been, but that did not stop how mentally in tune each of them had become to one another over the years. She felt his pain if he were sick, his anguish when he had thoughts of suicide, his joy when all was going well, and this — this whatever had happened — she felt as well. She had begged him to take her to Colorado but he had insisted she spend time with her family as it may be the last opportunity for that in a very long time. Perhaps there might have been something she could have done to prevent whatever was happening, that which she was now feeling. She quieted for a moment, just long enough to catch the last of the phone's rings. "Hello?" she could barely say into the receiver.

"I'm alright," Henry said. He somehow knew she had sensed the mishap. He was, however, unaware she was feeling it a day later than the event actually transpired. He listened for a time to her sobs. "I'm alright, Susan," he said again.

"What happened?"

"Just a little car accident," he said. He knew to minimize was useless, that she couldn't be fooled. So he opted to speak the truth. "Alright... they ran me off the road."

"I knew it," she said. "I knew I should have stopped you from going, or I should have gone with you. Maybe I could have sensed something."

"And maybe you could have gotten yourself killed." *What is this?* he asked himself. Did this girl think more of their relationship than that of an employer-employee? Did she have further interests, personal interests? Because if she did, he wanted to know. He had hired her for her looks, meaning he must have had a deeper interest in mind back then, a feeling he had set aside as being foolishness born of grief over the loss of his wife. But there it was, her going all spousal on him. He felt like a husband again. "I couldn't bear something happening to you," he told her.

Susan Burton dabbed at her tears with a tissue. "Where are you?"

"At Fetchenko's estate. One of our choppers is in your area," he told her, referring to the helicopter that had brought Tony Copeletti to his uncle's place. "I want you to hop it and come out here." He gave detailed instructions. "I'll see you in a few hours."

"What about the campaign?" she asked knowing they had events scheduled in the area.

"There is no campaign. Arthur's decided not to run me."

* * *

"So... what I'm hearing is true?" Nikki Fetchenko asked Henry Tyler after he made his call to Susan Burton. He had been sitting at her father's desk, looking comfortable — like he belonged there.

"And what is it you've heard?"

"I've heard that you are no longer seeking office."

"That's correct. Not my idea though. Your father's."

"I've also caught wind of a plan on my father's part to retire."

"That's also a fact."

"Who will take over for him? Would that be you?"

"No, Nikki. That would be you. I'm just here to help you get settled in," Tyler told her.

"What if I don't want the job?" she asked.

Fetchenko's voice came from behind her. "Then shut the operation down."

She turned. "I have the choice?"

"You do," he said. "But I do want you to learn the job before you decide to do that. It's only fair."

Phil Blackburn, who stood to one side of Fetchenko added, "And I'm the fellow who'll be teaching you about all the people you'll need to know inside out and backwards."

"Our staff?"

"Our enemies," he said. And he began. He listed them first, mostly older officials from the Senate, Congress, the Executive Branch, and the Military who stood against the organization. The two of them would spend the remainder of the day — him instructing, her learning — defining the strengths and weaknesses of each on his list as well as how and when to use those qualities. Her constant question was, "Why?" His consistent and persuasive answer went far in convincing her that she would be doing a job that was both needed and would be appreciated by many, and that she was the right choice for that job. It was his goal. It was his assignment. And Henry and Arthur left the office as soon as Blackburn took the conversation over, and left him to it. Arthur sought out Liz Harmon for a fun-filled afternoon in the garage where they would detail his '56 Studebaker, then make love in the back seat like a couple of teenagers. It wasn't the first time and it wouldn't be the last.

Henry settled into a chair in Blackburn's, really his and Blackburn's, office, leaned back and shut his eyes against the constant headache his recent accident had left him with. He waited for the din of the helicopter that would bring Susan Burton home. And when it finally came, he went into the courtyard to greet her. He held out his one good hand to grasp one of hers as though she needed to be pulled out of the chopper. When her feet touched the ground, he leaned in and kissed her softly on the cheek. It wasn't enough. She broke his grasp and threw her arms around his neck and pulled him close. He winced, his broken clavicle giving him cause. "How much trouble," he whispered in her ear, "would I get into, if I patted you on the ass? Would I get slapped?"

She pulled back and looked into his eyes. Nothing like this ever happened before. She blushed. "Is that what you want me to do?" she asked and smiled.

* * *

Antonio Copeletti began a violent cough after raising his voice in a deep Italian accent at Freddy Fontaine. Tony Copeletti tried to calm him. The old man shoved Tony aside, let his cough run its course, and then continued. "My nephew, Tony, will take my place, and you will respect him like it was me talkin' to you. You got that, Freddy? Or are we gonna have to teach you?"

"I got it, Don Copeletti," Fontaine said.

"Not me. Him!" He swung a hand in Tony Copeletti's direction. "He's your Don now."

Fontaine turned to face Tony. He bowed. "I serve you, Don Copeletti, as I served your uncle before you, that is, if it is your will."

"It is, Freddy. I will depend on you. Now come. Let us leave my uncle to his rest." The issue, if there indeed had been one, was resolved. Tony, as well as Freddy Fontaine, knew where they each stood. "Have a drink with me, Freddy, and you can fill me in. There's much to catch up on."

* * *

The limousine parked in front of the Royal Diner drew considerable attention, especially from the police. J.P. Ferelli watched as officers questioned its driver, and then asked his newfound friend, Deloris, for yet another favor.

"Whatever you need," she told him.

"That limo driver has money for me. I'd be grateful if you'd tap on his window after the cops leave, and ask him for it. I'll meet you back at your place." And he slipped out the back door and down and alley. On his way he called Davidson, told him to inform the driver that the girl would collect the cash, and cancelled the limo itself. Change of plans. It would be unneeded.

Inside the girl's apartment, Ferelli made another call. "You said fifty thousand," he told Vernon Pratt, the Fetchenko security staff man who had promised to gain him access to the estate.

"Well now... that was before I learned a few things," Pratt said.

"And what did you learn that's worth a raise?"

"For starters, I found out you paid Pauley Danucci a lot more than the fifty you wanna give me. And I learned — you know Senator, we have intelligence too — I learned you wanna kill Fetchenko."

"What of it?" Ferelli's mind had journeyed past caring if Fetchenko or his people knew he was coming. Now he almost preferred them to know.

"You come in here, they catch you, you squeal, and Senator, I'm a dead man. That risk is worth more, a whole lot more. Now... suppose you don't get caught. Suppose you're successful. You kill Arthur Fetchenko, and I'm out of a job. That's also worth more."

"How much more?"

"I'm told you pumped out a half-mil for Vinny Gotto."

"And you think your little bit of help is worth that? Gotto had to smuggle out hard info to me. All you have to do is open a door and stand back. Hell... far as I'm concerned, you do that, take the envelope of cash I hand you, and tuck your tail between your legs and head for the hills for all I care."

"My point exactly. I'll have to head for the hills. And I can't stay long in those hills on fifty-grand."

"How much then, Pratt?"

"Quarter-mil."

"That's absurd."

"It's the price. Call me if you're interested." And Vernon Pratt hung up. "How'd I do?" he asked Jacob Rain.

"Perfect," Rain said.

"Think he'll come up with it?"

"He has no choice. But it will slow him a bit, give us time to prepare."

* * *

"Uncle Henry," Nikki Fetchenko said when Henry Tyler appeared in the office she was now sharing with her father, "I had no idea you had something going with Miss Burton."

"Nor did I, my dear," Henry said and kissed her on the cheek. "You know, Nikki, we haven't had time to talk, not really. And I've been meaning to tell you how good it is to see you here. It's where you belong. But I understand your trip out was quite an adventure."

"From the looks of it,' she gestured at his sling and brace which kept his broken clavicle in place, "no worse than yours."

"This? This is nothing. My travel from innocence into your father's idea of life has been a journey which began many years ago, back when we were children. All my trips are like this one. You, though, you have it easy.

You're thrown in to swim or drown. Quick — painless, even if the sharks get you. And believe me, girl, these waters are full of sharks."

"She knows all about the sharks, Henry," Fetchenko threw in. "She's done considerable time with Blackburn already."

"Philip Blackburn. Well... you do know all about sharks then," Henry said. Nikki wasn't sure if the sharks he spoke of were those individuals Phil Blackburn had been filling her in on, or if he was speaking of Blackburn himself. "So, Nikki, how are you adapting to this new life of yours?"

"The life itself? Or the job my father's trying to stick me with?"

"Let's start with the job."

"Seems simple enough," she said and looked at Fetchenko. His slight frown said she should say more. "I mean, I know I'll need to keep a sharp eye on things, but providing I do that, I think I can handle it. There is one thing, though."

"What's that?" Fetchenko slipped into the conversation.

"I'm not sure about all of this interference, like the court thing in Madison, the one that cost me my job," she said, still not completely convinced that this organization was the proper vehicle for repairing such problems as that with the misuse of power — or lack of proper use of power — by those two social services workers who all but caused the death of Jacob Rain's son. "I've heard it said, 'we right the wrongs'. I'm not sure that works for me."

"Arthur?" Henry said, turning this one over for him to field.

"That wasn't common," Fetchenko said. "In fact, that was something we'll rarely do in the future. And that one, we got into for two very good reasons: it was Jacob's kid, and you were involved."

"Explain that," Nikki said, this time she being the one with the frown.

"Which part?"

"Me being involved."

Fetchenko smiled. "It was time. You were making a reputation. Sooner or later that reputation would have grown and our enemies would start looking at you, and they'd put it together. They'd soon figure out you were mine."

Jacob Rain entered, leaning heavily on a cane. "You hurt your wound again?" Nikki asked.

"Run into my desk. Not used to this office work you know. Anyway, I came up here to let you know they finally brought your car in from South Bend. Thought you might want to pick out a place in the garage."

Chapter Twenty-Nine

"It's not gonna happen," Freddy Fontaine told Lupo Varga. He stared over the top of his glasses as he sipped his coffee. He wanted to see Varga's reaction or he would have handled this by phone. Varga wasn't big; he was a small-time hood with connections that were bigger than him. That was his use to Fontaine. If Fontaine were to take over the old man's position as he thought he might, he planned on expanding. There was a market — untapped — and it was a lucrative market. The family, under Antonio Copeletti's leadership, refused to sell drugs in either Madison or South Bend. The old man still held with a choice he had long held with, to never do business in a town where you have to live. He referred to it as 'not shiting where you eat', and to him, and unfortunately to his nephew, Tony, it made good sense. It was unlikely Fontaine's plan to market drugs provided by Varga would go any further. That ended when Tony Copeletti walked in the front door of his uncle's mansion. "Tony Copeletti ain't gonna budge on this."

"You better try harder to convince him. I ain't exactly alone in this, Fontaine. Me and some others, big others, we got a lot invested. You better try," Varga warned.

Fontaine rose, took a last sip of his coffee and slammed the cup down on the table. "Ain't gonna happen," he said. He walked out on Varga without looking back. To look back meant fear. On the street, Fontaine wondered how much trouble this little encounter would bring, then dismissed it from his mind, convinced that it was Tony Copeletti's trouble anyway — not his.

* * *

Daniel Davidson slept on J.P. Ferelli's words. J.P. was likely right, Arthur Fetchenko probably would have him (Davidson) killed before he was ever sworn in as Victor Parker's vice president. And what Ferelli had said about Victor, that he was a dead man destined to be replaced by someone of Arthur Fetchenko's choosing should he win office, was true as well. It all made sense. It followed their original suspicions and the whole reason their little coalition had been formed in the first place. The power that Fetchenko could gain from his efforts needed prevention. But they had failed. At least until now they had. And this one final leap, why... that would put an end to what has been, and a beginning to an all new and extremely dangerous future for the country. Time to put things in high gear. But J.P. was not answering his phone, home or cell, and Davidson was at a loss as to how he would contact him, how he would get those wheels, the wheels that had been stopped by his enlarged ego over having been chosen as Victor's running mate, back in motion. He listened while a generic message informed him to leave a call-back number or await the beep. He waited for the beep. "J.P. This is Daniel. Call me. I can help."

Daniel Davidson got on the phone. He touched base with every old-timer he knew, both in Washington, and in many states, a handful at best, but still, a force to contend with. He successfully rallied the troops to fall in behind him and J.P. Ferelli with the intention of fighting Arthur Fetchenko and his people to the death.

J.P. Ferelli had to sneak into his own home. He hadn't thought to take the fifty thousand he had packaged and set aside in his safe to pay off Vernon Pratt before he left. It was an error, and he would not make more. His cellular, for instance. Everyone knew they weren't secure. He dumped it in a trash bin at a nearby Wal-Mart and purchased a throwaway. That would make him less likely to be tracked. Unfortunately, it meant Davidson's message would never reach him either.

* * *

Lupo Varga related the sad story of his failure to close the deal with Freddy Fontaine and the Copeletti Family to his grinning superior. "I don't give a fuck how you do it, Varga," the man said, his smile never fading, "but you close this hole. You take as many men as you need and you bring Freddy Fontaine's head to me, and if that don't do it, you'll be going back for Tony Copeletti's head. You got that?"

"I got it," Lupo said. He did not wish for battle with Copeletti himself. Fontaine? What the hell. He's nothing. But Tony Copeletti? Not a chance.

"Good!" And Lupo Varga's superior let his smile relax. "Now... get the fuck outa here."

* * *

It was time for action. Benny Bruno, an enforcer who had served the Copeletti family for decades — trusted — loyal — had been sent out to keep vigilance on Fontaine. He had reported Freddy's meeting with Varga to Tony, and had been asked to force all he could from Fontaine, and then he was to kill him. Disloyalty was never an option for a family member. Too bad too, Tony had been willing to overlook certain things where Freddy Fontaine was concerned, out of consideration for his uncle who really did like Fontaine. But this couldn't stand. And Tony himself had plans for the man, as his own second in command. He would use Fontaine as his uncle had — to fill in for him. That way he could be Don Copeletti at home while still keeping a finger on the pulse of security back at Arthur Fetchenko's place. But that was now out of the question. He called the estate. "How's Jacob doing," he asked of Arthur Fetchenko.

"He'll do," Fetchenko said. "How's Uncle Antonio?"

"He'll survive, but he'll retire. It's official, Arthur. He's put me at the head of the family."

"Did he give you any time?"

"He would, but I got trouble brewing here. With him in a hospital bed, I'm not too keen on leaving."

"Listen, don't worry about us. Jake can handle it. He'll have to sooner or later anyway. But you can do one favor for me, kind of a last duty."

"Anything, Boss. What's your pleasure?"

"Remember that old family mansion? The place on the lake back home? Martha Ferelli left it to me. You think you could find the time to get someone in there to fix the place up a bit?"

"You moving?"

"Sooner or later."

"I'll see to it. But if it turns out to be sooner, let me know. You'll need watching."

* * *

"Maybe I should have left this thing in South Bend," Nikki Fetchenko said as she slid her backside up the hood of her little sport car. "It makes me long for the road."

"It's here to do that. Why do you think your father keeps these cars around?" Jacob Rain asked waving an arm at Fetchenko's collection.

"I have no idea."

"They're here to remind him that somewhere out there, there's a life aside from all of this, a simpler life — freedom — you get what I mean."

"Sounds like torture to me," Nikki said.

"It is. It's a torture that keeps him from taking this too seriously. Otherwise, what he does here would eat him alive, no more Arthur Fetchenko, just a power devouring destructive and self destructive machine. He don't ever want to become that, and he don't want that for you either. So he had your car hauled here, to be your reminder," Jacob explained. He placed his hands on her knees and kissed her gently on the lips. Then he helped her down from the car. "We'd best be getting back. You've got a busy day." Jacob Rain knew their love for one another could not come between Nikki Fetchenko and her responsibilities, or he would have opted for playtime out here in the garage — alone.

"Just one more thing," she said and walked toward the car across from hers, the oldest of her father's collection. "Tell me what you know about this one. Liz said something about it having belonged to a gangster. How did it come to be my father's?"

"He stole it."

"He stole it?"

"Well... really... I stole it, from J.P. Ferelli. But your father made me steal it."

"How do you know it belonged to a gangster?" she prodded and moved closer to the car. Rain took her hand, placed it flat on the driver's door and ran it gently over the metal.

"Feel that?"

"A little dent?"

"From a bullet," he said and opened the door. "Look at the window. It's got to be an inch thick. Bullet proof. This old car has quite a history. It was made bullet proof by Al Capone. When the Feds locked him up for tax evasion, Roosevelt took it and used it as his limo while he was in the White House."

"So, how did Ferelli ever end up with it?"

"It seems, somehow, probably after Roosevelt was dead and gone because Roosevelt really did not like him, Thaddeus Frank got hold of it,"

"I'm sorry, did you say Thaddeus Frank? Thaddeus Frank, my father's grandfather? That Thaddeus Frank?"

"That's the one; anyhow, Thaddeus left it to Ferelli."

"So how is it my father ends up with it?"

"That's the funny part. Ferelli hires this company to transport the car out here from Minnesota where Frank had it stored. The service he hired was owned by Copeletti's uncle, or at least he had influence with that company. I end up getting a call to drive the truck that hauled it. It never reached Ferelli. Far as I know, he's still trying to find out where it went."

"So, my dad just took it away from him. Why?"

"To settle an old score."

"Well... just how long have the two of them known each other?"

"Since they were kids," Jacob Rain told her and pulled his ringing phone from his pocket. "Yes, Sir," he said. Then, "We're needed. We'll finish this conversation later."

* * *

"I just got off the phone with Copeletti. You're no longer filling in for him, Jacob," Fetchenko said.

"Did I do something wrong, Arthur?"

"No. Not at all. You're no longer filling in because you're replacing him as head of security. He's not coming back."

"Tell me his uncle didn't pass away," Nikki said.

"No, but he's bad enough off, and there's some trouble brewing Tony thinks will require his attention. He doesn't feel that he can leave now. Are you alright with this, Jake? Can you do this?"

"I'll watch your back, Boss. Don't you worry none."

Arthur Fetchenko looked down at his desk. Sadness seemed to take him over. "Maybe it's time for me to think more seriously about getting out," he said.

"Because Tony's gone?" Rain asked.

"We started this together."

"Henry was there too."

"But Henry hasn't been in the thick of it like Tony and I have, "Fetchenko said.

"I have," Rain said.

"I didn't think you'd want out."

"Why not?"

"Her," Fetchenko said and pointed at Nikki. "I can't see you leaving her, Jacob."

"No?"

Fetchenko grinned. He looked at Nikki. He looked at Rain. "Do the two of you really think you're hiding anything?"

Rain and Nikki looked at one another — sheepishly. "So... you don't object?" Rain asked.

"It's my fault she's stuck here, maybe for the rest of her life. She has to have someone. I guess you'll do since I don't have the time or energy to shop around for her," Fetchenko said and smiled.

Nikki Fetchenko questioned her own thoughts. Should she even concern herself with her father's opinion where matters of the heart, her heart, were concerned? Was any of this any of his business? After all, he had only recently arrived in her life anyway. Not his fault. She was clear on that. But still, she had made her own choices for a very long time, and she'd continue doing so. And her choice was definitely Jacob Rain. "I'm keeping him no mater who says what," she said.

"And that's why you've been chosen as my successor," Arthur Fetchenko said.

Chapter Thirty

A cab pulled to the curb in front of Deloris' apartment and blew the horn like it had come for a commoner. Ferelli parted the Venetian blinds a bit and looked out. He looked back at Deloris lying on the bed, half covered, half exposed. God, she was beautiful. Her eyes opened. She rubbed sleep from them. "Where you going?" she asked.

"What's your last name?" Ferelli asked her.

"Lawson."

"Deloris Lawson. It fits you," he said. He walked out the door, knowing he would never see her again.

"Where to?" the cabbie said when Ferelli opened the back door.

Ferelli settled into the seat, leaned back, and closed his eyes for a moment. This was it. This was the finish line. No more going back to his lavish DC home; that was surrounded by cops by now. No more senate seat, or committee meetings or benefits to raise capital for running for office; all of these held an end in handcuffs for him. But still, he needed a last look. He gave the driver his home address. "Just drive by. Don't stop," he instructed. He had hoped for a better end, but, deep inside, he knew he was embarking on a suicide mission. Perhaps the forces would be kind and let him take Arthur Fetchenko with him.

Ferelli slid down in his seat as the cab approached his house. Unmarked cars sat idling in the cool morning air, some occupants asleep, others merely groggy from a need for sleep, one sipping at a steaming paper coffee cup and paying no attention to anything but the steam. The cab motored by doing the speed limit — unnoticed. Ferelli reached into the pocket of his trench coat for his cellular. He poked at the numbers.

"Yeah?" the raspy, sleepy voice of Vernon Pratt asked.

"You about ready?"

Pratt was at a disadvantage. He had not expected this call to come to his home phone. He lived with a wife and two teenaged kids in nearby New Creek, not at the Fetchenko compound. And it was five-thirty in the morning, not time for work where Jacob Rain could monitor. "Is this Senator Ferelli?" he asked to buy time. He wasn't that sleepy. He knew who it was.

"I asked you if you're ready."

"What's the plan?"

"You have access to a limo?" Ferelli couldn't see himself taking a cab to his death — or Arthur Fetchenko's death for that matter. Both of them deserved more.

"I can get one. I'll have to go into work though." Pratt thought for a time. He couldn't make this sound like he was too anxious, that he wanted to go to the compound. He had to dispel any thought Ferelli might have of him turning this over to Rain, or Fetchenko. "Got my money?"

"Fifty," Ferelli said. "You'll get the rest when this is over."

"What if you die?"

"Then you lose. So you'll want to see to it I don't die, won't you?"

"Where do you want me to pick you up?" Pratt asked.

Ferelli had some unfinished business. And he wanted a ride in the country, just to clear his head — time to think — time to plan. "You know Cumberland, Maryland?"

"Yes."

"You know that little country market there?"

"Lazear's?"

"That's the one. Meet me there tomorrow evening. Seven," Ferelli ordered. "Come alone. Don't tell anyone."

"I'll need a driver. I never have limo duty. If I take one out myself, without it's normal driver, they'll get suspicious."

"Just the driver then," Ferelli said then hung up.

* * *

Deloris Lawson spent most of her afternoon, having been halted at the door of the café where she worked when she reported at noon for the closing shift, being interrogated by local police officials. The photo of J.P. Ferelli, shoved in front of her so many times that she finally gave in, she identified as the man who had spent the past couple of nights in her home. "Did you sleep with him?" her interrogator asked.

"Pardon me?"

"I asked you if you slept with him."

"I don't think that concerns you," she said.

"Look, Lady, I ask, you answer. Is that too tough to understand? For all I care, you could be having a three-way, you, him, and your best friend — man, woman, or beast. But this is an investigation and you'll damn well answer any question I ask of you. I'll decide if it concerns me."

"I slept with him," she said. "What do you want with him?"

"Now that doesn't concern you," the detective told her.

"C'mon. I gave you something. I just wanna know if I should worry if he returns, Detective."

"You know where he went?"

"He left before I was awake."

"That doesn't answer the question, Miss Lawson," the detective said.

Deloris looked at the file in front of her interrogator. Amie Blue was printed on it in black marker. "Is that who you are, Amie Blue?"

"It is," Detective Blue said. "Now, do you have any idea where Senator Ferelli was heading when he left your apartment?"

"I do not, Miss Blue." She thought for a moment. "But I do know he left in a cab."

Amie Blue rose. It was something at last, something they could maybe use. She approached the door, and then turned to look back at Deloris Lawson. "Should the Senator return, Miss Lawson, be very cautious? Call me. We have reason to believe he's connected to the murder of his wife. You can go."

* * *

J.P. Ferelli knew things, mostly things he had learned from television or the occasional movie, things that might let him go undetected. He took his early morning cab to a small suburb on the north side of DC and had the driver take him to a sleepy residential neighborhood, claiming the house he wanted dropped in front of was his brother's. From there he backtracked to a bus stop several blocks away and caught a bus bound for yet another suburb where he hired another taxi, this one to take him to Baltimore. That should throw any pursuers off track. At least that was his hope. And in Baltimore he hopped another bus, disembarking just past a car with a for sale sign in its side window, sitting at a curb. He used a bit of Vernon Pratt's money, two thousand dollars. For two grand, the kid gladly parted with his wheels; he didn't need to know what name to write on the title. Ferelli's only question was, "Will it make Aberdeen?" Let the cops look. Let them tear Aberdeen to the ground trying to uncover him. He'd be far away in Cumberland, Maryland — waiting for Vernon Pratt.

Eric Lazear, owner and manager of the market on the edge of Cumberland where Ferelli had made his way to on the day he shared a limo with Pauley Danucci and a handful of dead soldiers, was in the back alley throwing out trash when Ferelli drove up.

"Senator?" Lazear questioned, and rightfully so. Ferelli was dressed ten steps below his normal station in life, and driving a throwaway car to boot. "Is that you?"

"Good afternoon, Mr. Lazear."

"What are you doing way out here?" Lazear asked, looking first at J.P.'s attire, then at his ride.

Ferelli followed his glances. "I'm traveling incognito," he explained.

"Well... it's working, Sir. I nearly didn't recognize you."

Ferelli thought it too bad that he did, because now... he'd likely have to kill the grocer. He thought it best if no one could say that he'd even been in these parts. "How late are you open?" It was a Saturday and Ferelli recalled the sign in the front window setting an earlier closing time on Saturdays, and thought it to be closed entirely on Sundays.

"I'm already closed. Why? Did you need something?"

"I wouldn't mind the use of your phone."

"No problem," Lazear said and led the way. "You know, back when my father ran the store, we were open seven days a week. In those days, there were no chains to compete with, plenty of folks willing to put in an honest days work without breaking a man. That was something. I was just a kid, but I remember. Nowadays, you want to be open those kind of hours, you better be prepared to work 'round the clock — all alone."

"No doubt, your dad lived in a better time, Mr. Lazear."

"Please, Senator. Eric." He headed to his office. "Wait'll I tell my wife I got a second visit from you. She told me last time, if this happened again, and I didn't call her and invite her to meet you, she'd never forgive me. Too bad she's away this whole weekend, visiting her sister over in Morgantown. She'll just die."

"No... she won't, Ferelli said as he snatched a Philips head screwdriver from a bin and stabbed Eric Lazear in the throat. "You will."

Eric Lazear fell to the floor, blood spurting into the air with each beat of his heart, his eyes open — unblinking — staring into Ferelli's — begging to know why.

"I really did like you, Eric," the senator said. "But no one can know I was here, not even your wife." And Ferelli watched as the little life the man had left drained from him. Then he searched until he found the grocer's deposit bag, took the cash and threw the checks in the pool of blood beside him. This would go down as a run of the mill robbery, nothing more. Country cops will spend entire careers trying to solve it.

Ferelli looked at his watch. Five-thirty. Twenty-five and a half hours until his escort into the Fetchenko headquarters would come for him. Aside from one little thing needing his attention, he'd spend it right here. He pulled out his cell phone. He called Vernon Pratt. "Everything set for tomorrow?"

"All set."

* * *

Deloris Lawson panicked when it came closing time for the café. She was, again — as usual — alone. The others, most of them younger and all of them with dates, had left hours earlier. Normally it didn't bother her. But with the interrogation she had endured that day, where she learned that her recent foray into bedroom excitement had been with someone who was in all likelihood a murderer, the darkness beyond those café windows gave her a fright she was having trouble dealing with. Was he out there, in the dark, waiting for her? And if he was, would she be a sexual conquest or a murder victim? She paced. She wiped at tiny beads of sweat forming on her upper lip and on her brow. Then she threw open the door, walked onto the walk in front, locked the door behind her, and headed up the street toward her apartment. She would not feel safe until, after six blocks of walking, she came to the front of her apartment and found her neighbor, Tom Bourn, sitting on the steps getting some evening air. She barely knew Tom, knew little about him, but tonight seemed the time to remedy that. "Good evening," she said and smiled.

"Hi," Tom said. "I'm, Tom Bourn."

"I know who you are. I'm Deloris Lawson."

"I know. From the diner. I eat there now and then."

She began to sit, and then decided it was polite to ask. "Mind if I join you?"

"Not at all. I'd be glad for the company. I usually don't sit out at night, but the air in my apartment went down. It's hotter than hell up there."

"Mine's working. Wanna come in? I could fix us a drink."

"I wouldn't want to trouble you, Miss Lawson," Tom said, hoping it wouldn't stop her from insisting. She was quite a dish. Sexy. Alluring.

"Deloris," she insisted. "And you won't be putting me out. I'm all wound up from work, wide awake and will be for hours. You know. I'd like the company. Otherwise, it just gets lonely up there." She rose and started up the steps. Her short waitress uniform allowed for more than a glimpse of her well rounded bottom. Her stockings, thigh highs, her underwear, a lacy thong. And when he did not seem to get up right away, she turned and bent and extended a hand to help him. Her top, low cut, her bra, missing, her nipples, hard. He took his time getting to his feet, but get to his feet, you damn right he would.

She punched in her code at the security door and they went to her apartment on the second floor. She felt safe.

Chapter Thirty-One

Nikki Fetchenko enjoyed her evening walks with Jacob Rain in the courtyard of the estate, but she wanted more.

"This is all there is," Rain told her. "I'm afraid, if your decision is to take over for Arthur, you're stuck here just like he has been — inside the safety of the compound."

But that is not what she was talking about. She took him by the hand and led him into the brush at the edge of the lawn, into the darkness. "I meant more than a walk in the yard."

"What you got in mind?" he asked.

She pulled him along to the cliff face. "I'll show you." She looked the wall over for a moment in the moonlight, spotted a rock jutting out waist high, turned her back to it and hoisted herself up to a sitting position. She hiked her skirt up to expose most of her thighs and pulled him close to her, between her legs. She placed both hands around him, cupped his buns and pulled him to her with a jerk. "Get the idea?" She felt his erection grow. "I guess you do," she said. She kissed him hard on the mouth and let her hands slide around to the front of his pants — to his zipper. Soon his pants were around his ankles.

The whack, whack, whack of the chopper did not come long enough before it's bright landing light flooded the ground for Jacob Rain to pull his trousers back up. "Is that Jacob Rain's lily white ass I see?" came a voice over the chopper's P.A. system. It was the voice of Tony

Copeletti. He was on a quick trip back to the Fetchenko estate to collect the balance of his belongings.

"Son-of-a-bitch," Rain said and jerked his pants up.

"Son-of-a-bitch," Nikki whispered and yanked her skirt down.

Arthur Fetchenko and Liz Harmon, their garden door leading to the balcony off their bedroom having been open, heard all. "Thank God we don't get caught like that," Liz said.

"You mean with our pants down?" Fetchenko asked.

"Exactly."

"What makes you so sure we don't?" He thought of the last time they made love on their balcony. He had smelled the smoke from Tony Copeletti's cigarette that night.

* * *

It had been through his association with the late Colonel Randal Ferguson that J.P. drew what he needed to make this battle with Arthur Fetchenko his final battle. This had gone on long enough. Had it been a half-century? More? Less? Whatever, it had been long enough and it needed to end. So he needed armament. He needed explosives. Simple entry to Arthur's compound would not suffice. What was he to do? Sneak up behind everyone and cave their heads in with a rock. Sure he had a gun, one that had served him well over the years. But it was only a six-shooter, a snub-nose — great for shooting someone at point blank range, but not so accurate if any distance might be required. He needed a Glock — something with umph. Ferguson introduced him, some time back, to a man who lived near Cumberland, a gun dealer who dealt with much more than guns — under the table. That man's name was Parnell Piccinni — Triple P Hunter's Supply. Ferelli wondered what the third P stood for, Peter? Paul? Pecker-head? He dug into his wallet and pulled out the card Fergie had given him. He called Piccinni from Eric Lazear's office phone, his objective to obtained driving directions. Then he would set up a meeting for later in the evening.

* * *

With Tony Copeletti on site, Henry Tyler back and recovering from his recent ride down the side of a mountain, Phil Blackburn done with all of his funeral attending, and Jacob Rain and Nikki now in the building and fully dressed, it looked like the proper moment for a meeting. If Copeletti had left any unfinished business when he lit out for his uncle's place, the time to fill others in had come. Vernon Pratt could be reached at home if needed, but Fetchenko thought it unnecessary, since, at last word, Vernon had not heard from Ferelli other than his initial call and offer. Liz Harmon did the leg-work, and all were gathered in Arthur's office in little time.

"Before we get started," Fetchenko said, "Tony, how's Uncle Antonio?"

"He's recovering."

"That mean you're coming back?" Jacob Rain asked. "Because, if you are, I'll gladly step aside."

"No. You stay where you are. I couldn't do the things you can do." His reference, caught by both Rain and Nikki Fetchenko, evidenced by their downward looks, was to the scene he saw in the lights of the chopper. "But you and I will be working together, probably as much as and in the same way as Arthur and Antonio did over the years."

"Jacob," Fetchenko said. "Any word from your guy, Vernon Pratt? Any update on what Ferelli might be up to?"

"Not a word. I touched base with Vern this afternoon, and... nothing definitive."

"Blackburn, anything in the air?" Fetchenko asked.

"Only thing I've got is that Dan Davidson is rallying the old timers. His plan was to help J.P. get you since J.P.'s convinced him that you'll remove him from the Vice Presidents office should he get in."

"I will."

"I know. But there's a flaw in poor Davidson's plan," Blackburn said and smiled.

"A flaw?"

"Yeah. Seems Ferelli is so scared we're onto him, he's ditched his phone. Davidson can't catch up with him to help him come after you. Now Davidson and the rest of them are sitting on their thumbs, hoping to hear from Ferelli, or hoping Ferelli gets you all by himself. The rest of them guys are a bunch of pussies. Pardon the language, ladies. They won't act without Ferelli to lead the way. Might later, once we get him, but not now."

"And that's your assessment?" Fetchenko asked.

"That's it," Blackburn said.

"Henry, how ready are you?" Fetchenko asked, turning his attention to Tyler.

"Ready for what?" Henry Tyler asked.

"Ready for my retirement?"

Tyler did not answer. He simply shrugged his shoulders, his sign that one way or the other, everything would work out.

"You can't be serious, Father," Nikki said. "Isn't it me who needs to be ready?"

"You are. Your staff is in place, you have Phil Blackburn — he knows who all the bad guys are. You have Henry — he can make sure your decisions are in line with our agenda until you get a little more used to things, and you have Jacob Rain — he can keep you out of harm's way and, ah, well... whatever else. Copeletti's a phone call away, and so will I be. I'd say you're in good hands, and so is this operation."

Jacob Rain's cellular rang. He rose and moved to a corner of the room to take the call without interrupting the meeting.

"Surely you're not leaving right away, Boss," Blackburn said. "If Ferelli's serious, and the others can't find him, that could only mean one thing. He's gunning for you. You leave and he'll get Nikki instead."

"I go nowhere until I've dealt with that fool. Don't you worry about that. I don't know how long I'll have to wait, but I go nowhere until something's done about Joey Ferelli," Fetchenko said and pulled at the collar of his shirt like it had tightened on his neck while he talked. Nothing upset the man like talk of Joey Ferelli. Nothing.

"You won't wait long," Jacob Rain said and flipped his cell phone closed. "That was Vernon Pratt. Ferelli's made contact. Vernon will pick him up in Cumberland tomorrow evening about seven. How you wanna handle it?"

"Tell Pratt to let him into the garage. We'll deal with Joey on our ground."

* * *

J.P. Ferelli keyed the numbers he found on Peckerhead Piccinni's card into the phone on Eric Lazear's desk. His contact would be brief. Piccinni was well aware of Ferelli and his agenda. Ferguson had prearranged dealings with him, knowing the final blow to the Fetchenko operation would happen in someway similar to this. He did not, however, imagine he would not be part of it, nor did Piccinni. "I thought I would be dealing with Colonel Ferguson."

"I'm afraid that's not possible. Fergie's dead. Killed by the guy we're after now."

Piccinni didn't like surprises. He thought at first of hanging up, of canceling the deal. But Ferguson had ordered heavily. He would take the risk or suffer a large financial loss. He chose the risk. Times weren't that good right now. "Ferguson ordered lots of goods. You bring cash?"

"I did." Ferelli looked at the safe in the corner of the room. Still open. Might be more cash in it. Otherwise, the rest of Pratt's fifty was history and he'd have to shoot Pratt first thing and hope the driver could get him in. He jotted down directions to Piccinni's shop, just a few miles out of the city, and hung up. He checked the safe. Old Eric had been rat holing, probably from the IRS. "Sneaky bastard, there must be a hundred thousand in here," Ferelli said. He stuffed the cash in a bag and headed out to find the gun dealer's shop.

On his way past the lifeless body of the grocer, Ferelli looked down. "Care to come along, Mr. Lazear? Excuse me, Eric. I promised to call you Eric. Care to join me, Eric? No? Okay."

Ferelli got into his junker and made his way up a mountain pass. Piccinni's place was down a long dirt road at the summit, easy enough to find, but still dark when he pulled up in front. Piccinni watched from a stand of trees across the dirt road while Ferelli got out and approached the building.

"He looks harmless enough," Piccinni told an old hound sitting beside him. "Let's go, Boy." But the dog sat still. He always sat still whenever Piccinni told him to move. He shook his head and set out alone to let Ferelli into the shop. "See you found me," he said more to avoid scaring the shit out of his late night customer than anything else. "Hope you brought a lot of money."

"How much will I need? Ferguson never got around to telling me what the two of you agreed on."

"He ordered enough for five men. You got help?"

"Not anymore," Ferelli said. "Why? You volunteering?"

"Nope. I know who you're after. The colonel told me. I don't do suicide missions, Senator."

Ferelli shot him a curious look. Did this guy know too much? Was he safe to leave behind — alive? Or should he just shoot him, take what he wanted, and be on his way. A thought entered his mind. He was becoming like an old-time gangster, like Dillinger, like Capone. Capone, now there's something he hadn't thought of for a very long time. Capone's car, the one supposedly left to him (Ferelli) by Governor Franks, the car Arthur Fetchenko stole from him. He wondered if Arthur still had it. His blood began to boil at the thought. He reached into a pocket for his snub-nose. Where was it? Shit. He left it on the grocer's desk.

"You okay?" Piccinni asked.

"Fine," he said. "Let's get on with this."

The crate of weapons and ammunition caught Ferelli by surprise. "Christ, man. There must be enough for ten men. What the hell am I to do with all of that?"

"Not my concern, Senator. That there's your order. Take it or leave it."

Ferelli dug through the crate: grenades, four M-16 assault rifles, a couple of other guns he did not recognize. "What are these?" he asked.

"Those, my friend, are something nobody's gonna expect. They're M-79 grenade launchers. Those puppies will do some damage. Here," he said and handed Ferelli a cylinder shaped item that looked like an oversized bullet. "Here's the round. You put them in like this, take aim, turn off the safety — that's this lever right here, and pull the trigger. You won't even see where what you're aiming at went. Couple of these, carefully aimed, and your war is over."

"So what do I need with the rest of this shit?"

"Don't know. Don't care. That's what Ferguson ordered and that's what you're buying. Forty-eight thousand."

"But I can't use all of that," Ferelli complained. Not that he really cared. Win or lose, he didn't need the money. If he lost to Fetchenko, he'd be dead. If he kills Arthur Fetchenko, he'll take over his operation; to the victor goes the spoils. And Arthur has a lot of money, more than God.

"Then don't take it all, Senator. Just take what you need. The price is still forty-eight thousand."

Piccinni was getting on Ferelli's nerves. No wonder his middle name was Pecker-head. It fit. "Is there at least a Glock in the mix?"

Piccinni dug into the crate and came back with a Glock nine. He handed it to Ferelli. "Careful. It's loaded. That's the safety," he said and pointed.

"Help me load this stuff in the trunk," Ferelli said, tucked the Glock into the waistband of his trousers, and handed Piccinni the envelope meant for Vernon Pratt. It contained forty-eight thousand and change, the rest of Vernon's fifty gone to the used car purchase — the little actual cash from Lazear's deposit bag in the mix. He popped the trunk on his junker, and he and Piccinni hoisted the crate into the back. "Close that," Ferelli said and leaned down, hands on his knees like the labor had been too much.

"You're real fit for a fight, ain't you old man?" Piccinni said and put both hands on the old car's trunk lid.

Ferelli straightened and pulled the Glock from his waistband, flipped the safety off, and plugged Parnell Piccinni squarely between the eyes as he turned to face him. The old hound began to howl. Ferelli shot in it's direction. The dog tore off into the bushes across the dirt road. Ferelli took his envelope full of Vernon Pratt's money and jumped in the junker. He returned to Lazear's Market to spend the night and plan for tomorrow.

He would haul his purchases into the store, where he could sort them and choose from them which items he would take to Arthur Fetchenko's with him. He would refill the trunk of the junker with the body of Eric Lazear.

Then he called Deloris Lawson.

Chapter Thirty-Two

"Hello?" the groggy voice came on the other end of J.P. Ferelli's phone call.

"Deloris?" He wasn't sure he had dialed right. It didn't sound at all like the girl he had been sleeping with in Washington.

"Who's this?" Deloris asked.

"J.P."

Deloris swung her legs over the edge of her bed. "What do you want?" she asked.

"Tomorrow, I'll be taking over a large and influential political sector, and I'd like very much for you to join me. This unit runs out of a secure compound where all of your needs will be taken care of for the rest of your life. The place is a virtual paradise, Deloris. What do you say to that?"

"The police came for me today. I sat through five hours of interrogation. They told me you are being sought for murder."

A long silence followed. Ferelli had hoped this would not surface before he had Arthur Fetchenko on ice and himself in Arthur's chair.

"Senator?" Deloris said, thinking she might have lost the connection.

"I don't know what to say. Who did they say I killed?"

"Mrs. Ferelli."

"Well... that's simply not true."

Tom Bourn sat up and rubbed at the sleep in his eyes. "What's going on?" he asked. Deloris quickly slapped her hand over the phone's mouthpiece and shushed Tom. Fear shone in her eyes. "Who is that?" he asked. She shushed him again and lifted her hand.

"Is someone there with you?" Ferelli asked.

"It's the radio," Deloris said.

"You slut! You just wait." Ferelli shouted and hung up.

* * *

Jacob Rain laid in Nikki Fetchenko's bed, wide awake, waiting for the trouble that was on its way. He knew he should sleep, but how could he? For he also knew if J.P. Ferelli managed to take Arthur Fetchenko out, and found out that Nikki was Arthur's daughter, she would be next. Nikki did not take all of this so seriously as Jacob. She trusted, sometimes too much, almost naively. She trusted that her father could not be taken by Ferelli in the first place. She thought of Ferelli as a politician, not a serious threat. And Jacob Rain? Hell, to her he was invincible. He may be wounded, that's true, but killed? Never. But what she didn't realize is that J.P. Ferelli was cut from the same cloth as her father. Both men were equally ruthless when it came to any kind of battle, and what was now heating up, was some kind of battle. Nikki could sleep. Jacob would remain awake. He wished Tony Copeletti hadn't been in such a hurry to get back to his duties of replacing his aged and ailing uncle, but he had. He gathered his things and hopped a chopper soon after the meeting was over. Rain had worked with him forever, it seemed, and he would miss him anyway, but right now, until this thing was behind them, he would miss Copeletti the most. He wondered if Copeletti felt this inadequate when he first became head of security for Fetchenko. He doubted it. The job was much less in those days, not so many dangers. And, of course, there was no girl, no love of Tony Copeletti's life to watch over. Nikki threw a whole new twist to the job, that's for sure.

Nikki rolled toward Rain, opened her eyes a slit, and asked, "You still awake?"

"Go back to sleep," he said.

"Do you need to sleep with that gun?" she asked gesturing toward the loaded Glock on his lap. He was sitting, leaning on the headboard, reading. But she was right. The gun would serve them just as well if it was on the nightstand. He set it aside. Nikki closed her eyes. Jacob returned to his book, Cobb's Landing by Schwartz.

* * *

Arthur Fetchenko paced the floor. "I wish I could read that son-of-a-bitch's mind," he said.

"Well... you can't. So you might as well come to bed," Liz Harmon insisted. She folded back the sheet and blanket and patted the space next to her.

Fetchenko sat on the edge of their bed. "He's not this brave. At least he's never before shown it. Joey Ferelli's the type who lets others get their hands dirty."

"Maybe he's run out of others."

"Still, I would have expected him to tuck his tail, run on home, and forget about all of this without someone else around to do his bidding. You don't suppose he's not alone, do you?"

"I'm sure I don't know, but aren't your people supposed to know?" Liz more reminded him than asked.

"You're right. If he wasn't in this alone, we would have known."

"So you'll come to bed now?"

Fetchenko lay back on his pillow. "I don't know if I can sleep," he said.

"There are other things we can do."

"You mean one last roll in case I die tomorrow?"

"Well... I really don't think it'll come to that, but... have it your way. Just as long as I get laid."

* * *

Vernon Pratt knelt beside his bed. He crossed himself and began to pray. His standard, mumble jumble repetitious memorized and thoughtlessly mimicked Catholic prayers gave way to a serious talk with God tonight. "Protect me tomorrow. I go with Satan, Father."

"What the hell are you saying, Vernon?" his wife asked. "That's not how you pray." She stared at him for a moment, wide eyed. "And who's this Satan you go with tomorrow?"

"Senator Ferelli," he said and climbed into bed beside her. "I have to escort him to the compound."

"So?"

"He's going there to kill Arthur Fetchenko."

"So why escort him?"

"Because Arthur Fetchenko wants me to," Vernon told her.

"Let me get this straight. Ferelli wants to kill Fetchenko. And you're to bring the man who wants to kill your boss to your work because your boss told you to. Is that about the way it is?"

"That's exactly the way it is."

"I don't understand you guys."

"You don't have to, Linda. You just spend the money I bring home. I'll see to the rest," Vernon said, snapped off the light, and turned his back. He needed sleep, not questions.

* * *

J.P. Ferelli was a man over the edge. He had lost control of all common sense. He had always been capable of murder. He just hadn't allowed himself to cross that line until now. Martha didn't count. It wasn't like he pulled a trigger, or slashed out with a knife. He didn't do either of those things, and frankly, he didn't do anything at all to her. He had someone else do it. And she had been his wife; he had the right. She was after all, only a woman. But these other two, Eric Lazear the grocer, and Pewee Piccinni or whatever his name was, the gun seller at any rate, those were, to his surprise, pleasurable acts. And he reveled in the pride of it all as he drank cold beers from Lazear's cooler and propped his feet up on Lazear's desk. "Tomorrow, I will kill Vernon Pratt. Then I will kill Arthur Fetchenko. Then I'll take that operation of his over and I will kill no more. I will miss it though." He popped the top on another of Eric Lazear's beers and settled in for the night. He needed to be fresh for the battle.

Chapter Thirty-Three

J.P. Ferelli felt on top of the world when he awoke.
He hadn't felt so good, or so youthful, in, hell... he
couldn't remember how long. Maybe he never had. But
this was to be his day. All he had wanted since he was in
his mid-twenties and Arthur was first released from reform school and cleared of all wrongdoings, was Arthur's
death. He had been disappointed when the courts cleared
him, and even more disappointed when the Party, his
beloved D.F.L. Party, gave the son-of-a-bitch a job. Job
hell, a career. What an error. Epic, he called it then, and
since, Arthur had proven him correct. And many times
Ferelli had taken it upon himself to do something about it
if no one else would. All these years though, Arthur
Fetchenko had always managed to sneak around any attacks — slippery bastard. And he was always heavily protected. But today, that playing field was level. Ferelli had
armament. He had guts. He was on the mission he now
felt he had prepared for most of his adult life. He was
ready. This wouldn't be like all the other times, the so
many attempts that ended in failure. Sure, one or two had
done damage: the hit meant for Arthur but took his family instead, and more up to date, wiping out of that little
weasel Arthur was trying to slip into the Whitehouse and
that Henry Tyler, an enemy from way back. The first,
Ferelli almost regretted. A woman and her youngsters for
Christ sakes. What were his guys thinking? Oh, well. Collateral damage. Could happen to anyone. But the weasel
and Henry Tyler? That was pleasure through and
through.

J.P. washed up in the men's room of Lazear's Market, and then went to a cooler to find himself something for breakfast. Bologna? Not on your life. Ham? Maybe. There. Bagels and cream cheese, always great for starting a day off on the right foot — light, but not too. He sought out butter and a plastic knife. Then, when he had his fill, he reached for his cellular phone. He called Vernon Pratt.

"Let's move this up," he said.

"Senator?" Pratt asked. "Is that you?"

"Of course it's me. Who the hell did you expect?"

"At six in the morning? Nobody."

Ferelli glanced at his watch. "Is that all it is?"

"That's all it is, Senator," Pratt said.

Maybe Pratt was right. Maybe it was too early. Arthur might not even be out of bed yet, and Ferelli wasn't sure he could get all the way to his bedroom. "Well, how soon can we move, what's the earliest you can pick me up?"

"Ten? Ten-thirty?" Pratt guessed.

"Ten o'clock then," Ferelli said and hung up.

* * *

Vernon Pratt called Jacob Rain's cell. It rang several times, then, "Hello?" It was not the gruff voice of Rain.

Pratt almost hung up, thinking he had misdialed. "Who is this?" he asked.

"Who are you looking for?"

"Jacob Rain," Pratt answered. "Did I dial wrong?"

"This is his phone."

"Is he there?"

"He's here. Would you like me to wake him?"

"Who is this?" Pratt asked again.

"Nikki Fetchenko. Is this Vernon Pratt?"

"Yes, Ma'am."

Nikki shook Jacob. When his eyes opened, she handed him the phone. "It's Vernon," she said.

Rain sat up against the headboard, shook the cob-
webs free from his mind, checked the time on Nikki's
nightstand clock, and then said, "Pratt. What's up so early
in the morning?"

"The good senator is getting impatient. He wants to
be picked up at ten."

"He in that much of a hurry to die?"

"I guess," Pratt said. "What are my orders?"

"I'll wake Arthur and call you back. Stay by the
phone," Rain said and hung up.

* * *

J.P. Ferelli chose to use the next four hours wisely;
he would practice. In his crate of miscellaneous armament he had acquired from the late Pecker-head Piccinni
(he smiled to himself at the thought of the name he had
tagged the dead man with) he found at least a half-dozen
hand grenades. He had seen them in action in the movies
over the years, but having never been in the military, had
never thrown one himself. How accurate was he? He
thought it essential to know. Apples, tossing apples at a
particular target ought to do the trick. He pulled a five
pound bag off a produce shelf, smaller green apples,
about grenade size. They even had stems; he would simu-
late pulling the pins. With the first, he bit down on the
stem like he had seen done in an early war epic, John
Wayne probably, maybe Cagney. He pulled the apple
away with a quick jerk, nearly dislodging his false teeth.
He pointed one arm out in front of him, threw the other
behind his neck in a windup before the pitch. He studied
the back door of Lazear's Market for a moment, and then
threw the apple. It missed wide, about five feet. He
glanced at the produce counter — plenty of apples, no
problem, he would learn.

* * *

"Are we really leaving here, Arthur?" Liz Harmon asked over the top of her coffee cup. Arthur Fetchenko lowered his paper, and considered her across the table for an instant.

God she was beautiful in the morning. He could wake up to her every day for the rest of his life — gladly. And he would never feel the need to look back. He was sure of it. "You bet we are," he said. "Just as soon as I can be sure Joey Ferelli is out of the picture." Joey was the reason for all of this. Had there not been a Joey Ferelli, there would not have been a need for all of this seclusion in the first place. Ferelli was always the one after him and all that he loved. It was Joey who rallied the troops against Arthur at every turn. And it had been him who had orchestrated the attempts on his life over the years. But still, as ample as opportunity had been, as many chances as Arthur had been given, he somehow could not bring himself to kill Joey Ferelli. Not that he didn't need killing, and not that Arthur hadn't wished someone would come along and do it for him. It was just that, somewhere deep inside Arthur Fetchenko laid an ancient code which prevented him from killing Joey Ferelli, a code only he knew about and one that he did not understand. Always the conundrum.

A knock came on the door of Liz and Arthur's quarters. It was Jacob Rain, there to tell Arthur of his call from Vernon Pratt. "Gather everyone, you, Nikki, Henry, Vernon Pratt if he's in yet, Blackburn too, in the board-room in twenty minutes," Fetchenko ordered.

"Pratt's not in. I'll call him, but it'll take more than twenty minutes."

"Have him join us when he gets here, him and whoever he's using as a driver."

Jacob Rain left to fulfill his boss' orders, and Arthur Fetchenko and Liz Harmon showered and dressed. "You don't need me in that meeting, do you?" Liz asked.

"I'd like you to be there. This whole thing places you in as much danger as anyone else around here. You might see the need for something the rest of us overlook. Yeah, you better join us."

Jacob Rain's call to Vernon Pratt set the ball in motion. Pratt hadn't chosen a driver, and hadn't thought about doing so. Was there even one available? These things were usually planned well in advance — by security. It wasn't as though limousines were needed daily or drivers were sitting around awaiting instructions like some cabbie. The drivers the company employed were security staff members who happened to have a commercial license, not full time employees who only drove. "Who do you want me to use?" he asked Rain.

Jacob Rain was lost. He was out of his element in this new job of his anyway, having spent most of his former years in the field, on this duty or that. Copeletti was the one who knew the security staff and how they worked. "I don't even know who drives," he told Pratt. "I thought you'd take care of that little detail."

"I didn't think to. That was always seen to by Tony Copeletti. I guess I hadn't thought of it."

"Well... you get here as fast as you can, and we'll figure it out then," Rain instructed.

"Problem?" Nikki Fetchenko asked. She had been in his office waiting for him while he made his call. Then they were to go to the meeting with her father.

"Who drives?" he asked her. The only one he could recall seeing behind the wheel of a limousine was Vinny Gotto, and Vinny Gotto was dead. Rain ought to know; he killed him.

Nikki grabbed for the phone. She called Liz Harmon. She knew that Liz had scheduled such things in the past. "Would you appoint a limo driver and have him at the meeting? Thanks." And she hung up. "Don't get so excited, Jacob. There's always a way." she said and smiled.

Blackburn strolled into Rain's office, hair from his comb-over falling in the wrong direction. Phil was not old, just prematurely balding. Henry Tyler followed Blackburn in. Henry's hair matched Blackburn's, only earned from age. "Ready?" Blackburn asked.

"Ready," Jacob Rain said.

Nikki Fetchenko hooked an arm through Jacob's and together, they led the way to her father's boardroom.

* * *

"Whose voice did I hear in the background last night?" J.P. Ferelli had finished with his grenade tossing practice, felt confident that he had his technique perfected and he was able to do some real damage. He broke from his self training to call and give Deloris one last chance. She had been good to him, better than anyone in a very long time, better than Martha had been even in her younger days, and he felt Deloris deserved one more chance. He hoped a good night's sleep had changed her thinking.

"Did you kill your wife?"

"Of course I didn't," Ferelli insisted. "I don't kill people."

"They sounded pretty convinced, the cops," Deloris said.

"Well they would now, wouldn't they? Especially if they wanted you to tell them where I am."

Maybe he was telling the truth. Maybe the police were trying to manipulate her. He had treated her gently enough, not so much during sex, of course, but otherwise. He had been a gentleman. But still, she had to wonder why he was with her in the first place? What had he been running away from when he showed up at the café that night? The police for sure, but why, if he hadn't done something wrong. "What's this new office you mentioned last night?"

"Who was that talking in the background?"

She thought about lying to him, telling him there had been no one with her, insist that the voice he had heard was the radio. But this was a senator. They're smarter than that. Still, she would not divulge all of the truth. "A neighbor. I was frightened — that story the cops told, you know. Anyway, my neighbor offered to sleep on my couch, just in case. That's who you heard."

"He sounded much closer than the couch."

"Well he should have. He came running into my room the minute he heard the phone. That's all," Deloris told him.

"Are you sure that's all?"

"I'm positive. Now, what were you saying about me joining you?"

"I do want you to join me, Deloris. I'll be starting my new job in a few days. I'll send a car, and a crew to move you."

It would be his last words to her.

Chapter Thirty-Four

Phil Blackburn suggested Henry Tyler, given the fact he was still wearing a brace to keep his broken clavicle in place and a sling to keep the wounded limb close to his body, be safely tucked someplace out of harms way, perhaps even off the estate.

"Where the hell would you have me go?" Henry objected. "Hell... don't let the sling fool you. It can be used to hide a knife."

"A knife?" Jacob Rain laughed. "What you gonna do with a knife, Henry. You can barely move."

Even Nikki Fetchenko smiled at the thought. Henry was brains, not brawn. She couldn't see him fighting his way out of a girls' locker room if it was empty. And even Henry had to chuckle, inwardly of course, at the thought. "Alright, not a knife. A gun then."

"You do that, Henry," Fetchenko said. "You tuck a gun in your sling. Jacob, get him a small piece, something unobtrusive, something nobody will see. Only, Henry, don't shoot any of us or yourself with it." Then Arthur Fetchenko considered the group around the table. Liz Harmon, he wished he could send her away, but he had promised that her trip to Antonio Copeletti's South Bend estate would be the last time she would be exiled, trouble or no trouble, and he would keep that promise. He looked at his daughter, Nikki. She was to take over for him. He couldn't very well teach her from the get-go to hide from danger. She'd spend the remainder of her life hiding. Blackburn — the schmoozer — send him away? Probably not. He had turned in handy when Colonel Fergusson came hunting. Then there was Jacob Rain. With

Jacob to face, Fetchenko didn't see how Ferelli had the guts. Jacob was a foreboding enemy, a brick wall, the proverbial person you would not want to meet up with in a dark alley. That's who Jacob Rain was. Had Joey Ferelli gone mad? Likely. Arthur had always suspected that would happen one day. But to try it alone? That was over the edge, even for Joey Ferelli. "Philip, any chance he'll have help?"

"Word on the street is no. Having me sic the police on him over Martha's death was ingenious, Boss. He's disappeared so completely, even Davidson can't find him. Not that Davidson doesn't have the manpower to help, he does. He just can't find Ferelli to join with him. And Nikki, you'll want to pay special attention to this. Davidson, even if we get Ferelli taken care of, will be your foremost threat. Don't underestimate him. He's not quite the pussy he makes out to be."

"How do you know he hasn't contacted Ferelli?" Nikki asked.

"I don't. Best guess, that's all. Ferelli's cellular showed up, but not in Ferelli's hand. Our people have been able to establish the last contact he had with Davidson, they looked at both of their phone records — mobile, home, office — and found no evidence of them talking to one another before Davidson began assembling troops. It's a pretty good bet that he's alone. Now... what he'll be coming at us with, fire power or whatever, that's anybody's guess."

Vernon Pratt knocked on the boardroom door and entered. "Sorry I'm late," he said and pulled a chair from the table. "I hear that Green kid's to drive. Did you want him in here too?"

"Billy Green?" Jacob asked. Green, Jacob Rain considered stupid — not much drive, nothing to offer. Good enough wheel man, but not for this job. Too important. "I want you on this personally, Pratt."

"Pratt, bring us up to speed. You're the one who talks with Ferelli," Fetchenko said. "What's his plan?"

"Come in through the tunnel," Vernon Pratt said. "That's all I really know except he's coming here to kill you." Pratt looked at Nikki, then at Liz. Smooth, he thought to himself. And he looked down.

"Everybody knows that," Fetchenko said. He could see Vernon's embarrassment. Might as well be out with it — tell it like it is. That's one thing Arthur Fetchenko always admired in Vernon Pratt — his straight forward approach to things.

"Boss," Pratt said. "Why don't I just kill him and get it over with?"

Fetchenko smiled. "I need to face him. You bring him in. Take him right into the garage. We'll handle it from there."

"I don't understand," Pratt objected.

"Sure you do. You know who J.P. Ferelli is. And you know who I am. I have to give him a chance, and if he doesn't want this to end without one of us dying, then it'll have to be him or me. That's how it is. Him or me. Nobody else can shoulder that." Arthur Fetchenko shook his head from side to side and a sadness crossed his face. He shook it off. "Henry, you'll be in charge of the women. Tuck a gun in that sling of yours, and if Joey comes for one of them, you shoot him. But try to wound, not kill."

"The hell you say, Arthur Fetchenko," Liz Harmon said and stood, her voice stern, her attitude no-nonsense. "Where you go I go and that's all there is to it."

"And that goes for me as well," Nikki said.

"I can't have two unarmed women to protect, and Ferelli to see to at the same time."

"Then arm us," Nikki said.

"No! I won't."

"Father?"

"You're no warrior."

"She is, Boss," Jacob Rain threw in, almost mechanically. But it was true. Had it not been for Nikki Fetchenko's inherent abilities along those lines, he'd likely be dead. "Not that I want to see her in battle again," he added.

"As for me, Arthur, if you want me to retire with you, it starts with this. We end our life here together. And we do everything together in our future. You can't deal with that? You got the wrong girl. So get with it. We stand together and what happens... happens."

"What do you think, Rain?" Fetchenko asked.

"I think we've been out-voted and Joey Ferelli's out-numbered. Where do you want the rest of us?"

"Close him in. Set up in the tunnel. Once Ferelli's in, nobody gets back out until this is over." Fetchenko turned his attention to Vernon Pratt. "When does he want you to pick him up?"

"Ten."

Fetchenko checked his watch — 9:45. "You won't make that. Best get over there."

* * *

J.P. Ferelli paced. He had made up his mind. He had struggled with whether or not he should let Vernon Pratt live, maybe even make him his head of security after he was firmly seated behind Arthur Fetchenko's desk, but now, as he checked his watch and found Pratt to be nearly a half-hour late, he decided to kill him. He would do it in the limo, once he was in, not before. Hell... it'd be cheaper anyway. A dead man don't need money. He paced more, thought more, wondered what he'd run into at Arthur's place. He really didn't care so long as he was able to get to Arthur. He stopped at the crate he had hauled from Piccinni's shop. He dug through, sorting even more of what he would not use from what he would use, stacking his chosen weapons neatly in a corner of the market, getting a feel for what he would need to transport them from the store to the car. He wanted something accessible. Something from which he could do a quick-draw. Lazear, the dead market owner, it seemed, was an exercise nut of sorts or had been. In a corner of the office, Ferelli located just the thing — a duffle, stinky gym attire included. "Jesus, Eric. What a stench. No wonder you stuffed it in the corner," Ferelli complained to the dead man's spirit, still lurking about the store. He dumped the contents, went back to his pile of armament and began packing as neatly as possible, persuading himself as he packed that any item that would not fit would not be needed. As he finished, a shadow darkened the store. Vernon Pratt and his limo finally had come to pick him up.

* * *

Jacob Rain fitted Arthur Fetchenko, Liz Harmon, and Nikki Fetchenko with Kevlar vests. They wouldn't protect entirely, but they would stop anything ordinary from taking out a crucial organ, a bullet perhaps. It was the best he could do, unyielding as they all were about running head first into danger. That and provide each of them with a gun of their own — Nikki's, a Glock like his, Liz's, a revolver. They were set. They knew where they would meet up with their enemy, or enemies if Blackburn had been wrong. And the possibility of enemy turning into enemies was precisely why the two women, Liz and Nikki, insisted on standing beside Arthur. They knew Henry would not be allowed, not in his present condition. They knew that Jacob Rain would set up a blockade to prevent Ferelli from escaping, after which he might be of some help, but not at the start. They knew that Blackburn was to guard the yard, just in case any simultaneous attack had been planned. And that pretty much left Arthur

Fetchenko alone, something he could handle, but not if there were more than just Ferelli.

Everyone knew from the very beginning that Joey Ferelli's only possible entry would be through the tunnel from the New Creek side of the mountain. If not, why the limo. And Vernon Pratt was to get him in, and Vernon Pratt only had access through the tunnel. Rain had seen to that. And Vernon's driver? Too stupid to be trouble. The tunnel. That was Ferelli's way in, take it or leave it. So... that meant the battle would take place in the garage. Arthur Fetchenko took both women down — to get them settled in, their locations to be chosen more for their safety than for their vantage point.

Fetchenko's plan was a trap. The elevator was to be disabled by Henry Tyler from above as soon as Arthur and the girls were in place. That trap was not for Joey Ferelli — not exclusively. It was meant for both of them, and now, it would be for all of them. Arthur's plan? To reason with Joey Ferelli. He would try to talk this fight away. But if that could not be done, he was willing to kill Joey Ferelli. For old time sakes, for the terrible scar this would leave on the inside of him, he hoped it would not come to that. But, still, he knew it would.

The elevator doors opened. Fetchenko stepped out. Liz and Nikki followed. Fetchenko surveyed their surroundings; he chose places for each of the women. "Sweetheart, I want you at the back the Studebaker. Crouch down, keep out of sight, and neither of you shoot. Keep those guns on safety. If you need to defend yourself, do it. Otherwise, do not fire those weapons. Clear?"

"Where do you want me?" Nikki asked. She took a good look at the Glock she had been given, sought out its safety, pushed the lever to fire, then back to safe, just to get a feel for it. She had fired one once, Jacob Rain's. But never enough to get a real sense of how it should be handled.

"You get behind that old Packard. The damn thing's bulletproof. You should be safe there. On second thought, the two of you switch. Jacob tells me you know how to handle yourself, Nikki. You might come in handy."

"And I won't," Liz asked. She too pulled out a pistol, hers the revolver. "Where's the safety?"

"Exactly," Fetchenko said and smiled. "It has none. You just point and squeeze the trigger."

"And where will you be?" Liz asked.

"Right here." He stood in front of the open elevator door.

"That doesn't look safe."

"It's not supposed to."

* * *

Vernon Pratt pushed the back door to Lazear's Market slowly open, just like J.P. Ferelli had instructed him to do when he called Vernon's cell and sent him around to the back of building. He slid in as soon as his body would fit, hoping he would not be shot by the senator who, judging from his manner of speaking when he talked to him on his cell phone had exhausted all signs of stability. He felt the barrel of a gun touch the back of his head, cold steel, and he stiffened. "Where's the driver?"

"Where's my money?" Vernon asked. He always found the talk of money seemed to chill the nervous. And Senator Ferelli was definitely nervous. Vernon could feel the gun shake.

Ferelli handed an envelope around Vernon, the gun still pressed to his head. "Count it."

Vernon counted. Forty-eight thousand. "A little light," he said.

"The rest comes after I'm in. Now get over there," he pushed the gun barrel into Vernon's head harder, shoving him with it, "and pick up that duffel bag."

Vernon walked to the bag and stooped to pick it up. "What the hell you got in here? A dead body?"

"Why do you say that?"

"It's heavy, and it stinks," Vernon said.

"Vernon, are you on my side?"

"I don't know what you mean, Senator."

"It's a simple question, Son. Are you with me? Can I trust you?"

"Of course you can, Sir," Vernon Pratt insisted. "I came here to get you, didn't I?" he offered as proof.

"Arthur could have ordered you to do that. Don't you think I would know that?" Ferelli popped him lightly on the back of his head with the gun.

"Look. Senator," Pratt said. "Both Pauley Danucci and Vicent Gotto were close friends of mine. I have no intention of fighting on the side of the ones who killed them. I was loyal until they done that."

"Where's your phone?"

Vernon pulled it from his jacket pocket and handed it over.

"Gun?"

And Vernon handed it over as well. "I'll need those. I need the phone to get us in and I'll need the gun if I'm to fight beside you."

"You'll get the phone when we reach the estate. The gun, we'll talk about on the way. Now you haul that bag to the limo. Ferelli emptied Vernon's gun as they walked, unknown to Vernon who walked ahead.

* * *

Jacob Rain checked his watch. It had been just over an hour since Vernon Pratt had gone for Senator Ferelli. They should arrive any moment. Vernon was to call when they got close to the estate. Ferelli would be told it was their way in.

Rain paced. Then he checked his watch one more time.

His phone began to ring.

Chapter Thirty Five

Vernon Pratt pulled out his handgun and slid the chamber open. Empty. He looked at Ferelli. "No!" he said. And Ferelli shot him in the forehead, opened the door, and pushed him out onto the concrete floor of the tunnel.

Jacob Rain stepped from behind a cement column and sidestepped Vernon's tumbling body.

The limo driver, having heard the shot, opened the privacy window and looked back. Ferelli aimed a gun at him. "Keep driving. Any fuck-up's and you're as dead as your friend. You do exactly as you're told, get me through that final door, and you get to live." The driver started to close the window. "Open! You leave that open so I can keep an eye on you. You try to close it, and I'll give you a bullet in the back of your head for your trouble. Understand?"

The driver did not reply.

"I asked you if you understand," Ferelli said as he leaned over the seat and through the window.

"Yes, Sir." The driver slowed as he came to a metal arm jutting out on his side. On the arm was a keypad. He lowered the window and reached out to key in a code.

"Hand me that gun," Ferelli demanded.

The driver continued his reach. "I have no gun," he said softly.

"Do you want to die?" Ferelli shouted. And the driver handed his gun back. "Now open it. When you enter, you drive straight in, all the way to the far wall. And don't try anything. I've been here before. I know my way around."

The massive door began to move. Soon there was room for the car to fit through. "Drive," Ferelli ordered. But the car sat still. Ferelli reached and tapped the driver on the back of the head with his gun. "Drive, damn you." And the car began to move. As soon as it cleared the door, Ferelli ordered the driver to close it behind them. Then he plugged the driver in the back of the head, blood and brains filling the windshield instantly. The driver slumped over the wheel, his foot pushing the accelerator to the floor. The limo bolted across the garage, crashing into the concrete wall on the other side. Ferelli threw open the door, shoved his duffle out onto the floor, and dove after it, shocked that he heard no gunfire or saw no lead flying in his direction. He quickly unzipped the duffel and pulled out the M-79 grenade launcher. He grabbed a round, loaded it, took careful aim at the electric motor above the door, and fired. "Arthur? You down here?" he shouted.

"I'm here."

"You got anybody with you? I mean in here. I know the ones you probably got on the other side of that door aren't getting in."

"Nope."

"I figured you'd be alone. That's your style, always something to prove."

"And I figured you wouldn't be, Joey. That's your style, too chicken-shit to go it on your own, too good to dirty your hands."

"Don't call me Joey," Ferelli shouted.

"You were Joey when we were kids, and you'll always be Joey to me," Fetchenko said.

Ferelli glanced in the mirror of the limo. He could see the Packard, the car Governor Franks had left to him and Arthur stole. "That my car?"

"The Packard?"

"You know which car."

"That's Capone's car," Fetchenko said.

"The hell it is. It's Roosevelt's or was. And Grand-dad left it to me."

"It wasn't his to leave. He stole it, or got it with tax dollars, same thing. It wasn't his to give away. Damn little he had actually belonged to him."

"Oh what the hell do you know about it?"

"I know you don't have it," Fetchenko said and grinned. "Look, Joey, don't you think this old war has gone on long enough. Let's put down the guns and talk this out."

"Maybe, little brother, but first," Ferelli reloaded the grenade launcher and took careful aim, "we settle the issue of the car. If I can't have it back, then..." And he pulled the trigger.

"NOOOOOO!" Arthur Fetchenko cried out and ran toward the car.

The old Packard burst into flames and drove Fetchenko back. Then it exploded, knocking him to the floor and Liz Harmon against a nearby cement wall.

Nikki Fetchenko stood and took aim. She had a clear shot. She pulled the trigger. Ferelli fell to his side and rifled through his duffel for a handgun. He aimed it in Nikki's direction and fired. He missed wide, flinching as the pain from Nikki's shot to his shoulder caught up with him. He shot again, but Nikki had crouched back down behind the Studebaker. Arthur got to his feet, stunned, not knowing which way to look — at Nikki or at Ferelli. J.P. saw his opening and took it. He shot Arthur Fetchenko in the chest, the armor piercing rounds Piccinni had provided for his Glock easily penetrating the Kevlar vest. Fetchenko dropped to his knees, then to his belly. Nikki Fetchenko stood, clutched her Glock with both hands, advanced on Ferelli, took careful aim, and shot him from point blank range. Ferelli fell to the ground. He convulsed a bit, and then lay still. Nikki looked up to see her father, crawling toward Ferelli. Arthur Fetchenko grabbed J.P. Ferelli's limp hand. Ferelli opened his eyes and looked into Arthur's. "I'm sorry, Arthur," he said. Then he died.

"So am I, Joey," Arthur Fetchenko said. He began to cry, shaking violently with each tear.

Nikki approached him, placed her hands on her father's shoulders. "Who is he, Dad?" she asked.

"He is, or was," he sighed and sobbed a bit, then with quivering lip continued, "your uncle, Joey Fetchenko, my older brother." Then Arthur Fetchenko's crying was over, his pain giving way to a limp body. He slumped into darkness on the cold cement of the garage floor.

Nikki Fetchenko dried her eyes, put another bullet in Ferelli, this time in the head — to make certain, and then she went to check on Liz Harmon. If she were alive, she would have to be told that her Arthur was not. Nikki would see to it.

Chapter Thirty-Six

It rained the day of the funeral. But diplomats from everywhere, officials from countries most folks never heard of, senators, congressmen, kings and queens, and the President of the United States himself, attended. Nikki Fetchenko dressed in black satin, her elbow length gloves hiding her shaking hands, her hat and veil concealing her tears as she stood solemnly between two caskets, her father's and Liz Harmon's. Jacob Rain steadied her on one side, Henry Tyler on the other, while Phil Blackburn, Tony Copeletti, and two of Rain's men kept anyone from getting close to her. The service was short, sweet, and to the point, just like Arthur Fetchenko always liked things.

Afterward, a line formed, the dignitaries all wishing to express their heartfelt sadness and sympathy to all who were close to Arthur: Phil, Jacob, Henry, and the pretty creature dressed in black whose name none of them knew.

Then came Daniel Davidson — Senator Daniel Davidson — friend and confidant of J.P. Ferelli and enemy of Arthur Fetchenko, and along with him, a large number of the followers of J.P. Ferelli, friends of Colonel Randal Fergusson, and fellow enemies of Arthur Fetchenko and all who stood with him. "Well...," said Davidson. "What're you boys going to do now that the Fetchenko regime has finally been defeated? Hit the unemployment line?"

"Who says it's defeated, Senator?" Blackburn asked and smiled.

"Come now. Even a snake dies when its head is removed," Davidson said, mirth in his voice.

"Not this snake, Senator," the pretty lady in black said and stepped intrusively close to him. "Allow me to introduce myself, Senator Davidson. My name is Nikki Fetchenko. I'll be picking up my father's sword, so to speak. You and your people here," she looked from one to another to another, making sure all were paying close attention to her, "can get ready for a whole new game. Philip Blackburn will contact you early next week to set up a meeting at my estate. I suggest you take that meeting, Senator Davidson." She reached and shook his hand, a firm handshake to let him know she did not fear him. "It was good to finally meet you." And she turned, hooked an arm through Jacob Rain's, and walked away from the crowd of mourners.

Chapter Thirty-Seven

A bright morning sun, after the cave-like darkness of Albert & Sue's, nearly stopped Jed Walker dead in his tracks. The attack had left him with only one working eye and a diminished tolerance for light. His head began echoing his heartbeat. His doctors had told him the condition would improve with time but that time had not yet come. He grabbed his head. How much time? he silently asked.

Lee Walker was not bothered by the sunlight. It was the sudden rise in temperature as she stepped into the street that got to her. The heavy turtle neck sweater she wore to hide the hideous scar that had been left by shards of steel that flew from the old Packard when the grenade detonated was a far cry from the delicate spaghetti strap top she preferred. She tugged at her collar, stuck an arm through her husbands, and pulled him close. She would guide him to their car.

"It was a nice service," she said, referring to their recent funeral.

"The next one will be better. We'll plan it all out."

She smiled at him.

"You don't need the sweater. That scar's barely noticeable." Jed told her.

"Oh, and how in the hell would you know?" She said. "You only have one eye." Along with the round he had taken to the chest, he had lost the eye to shrapnel.

They walked, arm in arm, until they reached the car. She helped him into the driver's seat and plucked his sunglasses from the visor. "Put these on," she said. Then she walked around to the passenger's side and got in. A rusty old pickup truck drove slowly by — the honk of a horn — a wolf whistle. Lee Walker flipped him off.

"Making friends?" he asked.

"I already have one," she said and smiled. "And that's plenty. How far is it?" she asked.

"Five miles, according to Albert. He said the place still has the gate posts, but the gate is missing. We shouldn't have difficulty picking them out. As I recall, they were pretty tall."

"You were what? Six? They're probably four feet tall and covered with grass and brush by now." She said. "Which side of the road?"

""Right," he said.

"I'll keep an eye out."

"You'll have to. I'll need mine to drive with," Jed Walker said and grinned.

"Is that it?" Lee Walker asked motioning toward what appeared to be a stack of brick and mortar lying in a pile, almost blocking an overgrown driveway.

Jed pulled to the shoulder and stopped. He studied it for a moment. "Could be," he said. "It was so many years ago. He crept forward for a better look. "Could be," he said again and turned in. He stepped out of the car.

"Where you going?" Lee asked him and opened her door. Walker did not answer. He looked down the lane, and then began tossing bricks out of the way of the car. "I take it this is it."

"I believe it is. Only way to be sure is to drive in. As I recall, there's a corner at the end of the drive. The estate is around that corner — out of sight." He kicked a few more bricks aside, and then returned to the car.

"This isn't much of a road," Lee commented after the third mud puddle and the Studebaker's frame bottoming out in it. The grass in the center was tall, wheat-like seeds flying into the air as they broke loose from the stalk above the car's hood. Then came the corner. Around it a large stucco building appeared. "You say this is an old family estate?" The grounds were unkempt, but she could tell it had been a luxury mansion in its day. It was quite impressive, and in remarkable repair actually.

"Yes."

"I thought you were from humble immigrant beginnings," Lee said.

"I was."

"Tell me, how does a poor immigrant family end up with a place like this?" she was asking as she caught her first glimpse of the lake beyond the mansion, the view — spectacular — breathtaking.

Jed Walker stopped the car. He studied the house. He looked out over the lake. I told you I'd one day take this for my pay, he silently told Thaddeus Frank. Maybe now I can consider us even. "Somebody has to lie and cheat his way into the governor's mansion," he said. "Then they buy something like this with tax dollars. That's how a poor immigrant family gets something like this. What do you think of it?"

"It's... breathtaking — reminds me of a southern plantation. This was your grandfather's?"

"It was."

"The one whose picture hangs in Albert & Sue's with the dart in his eye, that grandfather."

"That's the one." He turned and looked at the corner in the drive. He pointed. "That's where the son-of-a-bitch ran me over, right there on that corner."

"But I thought he didn't have anything to do with the family. How is it the two of you ended up here together?" Lee walker asked.

"I wasn't here with him. I had come out here with my brother, Joey," Jed began to explain. "Joey was just getting his start in politics and this place belonged to some Farm-Labor bigwig at the time."

"You mean Joey as in Joseph Patrick Ferelli? That Joey?"

"He wasn't J. P. Ferelli in those days. He was just plain Joey Fetchenko. Anyway, I was six years old. I was playing in the sand over on that corner. The son-of-a-bitch came barreling in here drunk and driving like a madman. He mowed me right down. It's one of the clearest images of my early childhood. How's that for luck? I recall something from when I was six and it's got to be that."

"Funny you weren't killed. Did it do serious injury?"

"No. All I got from it was kidney damage," he said. "That and my black sheep status," he added.

"Black sheep status?"

"Yeah! The incident left me with a bed-wetting problem, unfit to the likes of my parents."

"It seems wherever you turn there's a bad memory, Arthur."

"Jed," he corrected. "And yes, it does seem my life has been a series of dark clouds, doesn't it? But you, what makes you stick around, Liz?"

"Lee," she corrected and smiled.

"Of course. Lee. So... what makes Lee stick around knowing the clouds are dark?"

"I take pride in weathering storms, and I like silver linings," she explained.

"Would you like to see the inside?" Jed Walker asked.

Lee studied the home's exterior: missing stucco revealing weathered lathe, shingles of random colors patching obvious leaks, ancient wood windows with cracked glass and pealing paint, and said, "I'm not sure."

"C'mon. It'll be fun. And I promise, it'll be in better repair. Copeletti hired a contractor and put him to work, inside first." He turned the knob and pushed the door open.

"It's not locked," Lee commented.

"This is Minnesota. Doors aren't often locked. People usually can't find their keys," he exaggerated and walked in. "Nice," he said as he looked around.

"I'll say," Lee Walker agreed. She surveyed the living room: large, lavish, flawless plaster walls, fresh paint, tasteful art hanging and on elegant table tops, massive Russian fireplace nearly filling one wall — neatly stacked fresh cut birch beside it, and a recent four-wide French door leading to a screened in porch which filled the entire front of the mansion and overlooked the lake. "I can live here," she commented, a smile on her pretty face.

"I'll bet you can," Jed Walker agreed. He opened the French doors and walked out onto the porch for a lake view. Lee followed. She came up close behind him and reached her arms around him, her firm breasts pressing into his back. "Why is it your brother hated you so much?" she asked.

"Heidi Lang," he said.

"Heidi Lang?"

"Yes. The girl my grandfather raped and murdered. Joey admired our grandfather and believed in him. He also believed that I actually committed those crimes and tried to blame them on our grandfather. And he believed what I did with my life was all about revenge and retaliation for me having to pay the price — reform school and all of that."

He turned to face her and kissed her lightly on the neck, then nibbled at her earlobe. "Enough of that talk," he said and nibbled more.

"You know that drives me wild," she said.

"That's why I do it," he insisted, and slid his hand up her back under her sweater, searching for the clasp on her bra. "No bra," he said. "How lewd."

"I suppose it might have been, say... fifty... seventy-five years ago," she said. "I could put it back on if you wish."

"Hell no. I like lewd." And he slid his hand around to her front brushing lightly over the scars left behind by the explosion, then he caressed a breast and kissed her passionately on the mouth, his tongue probing, hers following suit. He turned her, back to him, kissed her neck. She reached down and pulled her sweater up... slowly... until her breasts were exposed, his hands gently caressing them. She pulled the sweater over her head and let it fall to the floor. His hands slid down the smooth skin of her stomach and to the waistband of her tight button-fly blue-jeans. He found the first button and unfastened it, then sought out the next, then the next. He slid a hand inside her panties, coaxing the jeans down over her hips. She turned her neck, her lips seeking out his. He slid his hands further into her silk panties, pushing them down to expose a hint of pubic hair. The jeans slowly slid down her slender legs, gathering at her ankles like the pedals of a flower.

"Anybody home?" a voice called from the living room. "Sir? Ma-am?"

"Oh my God!" Lee Walker cried out just as the stranger approached the French doors.

"Oh my God!" the stranger yelled excitedly and turned to avert his stare. "Oh my God!" he said again as his head involuntarily turned back for a second look.

* * *

Introductions came with more than a modicum of embarrassment. Lee Walker's color matching her red sweater. Lou Larrabee, the contractor Copeletti had hired, was nearly as red-faced as Lee. Jed Walker dug deep into his bag of Arthur Fetchenko guises and came up with one that hid his discomfort — a virtual mask of authority. It would work fine with Lou Larrabee. This was a mansion. This man had to be wealthy, maybe royalty.

"Copeletti chose well. The place looks remarkable," Jed Walker told the carpenter.

"Thanks, but I'm afraid he didn't have to choose at all. I'm the only carpenter in town," Larrabee said.

"Fortuitous," Lee Walker said. "Obviously you weren't busy."

"Oh, I was busy, Ma'am. But I've been dying to get my hands on this place. When the chance came, I took it."

"Really," she said. "And why is that?"

"I lived here once. Been a long time ago now. You see, it once belonged to my grandfather."

"Excuse me?" Walker turned and asked.

"My grandfather, Governor Frank. He owned this place years ago. But that wasn't his real name. It was Fetchenko or something like that," Louis Larrabee said.

"And you lived here with him?" Jed Walker asked.

"Oh! Heavens no. I never knew him at all. He never was anything to us. You see, he raped my grandmother and left her for dead. That's the kind of guy he was. The sheriff found her and got her out of town before anything else could happen. She almost died at the time, but she didn't. And my father was born."

"What happened to her?"

"She committed suicide. Anyway, my dad went to see his father once, here at this place, but the great former governor would have nothing to do with him. It wasn't long after that, the next deer hunting season I think, Dad got killed by a stray bullet."

"So... how did you come to live here?" Walker asked.

"An aunt took me in after my father died. I was just fifteen and they were talking about sending me to reform school. I had difficulty adjusting for a while. Then she came for me, my aunt. Later her husband got killed in the mines and she lost the house. She took me here. The place had been vacant since Frank died — real rundown.

No one knew we were here really. She passed on when I was eighteen and the place just didn't feel right to me so I moved on. I kind of regretted that. I always wanted to fix the place up."

Lee Walker looked into her husband's eyes. She knew the truth, all of it. And all she could think was, Now there you have it — irony in its purest form. Lives had been altered. Hers. For she had almost been blown to bits by a grenade, and now she was no longer Liz Harmon from New Creek, West Virginia, she was Lee Walker in some unknown corner of Minnesota where she would hide for the rest of her life. And what about Arthur? He was no longer Arthur Fetchenko; he was now a stranger named Jed Walker when he had once been a king. Tony Copeletti and Henry Tyler, too, had had their lives molded by this one incredible lie. Every turn of events, the death of Maryann Danucci Fetchenko, of Little Tony, hers and Arthur's baby boy, the casting aside of their daughter, Nikki, for fear his enemies would kill her in retaliation. All of it. Every dim-clouded development in the lives of all these people and more, even Lou Larrabee here, caused by a lie told to protect a young girl named Heidi Lang from a corrupt and soulless public official. "Dear, I think it's time for your medicine and a nap," she said poking an arm through his to lead him into the house. "You two can talk later."

"Mr. Walker," Larrabee said.

"Yes?" Walker said and stopped to listen.

"I don't suppose you'd rent one of those cabins to me." There were four of them on the property, once used to house visiting politicians. "I have a wife and a little girl, and our place in town is a dump. This would be so nice for us."

"Take your pick." Walters said. "Get whatever you need to fix it up. Bill the materials to me. Your family can live here and you can be caretaker. We'll talk about your wages later, Louis."

"Thank you, Sir. Have a pleasant nap."

"It's Jed," he said and smiled pleasantly. "Call me Jed."

THE END

Look for more from America's dynamic new author.